ALL

THAT

WAS

ALSO BY KAREN RIVERS

Before We Go Extinct

All That Was

KAREN RIVERS

Farrar Straus Giroux · New York

For H., my first best friend, who was
(and always will be) a part of me

The author gratefully acknowledges the support
of the British Columbia Arts Council.

Farrar Straus Giroux Books for Young Readers
An imprint of Macmillan Publishing Group, LLC
175 Fifth Avenue, New York, NY 10010

Printed in the United States of America
Designed by Aimee Fleck
First edition, 2018
1 3 5 7 9 10 8 6 4 2

fiercereads.com

Library of Congress Cataloging-in-Publication Data

Names: Rivers, Karen, 1970– author.
Title: All that was: a novel / Karen Rivers.
Description: First edition. | New York : Farrar Straus Giroux, 2018. |
    Summary: While seventeen-year-old Sloane shares a drunken kiss with her
    best friend Piper's boyfriend Soup, Piper is murdered on a nearby beach,
    and over the next few days, Sloane and Soup are left reliving their past
    moments with Piper, wondering if they are responsible for her death and
    figuring out how to move on without her.
Identifiers: LCCN 2017011019 (print) | ISBN 9780374302467 (hardcover)
Subjects: | CYAC: Death—Fiction. | Best friends—Fiction. | Friendship—
    Fiction. | Love—Fiction. | Dating (Social customs)—Fiction.
Classification: LCC PZ7.R5224 (ebook) | LCC PZ7.R5224 Al 2018 (print) |
    DDC [Fic]—dc23
LC record available at https://lccn.loc.gov/2017011019

Our books may be purchased in bulk for promotional, educational, or business
use. Please contact your local bookseller or the Macmillan Corporate and
Premium Sales Department at (800) 221-7945 ext. 5442 or by e-mail at
MacmillanSpecialMarkets@macmillan.com.

PROLOGUE

What do I do now?

I'm under.

I'm gone.

I'm below.

Above me, there is the surface of the water, the sun streaming in like light through fog, except the fog is water and I can't reach the light. My hands twirl like ballerinas spinning in a music box. I never liked ballet. I didn't want to dance.

Someone has already found my body in the sand, seaweed draped over me, my eyes frozen open, staring at the sky. I want to blink.

Blink.

I can't.

Paralyzed.

So why am I still looking at myself, my hands pushing at the curtain of water, red blood ribboning into the sea? How can this be happening?

It isn't so much like being in the water as it is like being inside music. I can't hear it, but I'm a part of it. There's blood and fear and emptiness and death and me and we're locked together in an underwater song that's forever.

It's a bad thing but there is no good thing to balance it out.

It's everything and nothing and I'm in the water but I also am the water.

I'm in Sloane but I also am Sloane.

I'm also the jellyfish and the rocks and the girl and the boy on the beach, the girl struggling, the boy triumphing, and I'm sorry.

I'm the current.

I'm everything.

I'm nothing.

When the water closed over my face, it felt as soft as the velvet curtains that used to hang in the room where Sloane's grandma stayed in their house. They were pale yellow. We used to hide in there, wrapped up in them, thinking she didn't know we were there. "I sure miss those pretty girls," she'd say. "I sure wish they'd come in here and see me."

She's not dead.

I am.

Death turns out to be the moment when the present freezes in place and holds on, a slice of everything held between two pieces of glass, like on a microscope slide, with you in the middle.

I know you hate me, Sloane. It's okay. I hate you, too.

I love you.

I'm sorry.

But think about it: you're the one who gets to live.

I don't.

Am I a ghost? Is that what this is?

It's a riddle and an answer and a mistake, all at once.

This isn't what I thought it would be, but what is?

Nothing.

Life.

Love.

Death.

I feel like I can almost understand but the words get all jumbled up in me, like salty weeds tangling around my tongue, and I can't breathe and I can't breathe and I'm drowning, I've drowned, and I can't speak any of the words and I never will again. I'm here under the water but somehow I can see the blue of the sky, I can see Soup kissing you, I can see the birds who careen by on the wind, I can see people on the beach, police, a German shepherd dog, and it was dark when I died, and now it's light, and my body isn't here, but I am still here, I am here, can't anyone see me here?

You don't even know yet.

I'm going to miss everything.

I wasn't finished.

I'd barely even started.

The past and future are both leaving.

Gone.

I am the water.

I am the blood in the water.

I am the wind blowing above the water.

I am the salt in the water.

I am the molecules of everything touching the water.

I am you.

I am your blood.

I am your heart.

It's okay, Sloane. The dead don't stay mad. We probably can't.

Everything is too hard to hold on to.

Everything is drifting away from me, or trying to, but I can't let it.

I am so angry.

I am holding on.

I want to break through to you somehow.

I want to scream, LOOK WHAT YOU DID, YOU MONSTER.

I want to say, I LOVE YOU.

I'm the price that we paid.

I paid the price, but more than I owed.
More, right?
Did I really deserve this?
I twirl and twirl.
Blood in the water, an endless ribbon of blood,
is me.

PART ONE

NOW

WHEN MY PHONE RINGS FOR THE FIRST time since I last saw Piper, I ignore it.

The ice in my glass melts into my Diet Coke, turning it watery and thin. I take a gulp that hurts the whole way down, a stone that I've swallowed whole. I hold my breath. It stops hurting all at once, like a light going out.

Piper's mad and I'm not ready to talk to her. I don't know what I'll say.

"You're her spirit animal," Piper's mom once told me. I wanted to tell her that "spirit animal" is actually offensive the way she's using it. I also wanted to say that Piper's inner animal isn't a person, anyway. It's something furious and powerful, already extinct, so rare it couldn't even exist anymore—a clouded leopard or a Caspian tiger—beautiful and strange and pretty much impossible to understand.

I'm none of those things.

There are thousands of girls like me. Millions. I'm as common as a house cat.

The only thing that makes me different from every other girl is that Piper chose me. We've been friends for so long that we've started to look the same. We sound the same. We definitely, on purpose, dress the same. It messes with people, to see us together. I don't really know why, but it makes us powerful—twice as pretty, twice as special. But there's no guidebook for what to do when suddenly, you don't feel like being two.

You want to be one.

I want to be one.

Me. Without Piper.

Me, with Soup.

We said a boy would never come between us, but we were so wrong.

I kissed Soup.

Soup kissed me.

But what if it was a mistake? Maybe Soup just got us mixed up. He was pretty drunk and the lighting was bad and I was drunk, too, and no one said no. So it was my fault. He has an excuse, but I sure don't.

Me, alone, is terrifying, and Soup is Piper's boyfriend.

I take another sip of my watery drink and the blue sky sinks down around me and the sun burns my eyes and my head aches from a hangover I totally deserve and I stare at my phone and my skin beads with sweat and the day gets hotter and longer and worse.

Last night feels more real now that it isn't happening than it felt when it was happening. At the time, it felt like a dream. The house was tilting around me, all corridors and half-built rooms and echoing sounds of emptiness, and I was dizzy, spinning. Then the music that felt like it was inside me. Drinking and more drinking, the cough-syrup sweetness of the mix. Then there we were, me and Soup, dancing, slower than the beat, but also just right. The filth on the unfinished floor rose up around us, stomped into clouds, both of us shiny with sweat and grayed from the dust. And then there was his face and my face and I can't explain it, I definitely can't explain why I did it. I couldn't help it. It just . . . happened.

That's never happened to me before. I've kissed boys, but it's never felt like that kiss, like a force bigger than me, pulling my lips to his lips and taking over every part of me. I couldn't have stopped it if I'd tried.

But I didn't try.

I have to talk to Piper, but I can't because it's impossible to tell her the truth and I haven't thought of the lie yet. I can't be in love with Soup. And I won't be. Love is a decision, that's what Piper always said, before she changed her idea about that. But maybe she was right all along. If so, I'm deciding now. Love is chemicals: dopamine and serotonin, flooding your brain, making you more or less yourself. You should be able to take a pill to stop it, to lock into your neurotransmitters, blunt the signal.

There should be a cure.

But anyway, it's over, whatever "it" was.

The thing with Soup and me.

I shiver hard, but I'm not cold. Not even a little. If anything, it feels like I'm cooking. The backs of my legs stick to the paint on the sun-hot wooden Adirondack chair. I can feel my skin everywhere tightening from the heat, like a sweater shrinking in the dryer, the sun robbing it of everything.

"I'm sorry," I practice. "Please, Piper. Pipes, come on. I was drunk, so it didn't count. Maybe the alcohol and my meds . . . maybe that was . . . I mean . . ."

I lick my lips. They taste like a lie I'm telling myself, salty and wrong.

I don't always like Piper but I need Piper. Piper is part of me. Not being friends with Piper isn't an option.

I'd die.

But kissing Soup wasn't like kissing anyone else. It was something different. It was *everything* different.

It was everything I wanted all along.

I should go inside the house, where there is air-conditioning and Netflix, fresh ice and Diet Coke, but I can't seem to do anything but sit here and try not to think about Soup. I have a plan for my life and there's no room in it for a boyfriend right now.

I'm going to travel after senior year.

I'm going to go to film school in New York the year after that.

I'm going to be important. I'm going to really change things with my films. I know it.

I'll look back on this and I'll realize it didn't matter. I'll know that we made a big deal over nothing. Over a boy. We agreed a long time ago, boys don't matter.

There is so much stuff that *matters*. Real things.

Things like how flocks of birds are mysteriously falling dead from the sky, raining down on towns and farms in feathery hailstorms.

Things like how herds of antelope are lying down all at once, dead, on the grassy plains of Africa.

Things like how thousands and thousands of fish died at the same time in one lake in China.

Things like how polar bears are drowning because the ice is melting out from underneath them, leaving them wobbling on shrinking islands, and then swimming for their lives.

Everything is dying.

I hope you die, for real, Piper said. *Monster.* I could feel her spit hitting my cheek; I knew how much she meant it. Piper has hated plenty of people, but it's never been me. Not before last night. I didn't know how to answer. She was close enough to kiss and then she wasn't. Her eyes were tiny, angry slits when she spun away and vanished into the wall of music.

I don't know how she could see where she was going.

I hope she didn't fall.

I hate myself, but it wasn't *all* my fault. Soup should have let go first.

But even while Piper was yelling, we were swaying without meaning to, without wanting to; our bodies were touching in a way that felt like we weren't in control of them, our hands entangled, reaching for each other, her face collapsing.

Why does it matter so much?

It was only a kiss.

Whales are washing up dead on beaches everywhere, their corpses rotten and bloated. Sometimes they explode. It still doesn't seem like anyone cares.

If the elephants start dropping dead, maybe then the world will notice. Everyone likes elephants, right? Elephant zombies would really be something, their decomposing flesh dropping off in leathery sheets. They wouldn't be ignored.

I'll call my first real documentary film *The Zombie Apocalypse: The Future of Us*. It will make people notice. It will make them stop what they're doing and pay attention to what they've done to the Earth. What's more important than that?

Definitely not Soup Sanchez.

I flick through some photos and videos on my phone of me and Piper that I took over the summer. The selfies are always from the same angle, my arm reaching up with the camera, our heads together. Sometimes Soup is in the photos, sometimes he isn't. I've mostly avoided tagging along when they're together. It's hard to be the third wheel; it's hard to see her draped over his shoulders, her lips next to his ear.

I find a photo with him in it and I study his features, zoom in tight. He's an ordinary guy. Objectively, a little better-looking than normal. A *little*. But his nose is too pointy. His eyes are too close together. His cheeks are always dark with a beard that wants to grow in, making him look older than he is. My stomach clenches. I zoom back out again. In the photo, Piper is smiling so wide, it's like her face is splitting open.

I am a terrible friend.

I slide the screen off. Last night is already taking on a blurry quality, like an Instagram filter has been laid over the kiss, a vignette shadowing the outline.

"It wasn't real," I tell myself.

What's real is what is here right now: there is the green of the trees and the grass and the garden and the gardener and his music and the smell of fertilizer mixed with my sunscreen and the alcohol that's still oozing out of my pores. There is the beach just beyond that and the ocean with its dark depths and the swaying kelp and the smell of something rotten pushing through the smoke smell: sewage and decay. Farther out than that, a shadow in the distance, there is the island, glowing in the sunlight. There is the optimistic pink of my bikini, the way my skin has melted off and stuck me here, and I can't move and I can't do anything and I'm paralyzed with not knowing how to fix this thing that has to be fixed.

What's real is the future. My future and Piper's future and our plans. Next year, Europe. The year after, New York. That's when our real lives will start.

"I'm sorry," I say again.

"I hate you," she says, as clear as anything I've ever heard.

"Piper?" I say, swiveling around.

But no one is there, just a crow, so black it is almost blue, its head cocked, like "What is your problem, girl?"

"Sorry," I say. It disappears in a frantic flurry of flying. "Sorry!" I call again.

I don't cry a lot but I'm crying now. I don't think this can be fixed. I don't think she'll forgive me. And without Piper, what if I'm nobody?

Without Piper, I might not even exist.

* * *

The first thing I ever said to Piper was "Sorry."

The preschool was in a small red house with white trim that looked like a dollhouse. There were five steps leading to the front door, which had a huge door knocker shaped like a lion's head. It looked scary. My blood was rushing through my body too fast; my three-year-old heart was racing. I'd never been separated from my dad before. Mom always worked, but Dad stayed home with me right up until the day I started preschool. Everything was changing.

I've never been good at change.

My mom lifted the lion and knocked, and the sound of it hurt my ears. It felt like my brain was vibrating. She pushed the door open. I missed my dad so bad. I wanted to run down the street toward our house. I wanted to find him. To simply push back through the door and out onto the street and to get away, anywhere, anywhere, anywhere but here.

Then I saw Piper.

Her hair hung loose in shampoo-commercial waves. (Even then, I was easily seduced by good hair.) She was wearing head-to-toe purple, which to me, at three, made her look like someone from a movie. Her feet were slightly apart; she was taking up more room in the space than she actually took. It was like she was commanding the air around her.

In contrast, I felt dirty. Sticky. Small. My mouth was still sour from the chocolate milk my mom had let me drink in the car. I almost definitely had a milk mustache. My mom said goodbye and my knees went soft, like they did near the edges of high things or when something came on the TV screen that made Dad yell, "Look away!"

A boy came running up to me, disheveled and spitty. "You stink," he declared. He pushed me, hard, and I landed heavily beside Piper, elbow first, the pain rattling through my bone. She was lying down on the floor in a pool of rectangular sunlight, framed by the lines in the windows. The sun lit up the dust motes in a way that reminded me of home and I missed my mom and dad so intensely and my arm hurt so bad and I started to cry. I wanted to be anywhere but there.

I struggled off her and she grinned. Then she purred. I could see her invisible tail, her cat whiskers.

"Sorry," I mumbled, rubbing hard at my tears. I was scared of this magic half cat, half girl. Who wouldn't be?

"It's okay," she said. "I'm fine. Boys are dumb." Then, "Meow." Her teeth were tiny perfect squares.

"Meow," I said, deciding. I could have run away, but instead, I sat up and leaned toward her. I licked my own paw.

It was me and Piper against the world. Together.

* * *

There are a lot of ways to say "I'm sorry." I google the translations on my phone and start memorizing them. Memorizing stuff makes me feel like a better version of myself.

My mouth moves as I say out loud, crystal clear: "*Prosti menya*." Then, "Call me, Piper. Do it. Now."

The phone doesn't ring.

The wind pushes at the water in the bay in front of me, and white foam starts to break on the curved shore. The wind is hot. It's still so hot.

This summer, there has been a heat wave. It's September, but the sun seems unstoppable. Maybe it will stay hot forever. Maybe nothing will ever change. The heat shimmers over everything, blurring today with yesterday last week last month and forever. I lift my camera and point it at the sea, looking for whales. No fins break the surface.

I put the camera down.

I look at it.

I spin it on the table.

I think about everything it contains.

Things happen, or have already happened.

Sometimes I can't tell if something is a dream or real, if something happened or didn't.

Look.

A boy and girl set up their blanket on the beach in front of the house where the ground is layered with rocks the size of fists. It doesn't welcome sitters. It's lumpy and small and there's a rip current in the bay that makes it pretty dangerous for swimming. There are a lot of nicer beaches here. The best one is Smythes, with its silky-soft sand. Or Bay Beach, with its concession stand and lifeguards and music. This is a hard beach, alternating sand with surprisingly jagged rocks, rendering it unfriendly and usually empty.

There are also mosquitoes. The smell of decaying seaweed. The threat of raw sewage pushed in by the tide. The rope-and-driftwood swing hanging crookedly from a low branch on a leaning tree.

The blanket is one of those furry wolf blankets that probably smells musty and unwashed. The blanket looks familiar. Something about it makes me shiver, makes me want to climb out of myself and disappear. The girl has long, waist-length blond hair. Pretty hair. The boy has black hair. The girl is in a bright bikini. The boy is in trunks that look French. They are both thin and narrow-hipped, like models in an ad for Abercrombie & Fitch. The girl is barely sitting down before the boy starts to kiss her. It's hard to tell from here if she's enjoying it. His tongue is as fat and gross as a sea cucumber

20

launching itself into her mouth even as his hand grabs for her bikini bottom.

The girl pulls away and gets up from the blanket. It looks like she might come toward the house. I hope she does. I want her to. *Go*, I want to say. *Do it.* But instead, she runs into the sea, hopping on the rocks like they are hot potatoes, which they sort of are: some slippery, some even sharper than others because they are encrusted with barnacles. She is looking around, almost as if she is looking for help. There is something shimmery about the scene.

Something surreal. It is a mirage or a hallucination or both.

"This isn't really happening," I say out loud to myself, and I'm alone on the deck and no one is on the beach.

Am I going crazy?

Maybe.

The girl is so familiar.

It's like looking in a mirror.

Is it me?

She spins around and she's laughing in that fake come-and-get-me way that some girls do. It looks like she's acting, though. Something is off. But she's fine and it's a game and she's in control. I try to exhale.

There are jellyfish—a current from Hawaii that was created by the messed-up weather has brought thousands and thousands of lion's mane jellyfish drifting into the bay and up onto the rocks, their stinging bloodred tentacles splayed out like organ meat in the sun—which she has to step carefully to avoid. The girl hops over the rocks and kicks the water in the sea up in an arc, like a photo, like she's moving in actual slow motion and the water drops are following suit. Someone should be filming this or is or isn't or could be or didn't.

Then she wades out fast, in a half run, half skip.

The water is always so shockingly cold.

The girl splashes awkwardly in a messy front crawl. She probably used to be on the swim team. (I was on the swim team.) She probably took lessons at the pool, earned badges, tried hard. (Like me. Is it me?)

It can't be me.

She bobs in the distance for a few minutes and he shouts something and she laughs and goes under, coming up again like a seal, her hair now looking dark and sleek. The boy gets up and stubs his toe on something. Curses, sits down again. Yells something that the girl seems not to hear.

Then, finally, the girl comes splashing out again, safe, still alive, giggling, her body bright red from the cold water. She laughs and wobbles, hopping awkwardly over the rocky shoreline, not letting on how it was so icy it must have felt like needles piercing her skin, how now she probably can't feel anything at all from the neck down.

Numbness is necessary.

The boy is angry; his body language is clenched.

She laughs, pokes him in the shoulder.

He stands up, grabs the blanket. He throws it down again. She says something.

He pushes her.

Then he's on her and she's struggling and she's waving and shouting and someone is watching but she isn't coming and why isn't she going to help and no.

No.

I close my eyes, swallowing something bitter and acidic that's risen in my throat. My hands are shaking.

There is no one on the beach. The rising waves lap at the green-and-brown line of seaweed on the shore. It sounds like dogs drinking water, the slap of the waves against the stones.

I can't breathe. I have to bend over and force air in and out, in and out.

It takes a few minutes of concentrating before I feel okay again, before I can sit up.

The sky keeps pressing down on me, blue and judgmental. The angry sun shines right through me and how I feel.

"If no one saw, it didn't happen," I tell myself, my voice chopping up the sky into pieces.

"Stop talking to yourself," Piper would say. "You sound

crazy. You're one step away from being that guy on the corner shouting 'THE END IS NIGH.'"

"The end probably *is* nigh," I tell Piper's absence. "We're just too dumb to know it. Ask the whales. Ask the antelope. Anyway, I'm sorry."

"Too late," she says. "You're dead to me."

"People make mistakes." I plead my case to a june bug that has rattled to a landing on the arm of my chair. There are certain things I'd never say to Piper, not out loud, but the bug is a safe audience. "I'll never talk to him again," I tell it. "He's just . . . Soup. He's not important. Not to me." The june bug is unconvinced. It spreads its iridescent wings and vanishes, clicking. "You're right," I call after it. "I hate me, too."

It's easy to hate myself when Piper isn't here to tell me not to.

My skin feels prickly. I have goose bumps, even though I'm sweating, the hot wind blowing the sun into me like fire that my lungs can't quite breathe in.

She's thinking about me. I know she is. I can feel it.

That's how connected we are, whether we want to be or not.

I squeeze my eyes shut, tight. "Sorry, sorry, sorry," I murmur.

The phone rings on the table, making me jump.

I hold up the phone so that I can see the screen. *S Sullivan*, it says. So she's at home, not on her cell. Piper is always losing her phone and never seems to care. She's like Hansel or Gretel, whichever one dropped bread crumbs in the woods, except what she drops are brand-new iPhones. BlackBerries. Samsungs. None of them upsets her. She claims it's a Buddhist thing, to not get attached to stuff. Piper is Buddhist when it's convenient, but mostly the only thing she believes is that everything will work out for her in the end, and it always does.

It's not really fair.

The phone stops ringing.

If Piper weren't beautiful, she'd just be another smart geek, relegated to the social backwaters of Physics Club. She doesn't care about being smart.

She'd rather be me.

This is one of the fights that we're having without saying anything. This is one of the things that's come between us, ugly and true.

She wants what I have: a clear idea of what I want to do with my life and exactly how I'm going to get there.

And I get it, because I've spent a lot of my life wanting to be her.

"She's a bit mean to you, Sloane," my mom always says. "I think it's too intense, this thing with you two. You need more friends, a group of friends. I worry about you. You don't always have to dress alike, you know."

"She's not mean," I insist, even when I know it's sort of true. "I have plenty of friends," I lie.

Me and Piper are a *thing*. Piper and Soup are a *thing*.

Which means that me and Soup are nothing, like multiplying something by zero. No matter how many times I go back to that equation in my head, the answer stays the same.

The phone keeps singing again in my hand. I'm safe to not answer because she'll call back and call back and call back and then I can be the one to be mad, a bit standoffish, in control.

My grip is loose and the phone slips out of it and falls to the deck, which makes me think of that time when we were six, in first grade, and I held the class gerbil for the first time. "Don't squish him!" Piper squealed. She was scared of rodents. ("The way they wiggle," she said. "Yuck.")

I love animals, all animals, always, and anyway, he was the cutest. I kissed him gently on the nose, not squeezing, and he looked right into my eyes, like he loved me back a little. I didn't often feel braver than Piper, but she shivered when my lips touched his and it made me feel bigger and better. But it turns out that I loved that dumb gerbil to death: instead of squashing him, he slipped out of my hand and onto the floor. Piper shrieked and jumped and somehow pushed me, and I stepped on him by mistake. The furry crunch was the worst feeling I ever had.

The phone goes silent.

"*Je suis désolé*," I say dramatically. "*Es tut mir leid. Barkatu.*"

I reach for the silent phone, filling myself up with sorries until I have enough. Swahili and Slavic. They feel like poetry in my mouth. They'll protect me from Piper's anger, if she's still angry.

If.

"*Unnskyld,*" I whisper. "*Samahani.*"

I could make a documentary called *Sorry: The Piper and Sloane Story*. Documentaries often have subtitles. The subtitle of me is Piper.

I would interview people on the street. "Who do you want to apologize to?" I'll ask. "What do you need to be forgiven for?"

The only time I feel okay asking people questions is when I have my camera in my hand. The familiar weight of it anchors me at the same time as letting me be someone who is not quite me. I pick it up from the table right now—it's always within a few feet of me—and put it up to my eye. I hit record, and start filming the sky. "What are you sorry for?" I intone, panning the camera slowly across the sun. When I put the camera down, there's a huge sun spot over my vision. "I'm blind," I murmur. "I'm blind."

Is Piper ever sorry? She must be. Besides, everyone wants

to get this kind of thing off them, put it out there, save themselves, be forgiven. Even if they don't believe in God, which I don't. But I believe in karma.

And everyone is sorry for something.

The phone screen cracked when it dropped on the deck. I pick it up and run my finger over the long seam of the crack and it comes away with a line of blood. I lick it clean. It tastes like pennies. We are all copper inside.

A seagull flies by, crapping on the deck right next to my foot. I flip him off. "The bird!" I say to him. "I'm flipping you the bird, Bird." The seagull laughs. "You're a good audience," I tell him. "What are you sorry for?"

The phone rings. The seagull circles and then flaps away.

I look at the screen.

Philip Sanchez.

My heart drops all the way through the deck and onto the front lawn and rolls down the driveway like in a cartoon.

"I'm dead," I whisper.

Soup.

I take a sip of my horrible diluted soda. Mr. Aberley, the old man from the other side of the bay, is slowly rowing his half-submerged dinghy on his first trip to the island. He does it twice a day: at dawn and at dusk. "After breakfast and after supper," he says. "Keeps my girlish figure." He laughs his old man laugh, teeth exposed, showing his receding purplish gums. Mr. Aberley keeps himself impeccable, reads *Vogue*, dresses better than I do. But his teeth give the game away. I hope I never get old. Not that I want to die young, but still, his *gums*.

The phone rings and rings. My voice mail must be full. My heart is beating so hard, I press my hand to my chest.

No one ever calls Soup "Philip." He has been Soup ever since third grade when Mrs. Moffat helped everyone to "discover" their heritage and it turned out that he was a mix of every race anyone could even name. *You are like human soup*, Mrs. Moffat had said thoughtlessly, the racist cow, and it stuck, as things do in small schools, forever.

I slide my finger on the screen to answer, leaving a red smear, but my voice is stuck and nothing comes out.

"Hey," he says, without waiting for me to talk. "Sloane." There's a silence. Then, "Is Piper with you?"

I let the question hang in the air and then I say, more cruelly than I actually feel, "Actually, she's busy traveling back in time to stop your parents from making the fatal mistake of ever screwing without a condom." I don't know why I said it. I don't know how to unsay it. "Soup," I say, more softly.

"Wow," he says over me. "That's not what I was expecting,

I guess. I need a second to digest that. That's pretty harsh." He coughs. Then, "We've gotta talk, Sloane."

I can't decide how to respond, so I don't say anything at all. *I love you*, I think, but don't say. *I'm sorry. Anteeksi. Prosti menya.* I might be crying, or maybe it's only sweat running down my cheeks in salty rivers.

It takes him a long time to hang up. He breathes into the speaker, in and out, in and out. The sound of his breathing makes my own breathing slow down. I feel sleepy and warm. I can hear a car going by, then the lower roar of a bus in the far distance. Then finally, he clears his throat and clicks off without saying goodbye.

"Well, goodbye, *Philip*," I say to the echo in my ear that he leaves behind.

I pull more and more paint off the chair and drop it onto the shingles of the roof, where it looks like flakes of the sky, falling.

"The sky is falling, the sky is falling!" I whisper.

I put another cigarette into the cigarette holder and light it. I don't know when I became a smoker for real. The first time, it made me puke, but I kept doing it because Piper did and now I couldn't stop even if I wanted to, though the truth is, it's gross. It makes me feel like I'm coated in a sticky dust, the taste of it on my teeth, the scent on my skin. It's just one more thing about myself that I don't quite understand. How did it happen? When, exactly? The holder, which I stole from Grandma's jewelry box when she used to have a room downstairs, is made from an elephant's tusk. Her room had these white velvet curtains that had turned yellow from the smoke. Mom took the curtains down when Grandma moved out. She replaced them with blinds that go up and down at the touch of a button. She took Grandma's bed out and replaced it with a stair climber and an elliptical trainer.

Grandma won't miss it. She's completely out of it. She lives in an old-folks' home now, where she sits in a chair with an oxygen tank beside her and stares out her window all day, remembering something she can't articulate but keeps trying to say, phlegm swirling around in her lungs, her cough keeping her neighbor awake. The veins in her hands droop down like yarn. Sometimes I go there and sit in her room. Grandma doesn't exactly have conversations. It's hard. It makes me feel panicky, like I can't breathe, like I'm going to die.

The only sounds are the rustle of her polyester shirt as she reaches to push her glasses up her nose, the harsh sounds of her breathing in and out of the tank, and the sound of my sneakers, squeaking on the floor as I leave. Being there makes me too aware of my own racing heart.

It's obviously wrong to use ivory for anything, but it's not like Grandma went out and killed the elephant herself. Maybe the elephant didn't even die. Maybe someone just found the tusk, lying there, a hapless victim of some kind of elephant sickness or something. Maybe that elephant recovered and now is running around with one tusk, trumpeting at the sky, or whatever elephants do when they aren't being shot at for their ivory.

Probably not.

Elephants bury their dead. I try to make the fact of that in combination with the cigarette mean something, but I can't.

The things people are willing to kill for are so stupid.

I take another lungful and hold it in until it burns.

Then, again, after forever or a few minutes, the phone rings: *S Sullivan*. I'm flooded with relief. That's how it is with Piper and me. I clear my throat and I slide my sweaty finger across the screen and take a deep breath.

"*Anteeksi*," I say dramatically. I pull the middle syllable out nice and long. Then I exhale, a perfect smoke ring. I wait for Piper to say something back, something sharp and clever but forgiving, like that.

But instead, her mother's voice comes on the line. It sounds weird, tight, high-pitched. "Sloane, is that you? I need to speak to your mother. Can you put your mother on the phone?"

The way she says "your mother" makes my skin hurt and

a ringing start in my ears. She sounds like she did the day she flung open the door to Piper's bathroom, where the two of us had been bleaching our eyebrows, and calmly told us that Piper's father's plane had crashed somewhere over the Atlantic. I couldn't tell what were real tears and what was the bleach fumes, stinging my eyes. Piper's dad was pretty much a stranger to me. I'd only met him twice. But it was my tragedy, too, because it was Piper's.

"There were no survivors," Piper's mom said. She sounded like a talking head on CNN, like she was simply delivering news. It took me a minute to understand that I was crying and Piper was crying because Piper's dad was dead. Piper fell sideways into the bathtub, cutting her forehead on the shower tap, the beautiful bright red of her blood dripping into her golden hair. My head hurt for a week after that.

Right now, we are platinum blond.

I touch my stupid, ugly short hair. *Our* hair.

It looks better on Piper than on me. On her, it's gamine. On me, it just looks shorn. I know I'm supposed to say something now to Piper's mom but I don't know what it is. My brain is suddenly thick with fog. I can't find any words.

Piper's mom is crying now. She is crying hard. She is talking like she's not crying or maybe like she hasn't noticed that she is. The cry is more of a moan that I can feel underneath my skin, buzzing like static. It is unbearable.

"Stop," I say. "Stop doing that." I can't stand it. My eyes water and I can't blame bleach this time. She doesn't stop. "STOP!" I shout.

Piper's mom is supposed to be in Hong Kong. She's a flight attendant. She is not coming back until next Thursday, Piper said. She's working on starting a business over there, importing strings of pearls to North America. Pearls are cheaper in Hong Kong.

Today is Saturday. "It's only Saturday," I say, more quietly.

She says, "Sloane. Your mother." Then, "Please."

Mom has gone into work, but I can't seem to say that. My words are scabbing in my throat, dry and hard. I can't breathe. I cough. Tonight Piper and I are having a huge party at Piper's house. We are celebrating the start of our last year at Rogers. "The party," Piper said, "that will set the tone for all other parties." (But that was before last night, the biggest worst best party I'd ever seen.)

I have a terrible feeling. It's not that I'm choking, it's something else. Something inside me is collapsing.

My logical brain keeps trying to interrupt: maybe her mom found out about the party. I've already bought watermelons that are right now piled up in Piper's living room, two deep, absorbing the vodka we carefully injected with huge syringes. "Junkie melons," Piper said. She put the pics on her feed. "When melons go bad," she typed. "Support clean needle sites for melons." She drew sad faces on the watermelons.

"Sloane, *now*," Piper's mom says again, and a sound comes out of her that peels my skin away in sheets.

"Where is she?" I say, in someone else's voice. "Where is Piper? Is this about the party?" But I know that isn't it. I already know. I knew. Maybe I've known for this whole morning. I'm drifting entirely away from myself and up into the sky, where I can see myself below in the blue chair. Flakes of me fall onto the roof like feathers from a zombie bird.

I'm the zombie apocalypse.

I'm the dead.

Am I?

"Tell me." My voice is a tape recorder and the battery has run out. My words are thick and coagulated. "Tellll meeee."

"Sloane," she screams. What is left of my insides is made of glass. The glass shatters and falls up like sharp rain and maybe that's why the sky is falling in pieces all around me, bringing birds down with it, dead before they hit the ground.

The gardener starts the hedge trimmer and the roar fills up the world, which is now entirely a blue bowl of noise. I can't hear anything at all.

"I can't hear you," I say, panicked. "I can't hear you! What? I can't hear!"

I think she says, "Sloane, I need you." Or maybe she says, "Sloane, I need you to . . ."

And I say it, I say, "She's dead, isn't she? Is Piper dead? Tell me."

The word "dead" catches in my throat and I start to choke. I press the lit end of the cigarette into the flesh of my leg. I lie down on the deck. The wood is burning hot. My skin is bubbling off. Nothing is safe.

Nowhere.

I'm still holding the phone and I can't hear anything but a roar that's inside the blue sky of my skull, which is inside out. I smell flesh burning but I still can't feel it and so I press harder and harder until the cigarette breaks and falls away.

"I can't feel it," I say between coughs. I'm choking. My lungs are hands, grappling for air. "I can't feel anything."

The sky is crumpling up and I see a freckling of stars that can't be there, but are, and a halo of light that is coming from the sea or everywhere.

I'm talking in slow motion but I'm not talking, I'm screaming, but I'm not screaming either, I'm moaning.

I'm silent. I am silence.

"Sloane?" the phone squawks. "SLOANE."

I throw the phone up into the sky and it somersaults, mirrored against the too-blue brightness, down onto the lawn, where the sprinklers have come on with a *rat-a-tat* machine-gun fire. And even as it is midflight, still falling, a police cruiser crunches onto the gravel of the long, curved driveway.

That's when I know for sure that I'm right.

Then I hear her, her voice cutting cleanly into the mess of everything.

Look what you did, she says, as real as I am. *I'm the price we paid.*

And then nothing nothing nothing just the sound of my own scream curling around my head like smoke.

BEFORE

"THERE'S NOTHING WRONG WITH YOU," Piper says. She's leaning on the counter of the mall store where she's working for the summer. The store sells quirky fashion. She's wearing a baby doll dress and combat boots like it's 1993. She looks great, of course. She looks perfect.

I'm sitting on the floor in my going-to-the-gym leggings and an old T-shirt of Dad's from the eighties—FRANKIE SAYS RELAX, it says—over a sports bra that is digging uncomfortably into my ribs. From here, I have a good view of her legs and shoes. I have to awkwardly look up to see her properly, my head banging against a shelf labeled RETURNS AND GROSS, where they put the things that are brought back dirty or damaged, things that can't be resold.

"I can see up your nose," I tell her. "It's not pretty from down here. Why do I have to hide? Can't I pretend to shop or something?"

"I told you," she says impatiently. "I don't want to get fired. You never know when they'll be watching."

"I'm not sure *they* would appreciate me being behind the counter more than they'd appreciate me trying on that weird fairy dress"—I point to the rack of glittery pale pink wafting dresses that are moving in the breeze generated by a carefully positioned fan—"and maybe buying it."

"You'd look terrible in that dress," she says. "Pale pink washes you out." She goes over and takes it off the rack and holds it up to herself, squinting in the mirror. "Exactly zero people who have tried this on look good in it. You know what they look like? Adults playing reverse dress-up. Why do grown women want to look like three-year-olds in ballet class?"

"You'd look good in it," I say flatly, because it's annoying but it's also true.

She disappears behind the mirror-sequined curtain and emerges in the dress. She looks gorgeous. She's left the boots on, which somehow only make it look prettier. "Yeah, you're washed out," I lie. "Take it off. This sucks. The floor is cold. I could sit on a chair or something. I'll hold really still. I'll be a mannequin."

She shrugs, twirls over (literally), and pats me on the head, before vanishing back behind the curtain. "You're a good friend," she calls. "I'd die without you, remember? And today it would be death by boredom. Who goes to the mall on a Saturday in July when it's perfect weather? Only losers."

"I'm here," I point out.

"Exactly," she says. "Ha ha. I'm kidding. Anyway, stay."

"Woof," I say.

She comes back, dressed in her own clothes, and reaches up to the shelf behind the counter and changes the music from one satellite station to the next. The tinny pop hurts my ears. "You have terrible taste in music," I say. "How can we still be friends when you voluntarily listen to Katy Perry? It's an abomination."

She sticks out her tongue and hoists herself up onto the counter, where she dances, giddily, until she falls off, somehow landing on her feet.

"Oops," she laughs.

"Show-off," I mumble.

Piper's legs are as smooth as wax, brown from the summer sun already. My legs need shaving. They look like ghost legs next to hers. I need a tan, but I don't want to get cancer. We're all only one sunburn away from a fatal diagnosis. Not that it stops me from smoking, which fails the logic test, I know.

"I need a cigarette," she says, reading my mind. She takes

a few sips from a huge smoothie that I brought for her. "Oh, shhhh," she says, even though I'm not talking.

"I didn't say—"

She kicks me in the shin.

"Hey," I say.

"Can I help you?" she says. I can't see who she's talking to, but she's using her fake British accent, so I know it's a boy. Or a man. Someone male.

If I were filming this, I'd contrast it against a jungle scene. A lioness circling a dopey antelope. The dopey antelope not understanding until it's too late that he's been destroyed, the lioness already tearing the flesh from his neck.

"Um, yeah." I hear his antelope-y voice. "I'm looking for, like, a gift."

"Oooh, for your girlfriend?" she purrs. Even from here, I can tell she is doing that *thing* with her tongue. A pressing of her tongue against her top teeth. It's a new thing that she does that drives me nuts, and boys love it. I want to push the back of her knee so she falls over, laughing, in a heap next to me. I sit on my hands. This is Piper 2.0: The Sexy Years. Maybe a month or two from now she'll say, "I was acting! Couldn't you tell? I thought you were in on it. Boys are so dumb, amirite? So *obvious*."

But it's been at least three months now. Maybe more. Maybe it's happened gradually over the last year or even two and I didn't notice when it started. When people change, that's how they do it: too slowly to be seen.

Maybe I've changed, too. I pick at my cuticle. I put my own tongue on my lip but it feels ugly, not seductive. I look like Grandma, drool and all, not Piper, who always looks great.

"No, no," the man-boy says. "No girlfriend. I don't have . . . I mean, I do, but . . ." His lie is so obvious, I want to giggle. "It's for my, um, sister?"

Piper steps over my legs and goes around the counter. "Is she my size?" she says. And I know when she says this, she's spinning for him slowly. I know he's into it. I know he's into her. I know that's why he came into this shop—maybe on a bet or a dare from his buddy—and I know what he wants.

And I know that she knows, that she's playing. But I really don't like the game.

I slip my earbuds into my ears and dial up a podcast. I turn it up loud. I hope they can hear it. She'll be annoyed with me after, but I don't care. The podcast is called *Stuff You Should Know*. This one is about extinction. Did you know that over fifty million different species have lived on this planet at one time or another? Almost all of them are dead.

Gone.

Wiped out.

I close my eyes and let the voice in my ear fill me up. I find facts calming, even when they are terrifying. I definitely enjoy listening to podcasts more than I like watching Piper flirt another guy into buying a tiny cashmere sweater that she's modeled for him that he doesn't want (or have anyone to give to). When he returns that sweater, it's definitely going on the Gross Shelf, that's for sure. She accidentally on purpose drops a lace tank top over the counter. It lands on my head and gets stuck on my messy ponytail, my gym hair.

I take out one earbud. "So, do you go to school?" I hear him say.

"For now," she says. "I'm really a filmmaker, though." My stomach clenches. I'm *the filmmaker*, I want to say. Let me have at least that. "I'm hoping to make a movie about—"

I put the earbud back in before I can hear her taking everything of mine for herself. I close my eyes. The podcast ends and I let the next one start up without caring what it is. Trees. It's about trees. The floor is cold and hard under me and my tailbone is starting to ache. I'll get up and go, I decide. I'll skip the gym and I'll walk home. It's a perfect Pacific Northwest day. Hot, but not too hot. Maybe I'll stop for a frozen mocha from the coffee truck that parks near the mall parking lot. Better than mall coffee by a mile. I love those things.

Trees, the podcast intones, *have a symbiotic relationship with a fungus that grows hairlike on their roots and attaches them to other trees. If you looked at a map of trees' roots, you'd see they were all connected. You'd see everything that they share.*

There is maybe a fungus that has woven me to Piper.

Piper is the fungus, invading my roots.

It's symbiotic, of course.

But what am I getting?

It's more parasitic than that.

I turn it off and leave the earbuds in, so I can hear her still, but it's muffled. Her laugh—like a creaky gate—leaks through. She's always laughed like that, ever since I can remember. It's a little kid's laugh that she never outgrew. I smile because I can't help it. The creaky-gate laugh is contagious.

She steps back around the counter and nudges me with her boot while she rings him up. He must be able to see me, my legs, my shoes. He doesn't mention me. I wonder if he's averting his eyes on purpose. I wonder if he knows that I'm laughing at him.

"Thank you *so* much," she says. "She's going to look so hot in that."

He laughs nervously, then he's gone, $78 poorer. I hope it was worth it, the poor idiot.

"What was *that*?" I say.

She laughs, pulls my earbuds out with a dramatic hand movement. "Why are you mad?" she says. "I'm working, remember? This is my jooooooob."

I roll my eyes. "Did you get his number?"

"It's not like that," she says. "He wanted a sweater. For his girlfriend slash sister. For his sister, who is also his girlfriend." She pauses. "And his cousin." She laughs. "Come on, that was funny!"

I shrug. "What he actually wanted isn't exactly for sale," I mumble under my breath.

"What's *wrong* with you?" she says.

"There's *everything* wrong with me," I say, which is true, but I can't explain. It's not only this latest version of Piper, this tongue-on-teeth Piper, that's my problem. It's more than that. It's *me*. I'm changing. I feel like I'm growing out of my life. Nothing fits right and everything is an irritating seam that's pressing into my skin. If I were a tree, I'd be one that was painfully pushing out of my own bark, splintering down the sides. But without bark, trees die.

I don't know how to say it without sounding crazy. I can just imagine what she'd say: *Trees? What?* I can imagine her creaky-gate laugh, *at* me, not with me.

"I'm going to go," I say. "I'm going to the gym." I don't move, though.

She slides down next to me, our backs pressed against the canvas bags that she gives to customers who spend more than $100. They smell like rope and potatoes. Dirt. They were probably made by kids in India or Bangladesh for a penny a day, or worse. The last doc that I watched was about the factories where they make cheap clothes for Old Navy and the

Gap. It made me want to cry, all those young girls, our age. Younger. Hunched over sewing machines so we can have $5 tank tops.

I scratch my neck.

"I'm just bored," I lie. "I'm sorry."

"Maybe you're just *boring*," she says.

"Ouch. That's actually mean. Even for you."

"I was *joking*," she says. She makes a face, drapes her arm around my back, kisses my hair. "Take a joke. God."

I shrug her arm off me. "Don't touch," I say. "I don't feel like being touched."

"This *conversation* is getting boring."

"Sorry," I say automatically. Even though I'm not.

"Whatever," she says. Her head is bent over her phone, her thumbs moving across the screen, rapid-fire.

"Soup?" I say.

She nods without looking up.

I hate Soup.

I love Soup.

I have so many feelings about Soup that I can't share and I don't know what to do with.

I have no feelings about Soup.

Why would I?

He's Piper's boyfriend.

Soup, with Piper, makes me think of moths and how they

are always fluttering around the porch light. If they had a brain at all, they'd understand that the bulb was going to adhere to their wings, burn them up into nothing but dust.

I've had a crush on Soup since fourth grade.

"We could go to the beach when you're done with work," I say. "Have a fire or something?"

"What?" she says without waiting for an answer. "Oh my God, he's so funny."

"What did he say?"

She laughs and bites her lip. This stuff with her mouth is so awful. I'm fixated on it in an unhealthy way. I stare. I read somewhere about a wife murdering her husband because of the sound of his chewing. This is like that, but worse. "Don't *do* that," I say, before I can stop myself.

"Do what?" she says, still typing.

"Forget it," I say, even though she already has. My heart is beating double time, the anxiety sweeping over me like a stealth wave, catching me unprepared. "I'm going to go work out," I manage. I pull myself up and grab my gym bag.

"You're thin enough already," Piper says. "You're thinner than me."

"It's not about being thin; I just like it. I feel like sweating."

She shrugs. "Sure, okay, whatever. But don't get so small we can't share clothes."

"Priorities, amirite?" I say, laughing, or trying to laugh.

When I'm panicky, everything feels like an act. Fake. "Later, alligator hater."

She raises her hand in farewell, already typing with her other thumb.

"In a while, vile crocodile," she murmurs, but it's an afterthought. She doesn't even look up as I go, knocking the ballet pink dress off its hanger as I pass. It doesn't make any sound at all as it drifts slowly down to the floor.

From the escalator, going up to the top floor, I can see the rows of treadmills lined up at the floor-to-ceiling windows in the gym, with a view down to the food court. The sight of them gives me vertigo, and my vision trips and tilts. I try to steady myself by taking a long, slow breath in, but the air feels too manufactured to breathe, metallic and air-conditioned. I'm going to faint. The gray light of an oncoming spell shivers at the edge of everything, like the vignette feature in Instagram.

I force myself to look down at my feet. *See something. Feel something. Smell something. Touch something.* I call that the Four Somethings, and I use them to stave off panic attacks. It doesn't always work.

The escalator is moving so slowly but my legs don't want to move to take me up faster. I don't want to go up. I want to go down. My heart is racing. I have to get out of here; I can hear my own raspy breathing, too fast, too fast. When I get to the top, I'll turn around and go down the opposite way. I'll run to the exit, out into the heat. I'll skip the bus, run home, pounding the ground with my feet (feel something), dripping with sweat (smell something), squinting through the shimmering heat on the sidewalk (see something). I'll—

"Hey, Sloane!"

On the opposite escalator, I see Soup.

My heart skitters.

He's pretty much the last person who I wanted to see and the only person I wanted to see. Seeing him makes me hate myself.

I raise my hand in a half wave, force my face into something that might be similar to something friendly but probably makes me look like I'm about to puke.

"No!" he calls. "I mean, wait there! I need to ask you something! To talk to you!"

The escalator pushes me off at the top, my shoelace almost getting stuck in the mechanism. For a second, I illogically picture bare toes getting stuck in the corrugated metal. The crunch of flesh. Blood. Quickly, I aim for a bench, put my head between my knees.

Soup bounds up the escalator.

"Are you okay? What are you doing?"

"I'm not fainting, that's what," I say to the smooth brown tiles on the floor. There's a piece of chewed gum down there. A clump of mysterious hair, like someone cleaned out a hairbrush and just dropped it on the ground. My own ponytail is touching the ground. "People are gross," I add, lifting my hair up with one hand.

"What?" he says. He drops to his knees, his face peering around my calf. "It's hard to hear you. Man, it's filthy on this floor. Good thing this isn't a hospital."

I laugh without meaning to. "I don't think hospitals are that clean either. I saw a doc that did an undercover—" I stop myself. I'm sure he doesn't care. "Anyway, I'm okay," I say. "Low blood pressure. I get dizzy."

"Weirdo," he says. "But seriously, do you need . . . something? Water?" He rests his hand on my back gently and I lurch up quickly. His hand makes me think of the softness of chickens. It makes me want to scream.

The world tilts and then rights. Tibetan monks can control the rate of their pulse by thinking about it. I *will* mine to slow down. Slooooooow. Slow. Come on. "I'm fine. I'm just. I was on my way . . . I'm going to work out."

"Uh," he says. "Is that a good idea? I'm not a doctor, but I feel like fainting and working out are not super compatible." He sits down next to me. "Did you ever notice that malls smell exactly like hospitals?"

"And schools," I say. "I think it's cheap floor cleaner. Why are you so obsessed with hospitals?"

"I wouldn't say *obsessed*," he says. "Well, maybe I'm a little obsessed with smells." He sniffs my hair. "You smell like shampoo and cigarettes, honey and . . . Orange Julius?"

"Strawberry," I say. "Smoothie, homemade, organic. Not a mall drink. This body is a temple!"

He grins. "But you smoke. So your body is a pretty polluted church. And hospitals, malls, and schools all use the same pine-scented crap to remind you that you're going to die, so you might as well buy more stuff because everything is temporary."

I whistle. "Dark, dude. That's really dark. But you don't buy anything at school. What is school selling?"

He shrugs. "College costs money. They want you to go to college. Spend more. Get into the system." He leans back and looks at me through half-closed eyes. "Everyone dies," he says. "Get used to it, Sloane Whittaker." When he says my name, goose bumps rise on my arm.

"Riiiiiight," I say, tucking the hair that's escaped from my ponytail behind my ears. "Well, I've got to go outrun death with some running."

"A lot of people die on treadmills." He nudges me with his leg. "Think about it."

"You are *such* a ray of sunshine today. What's going on? You should go talk to your girlfriend. She'll cheer you up."

He laughs, his eyes crinkling at the corners. Not that I notice. I don't think Soup is cute. He's Piper's boyfriend. He's Piper's new best friend. I remember to be annoyed with him: I hate him.

I don't hate him.

But I don't have a crush on him anymore. Not since he started going out with Piper.

It ended then.

It did.

Even though Soup Sanchez has it all going on. Dark sense of humor. Artist. Smiling eyes. Quirky. Weird fashion sense. Odd enough to be interesting while still pulsing with street cool. Better yet, he doesn't know it. He has no idea that he's attractive. He hangs out with Fatty and Charlie and he probably thinks they're the good-looking ones: all-American, athletes, fast car-driving loudmouths. Future Frat Boys of America.

He's so wrong.

He's different and so much better.

I hate myself.

"I really, *really* have to go," I tell him. "The treadmill is calling my name." I put my hand up to my ear like I'm hearing it, then I feel stupid and pretend to be scratching my head instead, which is worse, because I probably look like I have lice. I don't know what to do with my hand, so I let it drop down by my side, awkwardly, like it's not really part of me.

"Right," he says. "I wanted to talk to you about Piper's birthday. See if you want to plan something? Like, I don't know, a surprise? A party? She loves parties. You guys are good at parties."

I raise my eyebrows. "Sweet," I say coolly, like I'd forgotten, which I hadn't. "First birthday that you've been together. Don't mess it up. You know she has high standards."

"I know! That's why I need you to do it right," he says. "She's . . ." His voice trails off.

"I've known her for a long time," I say. "I know what she's like. Anyway, you have to figure the gift out for yourself, Ponyboy. I've got the party covered."

"Ponyboy?" he says, and I should have known he wouldn't get the reference. I'd thought he was interesting enough to have read *The Outsiders*, but I guess if it's not on YouTube, he probably hasn't heard of it, just like every boy, ever.

"I'm more of a Sodapop," he says. "Or maybe I'm Bob?"

"Makes sense," I say, relieved that he knows the characters, after all. I don't know why it matters, but it does. It really does. "Piper is Cherry, then, and I'm what's-her-name, the friend."

"Marcia," he says, nodding. "Nobody remembers Marcia's name."

"Yeah, well, don't get stabbed, Bob," I say.

"Everyone secretly has a crush on Marcia," he goes on.

"She's really the hot one. But no one can see past Cherry's blinding obviousness."

I blush. For a second, I can't talk, which is ridiculous, like this whole ridiculous conversation is ridiculous. "Everyone?" I say at the same time as I say, "Ridiculous?" So what comes out is something like, "Ridicu-one?"

He stares at me, a smile twitching at the corner of his mouth. He's not very tall when he's sitting down, one of those guys who has all his height in his legs. I look into his eyes, which are brown and laughing. At me. I force myself to look somewhere else. Anywhere else. At his knees. At my own knees. "Are you blushing?"

"No!" I say. "Anyway, reading *The Outsiders* doesn't make you cool. You have to do more than that to win me over."

"Do I need to win you over? Besides, who says I read it?" he says. "It was a dope movie, though."

"Duh," I say. "Figures. I *really* have to go." I grab my gym bag and stand up. My arm feels like lead, the bag too heavy to carry the entire way to the locker room. My legs feel shaky and strange, like they always do after a panic attack. "Paint her a picture," I say as I walk away. "A portrait, you know?" I know that's what she wants, and I just handed it to him and she'll think he thought of it himself and go even more crazy for him. The perfect gift. She'll love it. He'll probably even get her to finally get naked. They've been together now for over a

month. Long enough. Most boys don't have that kind of pa-
tience, at least not the ones that I've met. You wouldn't catch
Charlie Nevers waiting three weeks or even three days. Fatty
is basically a date rapist in the making, always talking about
girls like they're only alive to be used for sex. I remind myself
that Soup is friends with those idiots. And staying friends
with them is an act of misogyny, if you think about it.

At the very least, it makes him an idiot, too.

"Too obvious!" he calls after me, but I'm pushing through
the gym door, the glass door squeaking loudly, the sound of
the gym's loud music pouring out onto the mezzanine. It's
pretty easy to pretend I didn't hear him. It's pretty easy to pretend that I don't care. I stopped caring the very second they
hooked up.

I did.

I really did.

It started in May. Summer, the season, began early. The sun
seared everything with a sharp, unrelenting heat. It felt cosmic,
like everything was heightened because this summer would
be our last school-vacation summer. Everything felt huge and
glittery and important and life-changing.

We went to the beach a lot, on our lunch break, after school, our skin browning dangerously under the UV rays, highlights in our too-long hair.

We sifted sand through our fingers, feeling the silky luxuriousness of our lives.

"Every grain of sand represents a possible future," said Piper. "Think about it. We can do anything. We can be anything. We can choose anything."

I blew a few grains of sand off my already-golden-brown knee. I took in a deep breath and felt like I could float away, light as a balloon. Everything felt so *possible*.

"You just blew away the future!" She laughed. "Those might have been our best ones."

"Goodbye, futures," I said. "I never liked you anyway!"

She laughed harder. When we were eight or nine, her mostly absent dad gave her a lobster for her birthday. The lobster was small and blue and cute. I was so jealous. My parents said no to a fish tank, no to any pets. My dad has allergies, but no one is allergic to a lobster. "Too much trouble," they said. "We wouldn't be able to travel."

But we never traveled. Mom's job kept her schedule full six or seven days a week. "One day," they promised. "You'll see." I could have had a lifetime of dogs and cats, hedgehogs and ferrets. I could have at least had a fish or a bird, a lizard. I would have even taken a snake.

The lobster came in a clear plastic cube. He looked like a toy, but when she ripped off the paper, he waved his little claw like he was saying hello. "For your tank," the card read. Piper's dad left the fish tank behind when he left her mom for "some skanky ho." Piper's words, not mine. I always kind of assume that there are two sides to every story, and I'll never know the skanky hos her dad was with, because he's dead now.

Either way, I try not to judge.

The fish tank had been against the wall of her room forever and the fish themselves never changed, ghostly white and huge and blank and slow. A man came to take care of the tank once a week. The fish seemed to never be quite alive, but never dead either. They spent their days swimming so lazily they could have been drifting on the current from the pump, aimlessly bouncing from one end of the tank to the other. The lobster, I supposed, was meant to make the tank cuter and more kid-friendly, to make it hers.

"It looks like a spider," she'd whispered to me. "I don't want it."

"What will you name it?" I'd said, desperate for something of my own to name. Anything. A puppy. A mouse. A ghost.

"Dad," she'd said. "I'm going to name it Dad."

That night, while we slept, the fish became something we didn't expect: murderers. In the morning, all that was left of the lobster was the shell and the claws, lying scattered across the bottom of the tank like a massacre. The fish had no teeth. They must have suctioned onto his body so hard that he was torn apart. I can remember the terror that had gripped me when I looked, how my heart had stuttered in my chest and I had tried not to faint or throw up or cry or all three.

"Oh no," said her mom. "Oh, that's terrible. Your father is an idiot. What was he thinking?" She hugged Piper tightly, even though Piper struggled to get free. She wasn't sad, I could tell. Just relieved.

"We'll have a funeral," her mom said.

We took the lobster's remains to the beach and threw them into the waves. "Say a few words," said her mom.

"Well," said Piper. "Goodbye, Dad." She lowered her voice to a whisper. "I never really liked you anyway." I choked on my shocked laugh, and when her mom finally walked away, we doubled over, clutching our sides. "WE NEVER REALLY LIKED YOU ANYWAY!"

The lobster wasn't replaced.

That was a long time ago. We were just kids.

And now we're on the cusp of adulthood. Childhood seems like forever ago, like something that has nothing to do with me anymore.

"God," Piper said, rolling over in the sand. "The future. I feel like it's *now*. The future is all over us. This is it. Every choice we make could change anything. Everything! We're *free*!" She flung her arms wide, accidentally punching my nose.

"Ouch!" Tears sprang to my eyes. "Jeez, that hurt!"

"Sorry," she said. "What was your nose doing there?" She got up, wobbly in the sand. Then she did a dance, her old ballet school training showing through. "We have it all!" she shouted to the waves.

I smiled because she was right.

I was happy.

She was happy.

In that moment, anything and everything felt possible. We had each other, and we could do anything. We could be anything. We could be everything.

And we would be.

We just knew it.

I took a long sip of my spiked blue Slurpee that tasted like drinking a summer sky, sweet and vast and forever. We lay down on our backs, the sand already summer hot. We stared up at the white clouds drifting by. Piper hiccuped. "I feel kinda drunk," she said drowsily.

"The sun plus alcohol is a bad combo," I said, but I was too lazy to move or to stop drinking.

"Do you ever think we should have less of a plan?" Her voice was slurred. "Less specitifity. Specifis . . . Specif . . . Oh, you know what I mean. I can't talk. Blergh."

"Specificity? Less?"

"I don't know!" she said. "I want to be surprised, you know? Like maybe not filmmaking, maybe fashion or . . ." She hiccuped so deeply, it sounded like she was going to puke. "Real estate."

"Real estate?" I was laughing, belly-hard. I could barely talk. "*Real* estate?"

She squinted at me. "Houses are nice."

"Houses are nice," I agreed. "I guess. But nope, not for me. You could, though. I'm going to be a filmmaker. I decided a long time ago. You know that."

"No houses," she said sadly.

"Why are you talking about houses?" I was still giggling. "You're hilarious! You can have a job with houses! The world is your oyster!"

"I *like* those tiny houses," she said. "Sooooooo cute."

"You are blotto. You need to stop drinking."

"Okeydokey." She poured her drink out on my bare leg.

"Hey!" I jumped up. "That's cold! And sticky!"

"Oops," she said.

"Look." I sat down again. "Filmmaking is all *I* ever wanted to do." I reached into my floppy beach bag and took out my

60

camera. I zoomed in on her face. "Tell me what it is that *you've* always wanted to do."

"I do don't love it, too," she said, sticking out her tongue and smiling. "I mean, I don't do love it. I love. I mean . . ." She was laughing, tears running down her cheeks. "I love *you*. When I grow up, I want to be *you*."

"I love you, too," I said, "but I don't think being me is a good career choice." I clicked the record button off. "Europe is big. Anything could happen. And then I have film school, but your slate is pretty much wide open. You can do anything."

"I hope we're not murdered on a train," she whispered.

"Well, duh," I said. "I hope not, too."

A bee buzzed lazily and slowly across my field of vision. I watched as it landed on my blue, sticky leg. It crawled slowly, its feet like tiny wings brushing my skin. Then, faster, it made its way off, into the sand and away, out of sight. "Fly, little bee," I said.

"You don't know how to make movie films," she said, suddenly not laughing at all. "Not real ones. What if it doesn't work out?"

"That's mean," I murmured. "I don't know everything yet, but I'll learn. And you'll figure out something, too. Right?" I closed my eyes. The sun was so warm and perfect on my face. "We're going to have a great time."

"Maybe I'll apply to film school, too," she said doggedly, not letting it go.

"Hmmm?" I was sleepy, the alcohol catching up to me all at once, the conversation suddenly exhausting. I replayed what she'd said in my head. I sat up, sand raining from my hair. "Seriously? You're joking. It's *my* thing. You don't want to make films. You've never said."

"I do! I totally do."

"So what are you saying? Are you kidding?" I felt uneasy. The sun was behind her, so it was hard for me to see her face. "Piper?"

"I don't know," she said. She hiccuped again. "This drink is so gross. Why do we drink this?" She burped. "Let's talk about boys."

"Ugh." I rolled my eyes. "Why waste our time on them?"

"You don't really think 'ugh,'" she said. She gave me a look, eyes half shut, a look that meant she thought she knew me better than I knew myself.

I glowered back. "The No-Boyfriend Rule."

She shrugged. "You're right—it's better—just me and you. I love you, Sloaney."

"Just me and you," I echoed, but the sun and the alcohol and the sound of the waves lapping at the shore were pulling me into a daydream and I stopped listening. I don't really *hear* what she was telling me. I didn't understand until it was too late.

* * *

The art show was when everything changed. Maybe it was changing before that, but so gradually it was hard to really pinpoint.

I didn't even know it had changed until afterward, but by then, it was done.

If I had known what she was going to do, would I have done anything different?

We arrived early so I could set up my video installation at the end of the corridor, in a dark alcove. In the gym, white walls had been erected, creating a corridor of art. Soup Sanchez's paintings filled one whole wall of the art room: all vibrant colors, spray paint, and Sharpie. The canvases glowed with energy and accolades. The smell of them made me dizzy. They were like something you could fall into, bottomless illusions. *Oh my God, I love him*, I realized.

I had lied to Piper about the No-Boyfriend Rule.

I had time for boys. I had time for Soup Sanchez.

I felt light-headed.

I'd always had a crush on him, but somehow seeing his paintings that night, something was different. Something changed.

My heart raced. I realized that I might be in love with him. Real love.

But what is love?

I tried to calm down, to remind myself that love is a chemical reaction.

Dopamine.

Serotonin.

"Hey, I didn't know Soup did art like *this*," Piper whispered. Her breath smelled like coffee and stale alcohol from yesterday. "He's talented, like whoa."

"He's always been super talented. Have some gum, your breath stinks."

I felt weirdly like crying. Or maybe it was Sharpie fumes that were making the room spin. The wall made my heart go quiet. My brain felt shivery and metallic.

"You should go for him," Piper said, like she was reading my mind. "He's basically your dream boy. Besides, he's cute. When did Soup Sanchez get cute?" She snapped her gum.

"Remember the pact. Boy-free for you and me."

She rolled her eyes. "You should embroider that on something," she said. "Throw cushion. Ironic T-shirt."

"Tattoo," I said. "*That* would be cooler. And, as you know, I'm the coolest."

She laughed.

I don't know why I didn't tell her. I'd told her literally everything for our entire lives. Like when I got my first period on the bus and left a huge bloody mark on the seat and an old lady yelled at me when I stood up and everyone knew and I thought I'd die from embarrassment. Like the time when I had to pee in third grade but ran to the toilet so late and accidentally peed on my math textbook, which I'd dropped on the floor.

But I'd never told her that I had a crush on Soup. I didn't want her to laugh at me. When it started, it felt embarrassing. But when I started to feel more, I just couldn't. It was good to have a secret from her.

Soup Sanchez was my secret.

In fourth grade, Soup and I built a liver out of clay together, molding veins and arteries, painting the whole thing an unappetizing brown. At his house, after school, the first time I'd ever been alone with a boy, I knew, I just knew that one day, me and Soup Sanchez, we'd be something. There was almost a light in the air around us while we worked. I knew then. It was a thing that I was so sure of, but I also knew I wasn't ready yet.

I thought about how to tell her, right then and there. To get it over with. "I do think he is . . . pretty great."

"Oh my God, you *like* him! Sloane and Soup, sittin' in a tree, K-I-S-S-I-N-G. Why didn't you ever tell me? You're blushing! I thought you didn't have a crush. I thought you said crushes were lame."

"Are you twelve?" I hissed. "He'll hear you!"

"We're best friends! You didn't tell me! You've been holding out!" She mock punched my arm, a bit too hard. "I have to know everything about you, always. That's our deal."

"Don't be crazy." I frowned. "Love is a chemical reaction. Crushes are the result of biology and boredom. That's what you always say! Boy-free! Et cetera!"

"That's not the point!" She paused, making a dramatic gesture with her arms. "The point is now *Soup Sanchez*!"

"Shut up!" I hissed. He was around somewhere, I wasn't sure where. I half expected to turn around and see him standing behind me. "I don't have a 'crush' on him! You're making me feel dumb! Soup doesn't matter! I totally do not *like* him like him! I think he's fine. He's cute. But he's not my type. He's not!" I was protesting too much. She was turning it into a joke and I couldn't handle it. I didn't want her to turn this feeling I was having into something cheap and stupid, embarrassing and awkward. I wanted to crawl out of my own skin. I stared at her. I wanted to turn my back on her and walk away. Instead, I put my arm around her shoulders.

"Enough," I said. I faked a laugh. I played with her hair until I felt her relax again.

I didn't need Soup.

I had Piper.

We had each other.

We were going to the year-end dance together next week in toothpaste-green circa 1987 prom dresses we found at the thrift store that still stank of ozone-depleting hair spray. Mine had a stain on the bodice, lipstick or a pink drink that someone probably regretted. Hers had a broken zipper that needed to be repaired.

But they were *perfect*.

We were perfect.

I grabbed her hand. "We don't need no stinkin' boys," I said. "Right?"

"Right," she agreed. She smiled at me. "Meow."

We walked a few steps like that, holding hands. We were both wearing denim shorts with white tank tops, plaid shirts tied around our waists, our long blond hair pulled shimmering straight with her straightening iron.

"Actually, I'm forgetting why it matters," she mused. "Why does it matter?"

"What? About boyfriends?" I shrugged. "We're better than that, that's all."

She pulled her hand away and twisted around, an expression on her face that I couldn't read. "Don't you ever get sick of always taking yourself so *seriously*?" Then she was gone, pushing through the crowd, disappearing down the hallway, out of sight.

Piper did that sometimes. She ran. I was used to it.

"I was kidding!" I yelled after her. "Sort of? It was your idea in the first place!"

I took out my camera and filmed slowly across the display of Soup's art, silently: a painting of a cola can hurtling through space, leaving a trail of sparks and feathers. A teetering pile of cars, a tiny house balanced on the top. A dog and cat sitting next to each other, between them a fish flopping in a puddle. A family portrait of him and his mom, an empty chair between them with a guitar and a cobweb, which housed a dead fly with tiny shimmering wings. I saved it. I'd look at it later, when I could be alone, when I could really see what Soup Sanchez was trying to say.

For the show, I'd made a video called "High School 2.0." It was mostly a sped-up clip of people walking between classes, in and out of the front doors, and then it slowed down to slow motion as kids texted on their phones. It had no voice-over, only classical music that Mr. Aberley helped me pick out. He has a huge music collection. Hundreds of records and CDs. My video was meant to be an ironic statement about how we're all the same, going through the motions, thinking we're different when we aren't, and haven't ever been. I'm not sure it really worked, but it was trying to be something. The whole thing had a layer of sounds from a chicken farm over the top, the endless clucking, the squawks of pain. I'd worked on it for weeks. Afterward, my dad said it was awesome, and Mom said, "Sometimes you worry me a little, but I love it." They were trying. My parents are like that: people who try really hard to be good parents. But I could tell they didn't get it. Piper is the only one who would have understood it, but she didn't even see it.

"In case it's not obvious, I'm mad," I said the next morning, when I finally found Piper in the hallway at her locker.

"Sorry," she said, not looking at all sorry. She was smiling, her hands fluttering to her hair and back to her books. "I'm totally sorry. I love you. I don't know what happened! I sort of lost it."

"I love you, too. But you hurt my feelings! I needed you to see it! Why did you leave? Why do you look so happy? I'm mad!"

She kept smiling coyly; something was weird about it. "I can't tell you."

"Try." I was annoyed. "Please."

"Okay, okay, okay, I have to tell you! I can't wait to tell you, actually! I'll tell you at lunch. Meet me at the Vee?"

I nodded as the bell sounded. "Meet you at the Vee," I echoed.

The Vee was a pie-shaped parking lot behind the 7-Eleven where we regularly went to buy snacks during our spare periods. It was about three blocks from school. Usually we walked over together, but that day, I looked everywhere and I couldn't find her in the usual spots. I walked alone. She was already there when I got there, sitting on the low wall that separated the parking lot from a small stretch of scrubby grass and trees. We called it the Park, because it was the opposite of a park, littered with broken glass and empty chip bags. It was a scraggly mess.

"Why didn't you wait?" I was mad. She must have been able to tell.

"I just *flew*! I feel like I can't keep my feet on the ground!"

"What the what? Why are you talking like the Good Witch from the school musical? What aren't you telling me?" I dropped to my knees and pretended to sob, to play along, because she was Piper and my best friend and that's what best friends do. "Is it drugs? TELL ME."

"Get up," she said. She was looking at me strangely. "Don't be weird."

"I was kidding around!" I felt misunderstood. "What is *wrong* with you?"

She looked down, bit her lip. I got up and sat next to her on the wall, putting my hand on a piece of chewed gum. "Oh, man, gross," I said. She looked up at me from under her lashes with a strange look on her face. Her lashes were fluttering. It was like her whole *being* was fluttering.

"You're officially freaking me out," I said. "Are you having a seizure?"

She shook her head, tossing her hair. "I want to tell you . . . I mean, I have to talk to you. I want you to be the first to know. This is sooo hard to say." I stared at her mouth. She flipped her hair behind her and I got a waft of apple-scented shampoo, her favorite coconut body spray. Her tongue kept darting out between her small, square teeth and tapping her lip. It was making me furious. I wanted to tell her so badly how irritating it was, but I didn't know why. It made me think of lizards and sex, in that order.

"I'm still mad," I said finally. "No matter what you say by way of apology. That was really crummy. I wanted you to see it."

She looked like she was *trying* to look downcast, but her smile kept breaking through. "Oh, your little film? Yeah, I am sorry, tweetie, but it's not that. It's so much bigger. You're going to forget about your movie when you hear."

I blinked at her, trying to decide which part of this I should address first. The use of the dreaded old nickname she had for me, "tweetie"? My *little* film? Or should I be a real friend and let her tell me, overlooking the other stuff?

"Spill it." I sighed. "Did you lose your V to that kid from One Direction? Should I call the tabloids? Is there something on your lip?"

"It's so much more than that . . ." She was whispering now. "You were kidding yesterday about how you have a crush on Soup, right? You said you were kidding?"

"What?" I had to lean my long blond hair toward hers so I could hear her better.

"Me and Soup Sanchez," she says. "Last night. When I left the show, I bumped into him. And we started talking. *Really* talking. Like you and I used to talk, you know? I mean, it's a thing. We talked all night. *We're* a thing. Me and Soup. I can't explain it. It just happened. Like kismet."

"What? Kismet?" I said. I felt like she'd punched me so hard in the gut that my breath wouldn't fill my lungs. I must have looked like a fish, mouth open and gasping, just for a second. "When? *What?*" And then, "When? Kismet?"

"You keep saying that! You should see your face!" She laughed. "I'm sorry. You're mad. I'm breaking the No-Boyfriend Rule and I'm sorry, but that was always sort of a joke, right? For me! Not for you. I know you mean it. I know it's important to you. I *totally* respect that. You should see your face! You look so weird! Please don't be weird about this." She grabbed my hands and pulled me to my feet. She twirled me around.

A car pulled into the parking spot and honked. "Idiots!" a guy yelled. I stumbled, almost falling into the brick wall.

"I'm in love!" Piper shouted. "The rules no longer apply!"

"That hurt," I said, rubbing my shoulder. "God, I think you made a bruise."

The thing with Piper is that she goes too far; she doesn't know when to stop. She never knows when to stop. My heart was skipping beats all over the place. I was dizzy. I took in a slow breath and then another. And another. *See something, hear something, touch something, smell something.* Do something. "Keep it together," I whispered to myself. Piper play-punched me in the shoulder where I'd hit the wall, right on the bruise. She was giddy, I could see it.

She was happy.

I wanted to hit her back. I wanted to run.

I won't panic, I told myself. *I'm not panicking.*

But I was panicking. My hands were shaking. Adrenaline overload.

I remember once watching a documentary about the earthquake belt that the island rests on. It showed in slow motion what would happen if the plates slipped, the way the whole island would be thrust not down into the sea but upward at a terrifying trajectory, before splitting open "like a zipper." That's what the narrator said: "Like a zipper."

Piper had split me open *like a zipper.*

My secret crush.

But I *told* her.

The tectonic plates of our relationship shifted, right then, at that exact second. I was thrust up toward the sky before falling back down again, shattered into a million pieces.

"Okay," I made myself say. My voice sounded tinny and strange to my ears. "Yay, you! You have a boyfriend. I'm so happy for you." My voice crackled on "happy" like a car that was driven into a tunnel, interfering with the radio.

I would be a good friend to her, no matter what. I promised myself. We would always put each other before boys.

I didn't want a boyfriend anyway.

Boys get in the way.

Boys put their own needs first.

Boys want you to put them first, too.

Boys change everything, and I didn't want anything to change.

Not yet.

"Thanks." She sighed and tipped her head onto my shoulder; the familiar smell of her filled me up. "I knew you'd understand."

I nodded. I wasn't crying. Not very hard. Not so much that she'd notice. If she looked, I'd say it was just rain on my cheeks.

We live in the Pacific Northwest. It rains so much here that it's literally a rain forest. The rain will come back. It always does.

But right then, there was just the sun: too bright, too hot, too everything, stinging my eyes, burning my heart.

After that, everything is just a bit harder, like I only fit into myself awkwardly, the wrong size and shape.

Instead of dressing in mint green, going to Piper's, helping each other style our hair, on the day of the dance, I go to Mr. Aberley's.

Piper and Soup are *together* now. Soup and Piper. Piper and Soup. It's the shadow behind everything I say and do. It's the bitter taste in my mouth.

I try to convince myself it doesn't matter. Sometimes it works better than others. The dance, the last event of junior year, it's a harder day than the others, which blend together and disappear behind us more easily.

There are two houses on this bay, ours and his. His is huge and old and he's lived in it since he was a kid. I like looking at the photos that line the hallway of him as a baby and a little boy on the beach out front. There's a thing about beaches that I love: how they never change, how history seems to pass through them. Beaches remain the same; only winter storms rearrange their furniture. Nothing is built there, nothing grows, nothing changes.

Mr. Aberley was married on the front lawn of his house, which unspools down to the water in slow, undulating lawn-covered hills. He raised his kids there: their rooms upstairs still have posters and kid stuff littering them; he leaves everything as it was in case they come back, which they won't. He lives there alone. His wife left him forever ago. His children won't forgive him for being gay. Love messes everything up, he's living proof. He seems happy, though. Happy-ish. He has a boyfriend named Jean Paul who is French and seventy-five and likes to mumble French swears under his breath when I appear. Jean Paul isn't visiting today, his Mercedes missing from the driveway, and I am relieved. Some people are easy to make small talk with. Other people are Jean Paul.

I knock on the door, but there is no answer. I know he doesn't hear well, so I open it up and shout, "MR. ABERLEY! IT'S ME!"

"Well, well, well!" he says, emerging into the front hall from one of the many doors that I've never been behind. I try to catch a glimpse of the room behind him, but he's fast for an old guy; the door snaps shut briskly. "Ms. Sloane," he says. "To what do I owe the pleasure? And where is your other half?"

"Ha ha," I say. "She's busy. Just me today. Sorry."

"Are you going to offer to do my errands?" He smiles. "Or climb a ladder on my behalf?"

"I'm scared of heights," I remind him, following him through to the kitchen, which is huge and ramshackle, with copper pots hanging in dusty webs from hooks above the restaurant-style stove. "And don't you have people on the payroll for errands?" He fills a bright blue kettle with water and puts it on for tea, without asking. He makes his own tea from the stinging nettles that grow on the island in thick clusters. He credits the tea with keeping him young. "Young" is a stretch, but I guess he does look good for ninety. And he's pretty spry, not like Grandma, and she's only eighty-four.

When I was little, I used to imagine that Grandma and Mr. Aberley would fall in love and that eventually Grandma would move out of our house and across the bay to live with Mr. A. That they would row out to the island together, morning and evening. That it would be a love story like in fairy tales. But Mr. Aberley loves Jean Paul, and Grandma insisted that she gave up love for Lent one year and decided she was better off without it. "Love will ruin you," she always told me. "Love will be your undoing." She'd pat me on the cheek. "Don't ever fall in love," she warns every time I visit her now, like an old crone in a fairy tale. I frown, trying to remember if that's what started the No-Boyfriend Rule. Grandma has a framed photo of Grandpa when he was young on her side table. She sits beside it all day long, sneaking glances when she thinks no one is looking.

"So what's new from the west side?" Mr. A says now, pouring the boiling water over the dried leaves. We both watch as the water slowly turns a brownish green in the glass teapot, the leaves swirling in the current.

"Same old, same old," I tell him. "BUT only two more weeks of school, then the last summer holiday of my life."

"Of your life!" he exclaims, rubbing his hands together gleefully. "Sounds exciting. Suicide pact?"

"What? No! I mean that after this year, it's not like school is going to be, you know, the structure. I won't have the structure of that. It won't be 'summer holidays.' It will just be . . . summer."

"Ah," he says, nodding. He smiles, and I have to look away from his old man teeth. He's proud of having kept his teeth, but he should maybe reconsider dentures. Not that I'd ever say that out loud. "I see. But you'll go to college, you'll have summer breaks."

"I'm going to film school," I say. "Different thing."

"Big change," he says. "Then one day, you're old, and everything is a break. Right now, for example." He laughs his old man cough-laugh. "I'm on spring break. Next up, summer break. Then fall." He starts coughing for real, bending over, rasping and hacking.

"Mr. A? Are you all right?" I ask. I don't know whether to pat him on the back or call 911. He raises his hand.

Finally, it stops. "I'm fine," he says. "Turns out, I'm an old man! Old lungs. Old everything. I forget, you know, until I look in the mirror. Or try to stand up after sitting for a while."

"Oh," I say. "Right." I take a sip of my tea, which is burning hot and tastes like the forest, green and dusty.

"This will fix me up," he says, lifting his cup with his trembling hand. "Now, Sloane, I've been meaning to talk to you about something."

"You have?" I say, spinning my phone on the table. "What? Do you have any of those weird English biscuits? This tea needs biscuits."

The phone buzzes. Piper. I switch the sound to mute, but I don't turn it off. I spin Piper on the table, my index finger over the image of her face. She's calling about the dance and I'm not going. She's going with Soup and if I went, too, it would be so awkward, I'd die. I cringe to think about it.

"No biscuits, alas. It's about the boat," Mr. Aberley says. He slides his glasses down his nose a little and looks at me over the top of them.

"Ohhhhh?" I say, stalling. His eyes are bright blue. It's funny how eyes don't age, not really, not like the rest of a person. I picture his eyes in a baby. In a little boy. He's every age that he's ever been. His eyes assess me silently. I blink to see if he will, too, but he doesn't.

"Well, for one thing, *asking* wouldn't kill you, would it?"

"I am SO sorry," I say. "I don't know why we didn't ask. We won't do it again. Mr. Aberley, we suck. I have no excuse."

He chortles in that way that only very old people can do.

"I don't mind," he says. "Not really. Thing is, the boat has a leak in the bottom and I'm too old to fix it. And I figure since you girls like it almost as much as I do, maybe you can patch it up. Wait here."

He gets up and does his old man shuffle across the kitchen, which takes long enough for me to glance at Piper's texts: "come over! help me do my face!" "Does this look good?" "Wish u would come 2" "Soup can be both of our dates! He'd like that. Hawt." I delete, delete, delete.

Mr. Aberley comes back, holding his brand-new MacBook Pro. I grab it from him quickly before he accidentally drops it. "Now look," he says, dialing up YouTube slowly, typing each letter with the deliberation of a sloth. I grit my teeth, trying not to be impatient. The video is called, fittingly, "How to patch a fiberglass boat." We watch in silence while a slow-talking man describes in painful detail the process of making a fiberglass patch.

"Gripping, Mr. A," I tell him when it's done. "Can't think why it hasn't gone viral. And the camera angles"—I whistle— "it's award-winning stuff."

"It's instructional," he says. "Not everything has to be amusing or beautiful, you know, except perhaps people." He contemplates this. "Amusing and beautiful. Which also isn't your job, you know. This idea that women must be beautiful is so archaic, yet people still buy into it. Why is that?"

"I have no idea," I say. "I don't care about beauty. But amusing? Sure. I'll try to be amusing."

"Hmm," he ponders. "I wonder if that's true, that you don't care. Is it possible to not care? I'm an old man and I still buy new shirts each fall. I must care, mustn't I?"

"You buy them for Jean Paul," I say. I make a heart sign with my hands, and a kissy face.

"Oh, hush; you'll fall in love one day, too, you know."

I groan. "Okay, Mr. A. We will patch your boat. I mean, I don't know anything about any of what I saw on this video, but I'm sure I can figure it out. How hard can it be?"

"Attagirl," he says. "I knew you had it in you. Maybe you can get a beautiful and amusing boy to help you."

I snort. "I watched that whole video, and not once did it say that you needed to own a penis to patch a boat," I say.

He frowns, then smiles. "Valid point," he says. "Fair. And I thank you in advance for repairing my yacht. Or our yacht, I should say."

"I'm a true hero," I tell him. "That's what you don't understand about me. And thank you for sharing your yacht. And for this weird tea."

I take a last sip of the murky drink and pick up my phone. "See you later, Mr. A?"

"Anytime, Ms. Whittaker," he says, already scrolling through his Facebook feed. He's a big fan of George Takei. He

81

clicks like on the latest post and chuckle-coughs again. "I'm forwarding this one to you. You should make these viral videos while you practice to change the world with your films. Ask your parents for a cat. Cats really sell these things." He laughs again. I stand and watch him for a second, and then I let myself out. It's pretty tempting to open one of those closed doors in the front hall, but I resist the temptation. Everyone has a right to have their secrets, even the weird old men who live across the bay.

After all, you never know when you might be asking them to keep your secrets, too.

The hardware store is cluttered and old-fashioned. The shelves are high and teeter above me, so crowded with mysterious things, they look like a trick of the eye. I wouldn't want to be in here during an earthquake, that's for sure.

I pause in front of the electronic rat traps. There are rats everywhere in this city. You wouldn't expect it. It's an affluent place, lots of big houses, nice lawns. The rats don't discriminate. I could make a film about rats, a short one, something that could go viral, prove to Mr. A that I can make something go viral. Cats, rats, whatever.

Once, when I was six, Mom was reading me bedtime stories on my bed and I glanced down to the floor and a rat's tail swept out from behind the closet door. I screamed and screamed. We moved after that. Not because of it, but right after. I still have bad dreams about that door.

After the earthquake, after the tidal wave, after any apocalypse, I bet the rats will survive. There are so many millions of them. Maybe, like most animals, they're misunderstood, demonized by people who have more imagination than sense.

"Rat on a Roomba," I murmur to myself. "Grumpy Rat. Or maybe Pirate Rat on a Roomba chasing a cat dressed as a clown . . ."

"Are you talking to yourself?" A voice, low, and right in my ear. I jump, my skin instantly prickling.

"Argh!" I say. "You scared me half to death."

"You're the one who was talking to the rat traps," says Soup, leaning away from me to straighten one on the shelf. I'd forgotten that he works here. He does it to get discounts on paint is what he told Piper, but I'm sure it's more than that. He doesn't have a dad. I don't get the feeling that his mom is very wealthy. I'm gleaning information about Soup via Piper, collecting it without meaning to. I don't have a crush on him anymore. It's not like that.

It can't be.

Love is a decision.

"I was thinking out loud," I say. "It's not a crime. I forgot you worked here."

He grins. "If you remembered, would you have shopped somewhere else?"

I consider his question seriously. "Yeah," I say. "Probably."

He clutches at his chest. "Ouch," he says. "Sloane Whittaker with the knockout blow."

I roll my eyes. "You'll bounce back," I say. All my words feel wrong and strange, like I'm talking around bubbles that are forming in my mouth, sparking like Pop Rocks on every syllable. "I have faith in you."

He clears his throat. I let the awkward silence grow. Finally, he breaks it. "Well, seeing as you're here, is there something I can help you find?"

"I have to patch Mr. Aberley's boat," I say. "Long story. I need a fiberglass patch and . . . honestly, I have no idea." I take my phone out of my pocket and open my list app, thrust it into his hand. His skin brushes against my skin and I jump back like I've been burned. His eyes look for mine, but I look away. He knows, he knows. I know he knows. I know.

He *has* to know.

He must feel this, too. Right?

But: Piper.

Piper comes first.

Piper is my best friend, even when she drives me crazy.

"Yeah, we've got most of this stuff," he says. "I can round it up for you. If you want to go grab a coffee or something and come back, I can get it packed up."

"Thanks," I say. "That great would be." He looks at me funny. That great would be? My words don't work around Soup.

This is a problem.

"Yeah," I try again. "Great."

"Great would be," he intones.

I practically run out the door, the bell chiming like applause. My heart is racing, galloping, somersaulting in my chest. And then I'm outside in the afternoon's shimmering air, gulping and gulping, trying to get enough oxygen to stay upright, to walk in a normal way next door, to order a mocha and to sit and wait, phoneless and shivering, even though it's not cold.

I get cold when I'm sad.

I get cold when something goes terribly wrong.

I get cold when I screw up.

"I'm a terrible person," I say to nobody. "I'm the worst." I gulp down the hot drink, not caring that caffeine winds me up even more, trying to warm myself up from the inside, trying to do what the sun can't.

* * *

When I get back to the hardware store, Soup is gone. "Had to get ready for the dance," says the lady behind the register. She looks like a stock movie character: *kindly older woman with sloppily applied lipstick but a heart of gold.* I hope she's got hidden depths: secretly, she is in charge of a cult, or she collects ancient human skulls. Maybe she knows how to translate hieroglyphics, has four ex-husbands, and breeds mountain dogs. "Ain't you going to the dance, hon? You're in his class, right?" I shake my head, my hair sliding around my face for emphasis. She smells like hair spray, but under that, something wet and woolly, an animal caught in the rain. Up close, I can see her pores. The thing with humans is that we're so *human*, I think. I'm dying to take out my camera and interview her. "What is the secret to happiness?" I'll ask. "How old were you when you fell in love?" Probably she'd kick me out of the store for being a nut. Unanswerable questions, answered. Actually, that's a great idea.

"Do you——" I start to say, but she interrupts.

"He had to go home and 'get ready,'" she says. "Isn't that a thing. What's a boy got to do to get ready, anyway? Put on a suit, that's what. Not like they have to put on lipstick, do their face, not like we do."

"Truth," I say. "It's harder to be a girl. One is obligated to be so decorative." I touch my hair, self-consciously. I'm not wearing any makeup. "Some people think, anyway. Not me."

"Oh, you're plenty decorative," she says.

I glower.

"In a good way, hon," she says. "Don't you gals want to be pretty anymore? What a world."

I shrug. "It's complicated," I say. On top of the pile of things Soup gathered for me, he's left my phone. I pocket it quickly without looking at the screen. Piper will probably be mostly ready by now. If I were a better person, I'd stop at her place, take a picture of her, tell her how *amazing* she looks, which she probably does. But I'm not that good of a friend. I'm not that good of a person. I don't know how to lie.

Not anymore.

"That's thirty-eight ninety-nine, then," the woman says, yawning wide. Her canines are pointy. Maybe she's a vampire. A monster. "He gave you his discount. Sweet kid, isn't he, that Philip. Now are you payin' by cash or credit?"

I hand her the Visa card that Dad gave me for my birthday for emergencies. A leaking boat is almost certainly an emergency, or would be, if it sank. She rings it through. "Have fun at that dance now!" she calls after me. I nod and wave. I don't bother to remind her that I'm not going.

I walk home the long way. The streets are pretty quiet, broken up by the occasional car or truck. I pass a young mom with a baby in a stroller and a toddler who is whining loudly. A middle-aged woman, hauling a growling Chihuahua on a leash. A boy on a skateboard, eyes hidden by sunglasses. I wish I had my headphones so I could listen to something funny or serious or scary, but listening without them seems rude, like a podcast would interrupt everyone else's silence. My feet make slapping sounds on the sidewalk in my flip-flops, which weren't made for long walks.

I walk and walk.

I try not to think about Soup and Piper, but thinking about anything else is a lie.

I don't know why I never told Piper he was my Manic Pixie Dream Boy. A long time ago we decided that we would only fall in love with MPDBs, as defined by MPDGs in books and films, girls whose major purpose is to be quirkily needy and make the boy hero fulfill his manly potential. But our MPDBs would be our quirky cheerleaders, our slightly befuddled but fun companions who would make us realize our dreams! Cue theme music! It wasn't serious, but it also was. And Soup Sanchez: cute, quirky artist? I don't know about MPDB, but he made me want to do better. He made me want to impress him.

I think I didn't want to explain how you can like someone but prefer the idea of them to the reality of them, but that's how I felt.

I think I was scared of what would happen if we got together.

I was scared of everything that would change.

"Love's just a chemical reaction." That was Piper's line. She said it so often, it was like her motto. "Love is for the weak. Biology makes you want to have sex: fact. We aren't at the mercy of our biology. We're different, you and me. Sex turns people into idiots."

I believed her.

I believed that she believed it.

I believed we were above love somehow, circling the crowd from the vantage point of something higher: birds or stars.

I was *embarrassed* to like Soup. Liking him was too human. Too normal. Too lame.

I was stupid to not tell her.

But I did tell her.

Didn't I?

So how could she be with him, if she knew?

I close my eyes for a second, stumbling on the curb. I drop the bag and things roll out and my knees hit the pavement hard, the skin tearing. I stand up and blood trickles from the cuts, which sting like crazy. I blink back tears and stop myself from calling my dad to pick me up. He'd drop everything and come. He always would. But I'm seventeen and I'm not a little kid anymore, so forget it. Even thinking about how nice he'd be about the whole thing makes me angry for some reason, like I want to put my fist through something glass and feel it shatter.

I pick the things up, hurry them back into the bag like I'm being watched, even though no one is around. A bus goes by and the air current it makes almost makes me fall into the road, so I lean away from it to right myself. A crow caws. The houses around me look blank and empty; suburbia has gone to work or to school, if they don't have the day off because of prom.

My phone beeps. I glance at it—the battery is almost dead and there is a series of texts from Piper—and turn it off. I start walking, ignoring how much my knees hurt. I start counting steps, like I'm my own Fitbit: one, two, three, eight hundred and fourteen, one thousand and sixty-two.

When I get home, I put the bag of stuff in the garage. It looks out of place there. Real tools among Dad's collection of antique cameras and lenses, all laid out on his pristine white "tool bench." It was Dad who bought me my first video camera when I was in third grade. It was Dad who taught me how to use it, how to edit films using the computer, how to make things more interesting with sound, how to interpret meaning from small moments. Dad's favorite is still photography. Up-close pictures of raindrops. Portraits of me and Piper. A million portraits of me and Piper. He helped me fall in love with film.

There's that word again: love.

It pollutes everything.

It changes you.

Would I be different without my camera?

The camera bench sits against the wall in front of a fancy MG convertible, which is parked on carpet patches. He only drives it on perfect sunny summer Sundays. Never on highways. Never in traffic. Never on weekdays. The car is so perfect, it looks like a piece of art. I climb into it, sit in the driver's seat, pretend to drive. I haven't learned yet. I'm old enough, but I haven't needed to. Piper drives everywhere we need to go in her mom's Volvo, which perpetually smells like a wet dog even though her dog, Margarine, a big fat yellow Lab, died in the spring. She let me record the vet putting him down. I'll never forget the way a film rose over his eyes, a matte glaze covering the brown gleam of them. She threw herself on the vet at the last minute. She screamed, "Don't!" but it was too late. Her mom held her arms back like she was in a bar brawl. She made me delete it after. She made me promise not to show anyone.

I never did.

I wouldn't.

This car does not smell like dog. I inhale the Dad smell of it, leather and air freshener and Armor All. I pretend to turn the key, press my foot down on the gas. Hard.

Where would I go?

You can never get far enough away from yourself, that's the problem.

And I could never escape from Piper.

And Soup.

And what I want.

I get out of the car and shake the floor mat so the dirt from my flip-flops doesn't give me away. I close the door gently so no one will hear.

In the kitchen, Mom and Dad are embroiled in a pretty raucous game of Scrabble, glasses of red wine in their hands.

"Sloane?" says Mom as I grab some water from the fridge. "I've been wondering where you were! I thought you were at Piper's, getting ready for the dance? But she called and said you weren't going."

"Are you okay?" says Dad. "I was really looking forward to that photo opportunity."

I roll my eyes. "Migraine," I lie, trying to look sick. "You'll have to take pictures of Mom or something. I don't know. Sorry."

"Oh no," says Mom. "I'm so sad you'll miss the dance! You had such a great dress. You know, I was going to dig out my own prom pictures; I think mine was similar, although it was bright pink." She shudders. "The eighties weren't kind!" Then she seems to remember my headache. "Are you going to take a pill? Should you eat something? Those pills make you puke, remember?"

I raise my hand in a gesture that might mean yes or no or who knows what and slowly go up the stairs. "TRIPLE WORD!" Dad yells.

"Shhhh," Mom says. "Not when she has a headache!"

He lowers his voice. "I'm powning you now," he says. "You're goin' down, Whittaker."

"You wish," she says. "Take THAT!" They laugh. I can hear the glug glug of more wine being poured. I can't imagine why they are so happy. I don't understand why this is enough: this small town, their small lives, a car they only drive on weekends. I'm going to be so much more than them. I'm going to live so much bigger than this. Maybe I won't be as rich, but at least I'll *do* things.

I go into my room and shut the door, turn the fan on to drown them out. I climb into bed and plug my phone in. It takes a few seconds for the apple to light up on the screen. Slowly, my apps load, the notes on top, still open. I glance at the app, meaning to close it. It's the list of supplies to fix Mr. Aberley's boat, but then I notice that Soup has added something to the bottom of the list, highlighted it so I can't miss it.

At the bottom of the shopping list, Soup has typed, "I'll help you fix the boat. I know how to use this stuff. Tomorrow at 11? C U at the beach. x."

I stare at the "x."

The "x" was obviously a mistake.

A typo.

Wasn't it?

I hate the way my stomach drops. "Boys are a weakness!" I whisper. "Don't be weak, Sloane. Real girls don't need MPDBs to prop them up."

My phone buzzes, startling me. The buzzes come fast and furious as I scroll through all the texts I missed when the battery died. Piper and Piper and Piper and Piper, always Piper. I close my eyes and the phone keeps vibrating with her and everything she has to say.

Mom always said I should diversify my friend pool. She's a lawyer. That's how lawyers talk. "I don't need more than one friend," I always insisted. "One is plenty!" But now I wonder. If I had more friends, would I have gone to the dumb dance? Or would I have someone here, right now, with me? Someone to hang out with, making fun of prom in general, rolling our eyes at the Instagrams of everyone's corsages, pretending we didn't want to go in the first place?

I blink back tears and scroll through the texts. "Where R U?" Then, "Want to c my dress?" Then a photo of her dress.

Then a close-up of her face, an exaggerated sad pout. "I missssssss u." Then another photo, this time of her shoes (Converse high-tops). Then one of her front driveway, Soup's car. Then one of Soup coming up her front walk, grinning in his cocky way, carrying a rose like a romantic cliché.

She'd never even noticed him before.

Would she have "bumped" into him after the art show if I hadn't admitted that I liked him?

"She competes with you," Mom said once. "She's always trying to be a better Sloane than you are. She wants to out-Sloane you."

"That's stupid," I said, then. "Clever, but stupid. She doesn't want to be me. She wants me to want to be her." I paused. "It's complicated, Mom, but we both understand it. I think."

"Not very convincing," said Mom.

"Ha," I said. "Whatever. It makes sense to me. Sort of."

"Clear as mud," said Mom.

"She's my best friend, Mom! Give me a break!"

"She was never interested in filmmaking before you got your camera," Mom said. "Before you started filming every-thing. Doesn't that make you feel weird?" She batted at my camera, which happened to be rolling. "Stop filming me!"

"Two people can like the same thing!" I said, then, slam-ming a door, I yelled, "It's not a crime!"

/end scene

It's not a crime.

It *is* a crime.

Soup was mine, even though he wasn't.

I turn the phone off.

I turn Piper off.

I climb into bed and close my eyes. I want to fall asleep so that I'm not here, watching them dance in my imagination, laughing; watching them kiss, watching her do that *thing* with her tongue. I miss the Piper who chose those hot-pink sneakers with me to wear with the dress. I miss who we used to be, before I became a liar and she became one of *those* girls.

"Having boyfriends at our age is just a nod to the patriarchy," she said once. "It's not about anything but us learning to be cute and sexy, learning to want boy approval. It's about being who they want us to be, molding us into being people who care only that we look good for men."

"That's not us," I said. "We won't ever be those girls."

"Never," she said.

We had so much power then, when we didn't care.

I didn't want to be one of those girls.

I still don't want to be one of those girls.

I won't be one of those girls.

Soup Sanchez doesn't matter.

He signed with an "x" and that makes my heart hurt.

But it's only a typo.

And the pain is probably heartburn.

"I'm one of you," I mumble to the rats that start swarming into my dream. "We're the same. We're all the thing we don't want to be."

And they agree. Of course they agree. Who wants to be a rat? They flick their scaly tails and shuffle into the darkness, always mostly hidden from view.

I don't think that Soup is going to show up but then he shows up. I've been waiting, leaning on the boat's hull in the gravelly sand, collecting the white twirls of broken shells that the waves have tossed above the seaweed line. The beach smells tidal: salty and dank. It's not quite warm yet, the day hung with a thin gray haze that's stuck over the ocean with no wind to blow it clear. The sun is a shiny disk, trying to burn through but failing.

I raise my camera and film Soup coming toward me but then I feel shy and quickly put it away. Not everyone likes being on camera. Plus, he's Piper's. Not mine. And a part of me knows better than to capture this moment, in case she sees it and sees through me and what I'm really doing.

My tongue is stuck to the roof of my mouth, not prettily dancing against my lip, manipulating the narrative. I hang my head down, digging for nothing in my bag so he can't see my face.

I'm blushing, I know I'm blushing.

My stupid face always betrays me. I press my hands to my cheeks, hoping to cool the color away.

Last I heard from Piper, they were heading downtown for late-night food. She sent a photo of them together, waiting at the bus stop, both looking glassy-eyed drunk. Their eyes glow red from the flash. The whole thing is out of focus.

There was nothing this morning.

She's waiting for me to ask and I can't ask because I'm waiting for her boyfriend on the beach in the fog with a bag of patching supplies and a guilty conscience.

"Hi," Soup says. "Sorry I'm late. I had to wait while my mom finished telling me about how alcohol will destroy my life." He pauses. "She's probably right." He does look a little green. I want to reach out my hand and push his sweaty hair off his forehead because there is something wrong with me and I'm the worst.

"Yeah," I say instead. "My parents think that I don't drink but everyone drinks, right?" I raise my thermos at him. It's actually just water, but he blanches.

"Too soon," he moans. "Are you seriously drinking already? It's not even noon."

"You sound like my dad," I say, making a face. "Cheers."

He fumbles open the bag of stuff and spreads tins and paintbrushes and a stir stick out on a log.

"This isn't hard," he says. "It smells really bad, just a warning. It will probably make me puke." He looks terrible. "I hope not, but no guarantee. I'm pretty sensitive to smell." He laughs. "That made me sound like a delicate flower, right? I'm tough." He pauses. "Don't tell Piper that I'm a delicate flower."

"I won't." Because I'm not going to tell her about this ever, I think. "Do you, um, use fiberglass for a lot of things?" I say. "Like, art?"

He laughs. "No, I strictly paint," he says. "But I help my neighbor patch his thrasher car with this stuff. It takes a beating. I bought my car off him. It used to be a beater but we fixed it up pretty well."

"Oh," I say. I know literally nothing about cars except that I don't know how to drive one and I probably should. When people start talking about cars and driving, I feel like I'm in kindergarten, listening to the big kids talking. "I can probably do this patch by myself, you know. If it's going to make you sick." I take a sip of water, which I know he thinks is something else, and I feel too dumb to explain that I was kidding before. Jokes you have to explain are too awkward, which is fitting, because as it happens, I'm the most awkward person alive on this beach. "Then you won't have to explain to Piper why you were here."

He laughs, looking startled. "Why? Would she be mad?"

I shrug. "Who knows?" I fidget with my camera. I polish the lens on my shirt. You are the worst, I tell myself. You are so awkward, it hurts.

Soup is not awkward. He isn't capable of awkwardness. He starts undoing jars and popping open a tin of something that does, in fact, smell putrid.

My phone buzzes. Piper. Of course. "R U mad," it says.

I quickly answer, "No. Helping Mr. A. Call you l8r."

"Piper?" Soup says.

I consider lying to make it *less* awkward, but instead give in to the inevitable. "Yep," I say.

"She'll have a headache," he observes, not a shred of discomfort about him.

You signed with an x! I want to scream. *What did it mean? I love you, too!*

For a second, he looks like he wants to say more, but he doesn't. I step into the boat and look down at the hull. "I don't even see a hole in this thing," I say. I rock it back and forth slightly and it shifts in the sand.

"Careful. You might split it."

"I'm not that heavy!" I say.

"I wasn't saying you were heavy, but it's already cracked, right?"

"Right," I mumble.

"We have to flip it over," he tells me. "Then we can do a big patch all the way along that bottom seam." He points. I jump out of the boat and land on my butt in the sand. "Graceful," he says. "You should consider the ballet if this film stuff doesn't work out for you."

"Ha ha," I say.

"Hey," he says as we lift the end of the boat and turn it over. "Can I ask you something?"

"Okay." My heart does six full somersaults in my chest. "Sure."

"I know Piper hasn't had a boyfriend before," he says. "This must be weird for you."

I shrug. "Is that a question? It seems more like a statement. Ms. Cabrello is always so sure that questions are supposed to go up at the end? Like this?"

He laughs. "It's a statement with a built-in question, which is, Is this weird for you?"

"Huh," I say. "Well. It is what it is." I realize that doesn't sound very convincing, so I add, "I didn't think we'd stay single forever. We aren't nuns. I guess neither of us had ever met anyone who . . ." I pause. After all, this is a lie. I'd met Soup. He'd be worth it. I didn't act on it because I'm an idiot. "I'm an idiot," I accidentally say out loud.

"No, you aren't," he says. He looks confused.

"Sorry," I say. "That was two different thoughts. Forget it.

It's fine. It's good! I like you. What's not to like?" My voice cracks. "I'm so happy for Piper. And you. For both of you," I babble on. "If I had champagne, I'd raise it in a toast. Really. I'd write a speech, I'd . . ."

"Okay, okay," he says, and laughs. "I get it. Fine. But I think that we should know each other a little. We should know each other more because then it's not awkward. We should be friends."

"Friends," I echo. Behind me, a seagull laughs. *At* me, not with me. "Sure. We can be friends." I hit the word too hard, and it comes out mad or sad or both, because it is.

He gives me a funny look. "Okay, so we're friends, then." He gives me a hug. I don't know where to put my arms, so I leave them hanging down by my sides. I feel like an ironing board, I think absurdly, then I giggle.

"What's funny?" he says.

"Nothing, this, you," I say. "Everything. The world."

"You're pretty weird," he says. "I respect that about you."

"Well, *gosh*," I say, taking another long drink. "That's super. I aim to amuse." I'm doing it on purpose now. Acting, but don't know how to act. I don't know who I am. The water tastes like stale ice cubes. "You're not marrying her, you guys are maybe hooking up or whatever. For now. Don't get crazy."

"I just want you to know," he says. "I wanted to say that I like you, too, Sloane."

"That's good," I quip. "Because Piper and I are a package deal."

A silence hangs between us, which is interrupted by a bounding dog, who lifts his leg and pees on the bow of the boat. Soup laughs. "It's a metaphor!" he says.

I don't ask him what for. Instead, I reach over him to the concoction he's made in the bucket and start stirring.

"We add this to that, right?" I say, even though I know it's right because I watched the video three times.

"Yep," he says. "Here, I'll do it." He takes it out of my hand, which is annoying.

"I can do it," I say, grabbing it back. It wobbles on the log, nearly spilling in the sand.

"Hey," he says.

"I watched the video, I know how to do this," I say. "Let me do something."

"Fine," he says, and for a second I think he's reaching out to hug me, but his fist comes up. "Fist pound!"

"Fist pound," I mumble, knocking my ring against his finger.

"Ouch." He shakes out his hand. "You punch like a boy."

He picks up the tools and starts stirring, ignoring what I said about fixing it myself. I can't bring myself to fight for it. Instead, I lean against the log and watch him. He's right, it smells terrible. He doesn't look up; he's focused on what he's doing. It gives me too much time to stare, to think, to wish. The whole thing takes less time than I thought it would, and before I'm really ready for it to be over, he's spreading the fiberglass along the crack. Then he's done.

My phone buzzes again. "Thanks for the help," I say. "I guess this was good, getting to know each other? And now we're super-good friends."

He gives me a funny look. "It was good, Captain Sarcastic," he says. "Yeah, it was fine. See you at school."

I nod. I start putting the supplies back in the bag. I want to say, *Were you ever looking at me that way before? Did you ever think of asking* me *out? Is there something here? Do you like me?* But I don't do it. It was probably only in my imagination. He never even noticed me. That happens with Piper. I'm Piper's friend. I'm not anyone someone would see, not when they first look, not when she's around, filling up the space with her Piper-ness.

I take my phone out of my back pocket and text her. "On my way with saltines and ginger ale," I type. "C U ASAP."

She texts back a kissy face.

"Gotta go," I say. I raise my hand in farewell to avoid another painful hug. I walk away carefully up toward the house, avoiding the barnacles on the jagged rocks, not looking back to see which way he decides to go, the smell of the fiberglass hanging in the air like the fog, like everything I didn't say.

"Sloane!" he calls after me, but I don't slow down. The crunch of my feet on the rocky sand swallows whatever he was going to say and everything I feel.

"He takes my breath away," Piper says. She's lying on her bed, fresh from the shower, wearing yoga pants, a wrap top. "You know?" Her voice is breathy and almost unfamiliar.

I try to take my feelings (non-feelings) about Soup and remove them from my feelings about Piper, doing human math, to decide: Is Piper changing or am I? The differential of who Piper is now and who she used to be is Soup. The inverse of me and Soup is her. Math is hard, says Barbie. "I have so much math homework to do, I can't stay. If I flunk this math final, I'll have to repeat it next year and it will wreck everything."

"You'll do fine," she says. "You always say that you're going to fail and you get, like, a B."

"Yeah, well, you always say that you're going to ace it and then you do," I point out.

She giggles. "Well, sorry. What? Anyway, why are we talking about math?"

"Because I can't stay long," I say. "Are you going to puke, or do you want some more ginger ale?"

"I don't know. I can't decide," she says. "I feel strange. Floaty. Is that love or a hangover?" She sigh-smiles.

"Someone probably put a roofie in your punch," I say. "Do you have blank spots in your memory?"

"Not even a little," she says dreamily. "I remember every detail; want to hear?"

"No," I say, too quickly.

She leans up on her elbow and gives me a confused look.

"I mean, of course," I say. "I was kidding. But quickly because math."

"Oh. Math is priority one. Gotcha. Well, first of all, the photographer took a million photos of us. He kept telling us that we were the most interesting couple at the dance. That says something, don't you think? Anyway, Soup is so deep."

"Deep how? Did you talk about the *meaning of life*?" I mean it sarcastically but she doesn't seem to notice my tone.

"Yes! We totally did. We're so on the same page. He's like me. He wants to spend his life being creative and moving around, traveling, you know?"

"Um, you mean like what *I* want?"

"Yes! Like you, too. Basically, he's like the boy version of you, which makes him so perfect for me. Oh God, I'm going to hurl again. Be right back." She leapfrogs off the bed and over me, barely making it to the toilet before retching. I follow her in to hold her hair. She spits into the toilet and sits down on the tile floor.

"He's a really good kisser," she goes on, like she hasn't just been throwing up. She wipes her mouth with toilet paper. "He's so good. We need to find you a boyfriend now. It's time."

"Why is it time?" I ask irritably. "We had a deal."

"It was a dumb deal," she says. "We made it when we were, like, fourteen and we didn't know. Now I know."

"I don't want a boyfriend," I protest.

"I know just the guy," she says. "You'll see. I met this guy at work and he'd be great for you. Perfect, even. Not a boyfriend. Maybe a friend with benefits. You don't even have to be friends."

"No!" I say. "I don't want a boyfriend. I have to go. Math o'clock."

"Fine," she says. She yawns, leans her head over on a pile of towels. "God, I'm so tired. Are my lips swollen? They feel swollen."

"No," I lie, even though her lips do look chapped. There is something in my veins that's like poison; I can feel it creeping through me, envious and deadly. "Yes," I add. "Maybe." I try to smile, try to laugh, to remember how to be normal. How to be myself.

"I fixed Mr. Aberley's boat," I say.

"Oh, great!" she says. "I would hate to sink in that water." She shudders. "Can you imagine? All those jellyfish."

"And it's cold," I say. "But you can swim. I mean, we'd survive it."

"Right," she says. "Maybe. You would. You're a better swimmer than me. I'd drown in five seconds. I hate being cold."

"I'm a crummy swimmer," I say. "Remember when I couldn't get my sixth badge? I took those stupid classes eight times before I gave up. Maybe I should go back and get it now. I'd be, like, the oldest one in a class of ten-year-olds."

She laughs. "You'd get it now. You're good!"

"Aw, thanks," I say. "Flatterer."

She yawns again. "I'm going to nap. Want to stay?"

"Nope, I'm going to study," I say.

"Math," we say at the same time.

"Booooooring," she says. "Later, gator hater."

"While, vile 'dile," I reply. I help her get into bed, tuck her in, kiss her forehead. "Happy dreams," I whisper.

She laughs. "You're the only one who ever says that to me. You're a better mom than my mom."

"Ha, don't ever forget it," I say, leaving, pulling the door shut tight behind me. I stand there for long enough to hear her making the sound she always makes in her sleep, a lip smacking that used to make sleepovers with her pretty hard to sleep through (not that it stopped me). "I love you," I whisper as I leave. But I'm starting to wonder if it's even still true. Can you stop loving someone? And do you know when you have? Or does it happen all at once, like a tree falling over?

If a tree falls in the forest, does anyone hear?

I am sitting on a log named Seth and I am drunk and it is Piper's birthday and Soup has given her a spray-painted portrait of herself and he is here and she is here and his stupid buddies are here and I know that I'm drunk. I'm at the point of being drunk where the best thing to do would be to rewind time and not drink the last thing that I drank, which was a beer. I never drink beer. I'm trying to talk to the log we call Seth and the log isn't answering because logs don't talk.

"I'm a mess," I tell Seth. "Why do we call you Seth? I can't even remember our own stories."

Seth rolls his eyes.

Logs don't have eyes.

They have knots.

Seth rolls his knots, I amend.

It is a party.

Piper's party.

We are on the island. This was my idea and it was a terrible idea because it's impossible to leave without swimming or stranding people. My mouth tastes like a field of corn rotting in the sun, and something worse: manure or death. I lie down in the wet sand. The tide is high enough that it is licking at my bare feet and I'm probably cold but I can't tell. The music from the party is above me like a thin layer of wispy clouds, between me and the stars. I can hear loud laughter emerging from behind the rock that separates me from the fire and the group. Soup is playing the guitar. I close my eyes. He's really good at it. Well, duh. Of course he is.

When I open my eyes, Piper is beside me. Her face swims in and out of focus. "Sit up," she says, and I do. Talking seems like too much trouble, so I lean on her. "You're wasted," she says. "Thank you for this, it's a perfect party. Drink some water." She puts a metal bottle in my hand.

I nod, because opening my mouth to talk feels impossible. I try to sip water without opening my lips: also impossible. I open them a crack. The water is delicious.

"This is the best water," I slur. "The best ever."

"You're the best," she says. "Always and forever."

I nod again. I am the best. That's me: the best.

Me and the water.

Then I shake my head. Wait, no. I'm not the best.

I'm the worst.

Remember?

I should tell her. I should say it out loud. *I love Soup*, I should say. *I'm sorry*, I should say.

Then she'll give him to me. A birthday present.

It's not my birthday.

"It's not my birthday," I say out loud.

"No, it's Piper's," says a voice, which is a boy's voice and not Piper's voice.

I look beside me and she has morphed into Charlie Nevers. Weird. Never, Charlie, never. That's what we used to call him. He is Soup's best friend for reasons I can't even begin to figure out. He was one of those jockish, terrible, loud boys when he was little and he has grown up into being the kind of boy who makes you aware that you're not much more than a collection of body parts that he may or may not find attractive. I am breasts. I am hair. I am a body. A girl.

I laugh to myself, a mumbled choking sound. "I am a body."

Charlie Nevers leans back on Seth. *How dare you touch Seth?* I think-yell.

I feel Seth shift into the sand.

"Rude," I mumble.

I can smell cheap boy cologne and smoke. I squint at him in the moonlight. He is talking. My voice is rising and falling in cadence with his, like music. What am I saying? He closes his eyes and takes a breath, lets out a low whistle. Then he says, "Do you ever look up at the stars and feel totally insignificant?"

"Deep," I manage, meaning for it to be sarcastic.

"I have hidden depths," he says. "You probably didn't know that about me. Anyway, now that Soup and Piper are hooking up, I've been thinking—" His sentence stops before the end, abrupt. Definite.

I pull myself up. I glare at him. I don't know whether to laugh or throw up. Too much to drink, too much. "No," I say. "Ablosutely not."

"I didn't ab-lo-sutely finish," he says. And then before I can do anything or stop him, his mouth is on my mouth. His tongue is touching my tongue and I'm biting down, I'm pushing, and it's like a music video, all broken images and static and I'm kicking him and I'm screaming and then there is Soup, pulling Charlie Nevers off me, and Charlie is wiping his mouth and saying, "That ho bit my tongue." And then Soup is flattening him and Piper is screaming and I'm so cold that what I do is I get into Mr. Aberley's boat and I push it and push it, wading out to my knees, and then I start rowing and I go home, leaving the bright fire of the island, the rising smoke, the loud voices, and Charlie Nevers behind.

"Goodbye," I say. "Goodbye."

* * *

"Are you coming?"

Mom pushes open my bedroom door, tentatively. She's using her extra-quiet voice. Her migraine voice. I have a hangover, not a migraine. I deserve to feel terrible. I deserve to have a headache. The room spins.

"I'm looking for my pants," I lie, sitting up. Then, "Mom?"

"What's wrong?" she says, stepping over a pile of clothes on the floor. She climbs up onto the bed awkwardly, perching on the edge. "Whoo, you stink. Campfire? Maybe you want to skip yoga and take a shower instead." She laughs. I don't. My bed is tall and her legs don't quite hit the floor. She looks like a kid. "What's going on?"

"I can't find my yoga pants," I say, then I start to cry.

"Sloaney?" she says. "Is this about the party? Did something happen?" She tentatively pats my shoulder like she's not sure where to touch me, or if she's allowed. I lean into her and we both fall backward onto the duvet. She struggles to sit up, pushing her hair back behind her ears as she does. She isn't a lying-on-the-bed kind of mom. "Do you need to talk? Is this where you tell me you're pregnant?"

"Ha ha, Mom," I say. It's an old joke of Mom's, that whenever I say I need to talk, I must be about to tell her exactly that. "I mean, *Grandma* . . ." I poke her in the ribs and she laughs obligingly. "I'm still a virgin," I add for good measure, wondering if it's still true. I think about Charlie Nevers and his tongue. My memory contains a huge black spot. There he was, trying to be deep, looking to get into my pants, and I was fighting, and then there's a great, cavernous blank.

"I know you're a virgin, Sloaney," she says, which is sort of offensive. She doesn't know half of it. Or even a quarter. She smells like some kind of vanilla perfume, toothpaste, the brisk, efficient scent of someone who is a good mother.

"Mom," I say quickly so I don't chicken out. "I feel like maybe something is wrong with me."

She looks at me. "What do you mean?" she asks.

"I don't know. I'm anxious," I admit. "I'm really anxious. Like in too much of a way, not a normal way. In a bad way."

She frowns. "Is it Piper?"

"What? *Piper?* This is nothing to do with Piper! God, Mom. Why do you do that?"

"Do what?"

"When there's something wrong, it's always Piper's fault! You always do that! Maybe this is about *me*, not her!"

"I'm sorry!" she says. "It's just that sometimes she's pretty, you know, *strong*. She's a strong influence in your life. And maybe her choices are a bit uncomfortable . . ."

"MOM," I say. "Stop. Please."

She stands up, awkwardly thumping onto the ground from the height of the bed. "Ouch." She rubs her ankle. "This bed is crazy. Why is it so high?"

"I have no idea," I say as coldly as possible. I roll over and face the window so I don't have to look at her.

"Oh, Sloane, I'm sorry. I did that wrong, didn't I?" she says. "I'm always making mistakes with you. Parenting is harder than you'd think, it turns out."

"That actually doesn't help either!" I say. "This isn't about your *parenting*! You don't need me to give you an A in parenting! You're fine! I wanted to . . . I was trying to . . ." I start crying harder. "I'm just really anxious!"

She takes a deep breath. "It's pretty normal, I think," she tries. "This is your last summer holiday. Maybe you should get a job to fill the time, so you don't sit around and worry so much. I can understand. It must be a lot of pressure. Twelfth grade is looming. You're going to be graduating. Everything probably feels like pressure, like a big deal. Maybe there's even pressure on this *summer* to be perfect. Is that it?"

"Mom," I say. "I think it's not only that." I relent. "Maybe it is a little that. But sometimes my heart beats really fast. I can't breathe. I forget how to breathe. How can I go to Europe if I can't breathe? How can I do anything?"

"Oh," she says. "Well, to start with, you *are* actually breathing."

"I know, but if I don't think about it, it all goes wrong. I can't do it properly."

"When that happens to me," she says, "I hold my breath.

Then, when I can't stand holding my breath any longer, the breathing seems to click back to normal. Does that sound crazy?"

I shake my head. "No, it sounds like it sort of makes sense."

She smiles. "See? I'm not so bad at this!"

"Yay, you," I say weakly. "I'll have the trophy engraved right away, Number One Mom!"

"Seriously," she says. "Do you want to talk to . . . someone? A therapist?"

I shrug. I do, but I also don't. "No," I say. "Yes." Then, "Maybe."

"When you do, please tell me, honey. I'll set something up for you." She lays her hand on my forehead, like she used to when I was little and I was sick.

"How's my temperature?" I say.

"Normal," she says. "And it's yoga o'clock."

I roll my eyes. "Okay, okay. First, I have to change."

She steps out into the hallway while I change my pants. The ones I'm putting on smell musty, but yoga is mostly an exercise in farting and sweating. It may bill itself as something scented gently with patchouli and flowers, but once you've done a couple of classes, you learn to hold your breath. Maybe that's why breath holding soothes anxiety. It prevents the smells from filtering in.

"I want you to know you can always talk to me," Mom calls from the hall. "About anything."

For a second, I hesitate, hovering between moods. Choosing. I could tell her about the party. About Charlie. About how I felt. About how I fought. But I can't and I won't and I don't and I'm so mad, for a second I forget that it's not her I'm mad at, it's me.

"Forget it," I say as I join her. "I'm fine. Yoga will be good. Helpful. Calming. Hippies do yoga, right? And they're always calm! No one ever says, Hey, look at that agitated hippie!"

She smiles. "It may have something to do with the pot, too. NOT that I'm advocating for that. Don't do that!"

"Mom, it's fine. I'm not. I hate the smell of it, for one thing."

"Me, too," she says. She looks at her wrist, where she wears a Fitbit that doubles as a watch. "Okay, we have to run! I love this class. This class is the best. But if we're late, we miss my favorite part."

"Sure, Mom," I say, letting her off the hook. "Hurrying."

My heart skitters a bit, but the wave of panic doesn't come. I follow her down the stairs to her car, which is a sensible Mom-style white Land Rover. It still has that new car smell. The window is down, so I push the button, and the way that it firmly closes makes me feel safe. I turn on the radio and lean

117

back. The car rolls softly on the road and Mom hums and the green leaves blow brightly against the blue sky in the hot wind and the air conditioner silkily cools the car and my heart beats normally and I hold my breath and then breathe and everything is okay. It is okay. I swear it.

I'm okay.

I dig my nails into the palm of my hand and check my phone again.

Nothing.

I shut it off and let it drop onto the floor.

The tires crunch on gravel as we pull into the yoga studio.

"All set?" says Mom cheerily.

I grin, which probably looks like a rictus, which is fair because I feel dead inside. Piper still hasn't called. Not to say "R U OK?," not to get mad at me for abandoning her, not for anything.

She has Soup now, so she doesn't need me.

Something jiggles at the corner of my memory from last night, in combination with the wave of hangover nausea. Soup, his fists raised. Soup, pushing Charlie into the water.

I step on my phone on purpose getting out of the car. I like the way the glass feels when it cracks under my weight. "What's wrong with me?" I whisper again, but Mom is already pulling open the wooden doors, gesturing at me to hurry. I grab my mat and open the car door, the heat of the day flowing over me like a tidal wave. Sweat beads up on my face. Something about it being hot makes it hard to breathe, like I'm inhaling water.

I follow Mom inside, drowning, trying to get to the surface and failing.

Piper is lying on her back on my bedroom floor. Her legs are splayed open, like a broken doll or a *Vogue* model. She's wearing cutoff denim shorts and a tank top that's too big. She has sunglasses on.

"Too bright in here?" I say, nudging her with my foot.

"Everything is too bright," she says dreamily. "Everything is soooo bright."

"You sound high," I say shortly, feeling mean, wanting to pick a fight. "Take them off." She hasn't even *mentioned* what happened with Charlie. She hasn't said a thing.

She sighs, rolling over dramatically. She takes her sunglasses off. Her eyes are red and bloodshot. "Two-day hangover!" she says. "Whooo!"

"You must have been so wasted," I say flatly, not caring, but knowing what my line is. It's not her fault that I'm mad. She doesn't even *know* that I'm mad. I pull the curtains closed. "Better?" I say.

"Thanks," she says. "Better. God, I spent all day yesterday throwing up. It was the worst."

"Gross," I say supportively. "Fried food and fountain Coke?"

"Soup brought me some on his way to work. I had to call in sick. Ugh." She sits up and does that terrible thing with her tongue. "Sooooooooo . . . ," she says. "ANYWAY."

"Tell me," I say. My heart hurts, like it's stretched too far, like my calves do after a long run: a charley horse in my chest. I rub it.

"Are you feeling yourself up?" she asks.

"Totally."

She laughs. "Laughing makes my head hurt! Don't make me laugh!"

"Sorry not sorry," I say. "Stop stalling and tell me!" I pretend to be giddy but I'm not giddy because I'm a terrible best friend and I hate myself for feeling this way but I hate her for making me feel this way and it's complicated, so complicated. Downstairs the vacuum roars to life, as the cleaning guy, Elvis, starts his shift. I wonder what he's vacuuming up. I wish he could vacuum up my memory. I wish he could vacuum up my feelings. I wish I had a dog. A dog would understand me. Animals have a sixth sense. He'd be lying on my bed right now, between me and Piper, protecting me from what she has to say. As it is, I only have my camera. I pick it up off the corner of my desk and turn it on.

"Rolling," I say. "And . . . action."

Piper crawls up onto the bed like a dying man in the desert crawling to an oasis and drapes herself over me like she has a billion times before. She's a person who likes touching. The camera tilts.

"Get off me," I say. "Please. It's too hot for this and I'm trying to film."

Her skin feels cool and she smells clean. Like Neutrogena and Ivory. Pure. But she isn't.

"Sweetie," she says. "My tweetie bird"—*again* with that terrible nickname that I've hated since she coined it when we were six—"we did it."

My ears ring a little bit. I'm breathing too much, too fast, like I've been running. "It?" I play dumb, slightly stuck on "tweetie bird," but totally stuck on "it."

"Me and Soup," she says. "*It*. We had sex. And it was dreamy. It was perfect. It was amazing." She bites her lip. Her face is right over mine now. "It was *great*. They don't tell you how good it feels." She comes closer, grinning, and I turn my face, fast. Her lips land on my cheek. "He made me a portrait." She frowns. "Wait, you'd left by then, I guess? Did you even see it? I have to show you." She takes out her phone and scrolls through, laughing at her own pictures. I don't try to see them. "Here." She thrusts it in my face. I get a glimpse of green and red and blue and lips before she takes it back again. "Amazing, right? He's so talented. I think talent is sexy. There's a name for that, I think. When you're attracted to what someone does and not only what they look like. Anyway, Charlie took everyone off the island in his dad's boat but he left us the dinghy, which was nice of him"—she shoots me a look—"because you stole our ride."

"Yeah, sorry," I say. "I knew Charlie had a boat. I knew you wouldn't, like, die out there. So please be over it."

She waves her hand. "It was a big deal to Soup because of their fight," she says. "He didn't want to ask. But anyway, it is no matter."

"No matter!" I repeat, laughing. "You're the lady on *Downton Abbey*. Should I get your hat? Your gloves? Your manservant?"

"I've never seen it," she says, ignoring me. She stares into the lens of the camera and blinks. It's not an ordinary blink. It's a seductive blink. A pretty blink. I cross my eyes and she doesn't notice. She bites her lip. "Do you have to film this part? It's sort of personal."

"I'm not filming," I lie.

"I can see the red light!" she says.

"Fine," I say. "I lied." I turn it off.

"Oh, you can film it," she says. "Do it. I might love watching this later when I'm old and bitter."

"I'm sure this will be the highlight of your life," I say. "That time you had a two-day hangover and lost five pounds from puking."

She makes a face. I pick the camera back up and hit record. "Okay. Filming the most memorable moment of your life, Piper Sullivan. And . . . action."

She smiles and gives the lens a look.

"Are you flirting with me?" I ask.

"Stop!" she says. "I'm being serious! Anyway, cut that bit out. So me and Soup were alone. Soup had brought sleeping bags and hidden them up on the top. It was soooo romantic. He set them up on the beach. I didn't want to remind him that the tide was coming up because it would have wrecked the moment, you know?"

I grunt.

"We lay in the sleeping bags, watching the stars. I showed him where some of the constellations were and how to find the North Star. I think he was *pretty* impressed."

I make a sound.

"What?" she says.

"I didn't say anything!"

"Then we took off our clothes. It wasn't awkward or anything; it was like our clothes slid off us . . ." She sighs dreamily.

"We were just touching and touching and I didn't even think about telling him to stop and it was"—she pauses—"amaaaaaazing." She sits up, and then in her normal voice, she goes, "I'm not kidding, you have to do it."

"I have to have sex with Soup?" I say. "Gross. No thanks."

"No," she says. "You have to have sex with *someone*. I can't explain. It totally changes you. It's totally changed me. Don't I look different?"

"You look like you have a weird lip condition," I say. "Stop licking your lip." I contemplate her face. "You also look dehydrated."

"Do I?" She sits up, pushes her hair out of her face. "I drank gallons of water yesterday. I feel so bloated." She puts her hand on her flat stomach. Her tank top is slipping off her shoulder.

"You keep doing this tongue thing," I say. "It's . . . weird. Stop doing it."

"I do not!" she says. "Why are you being unpleasant? I thought you'd want to know, you know, the juicy deets."

I roll over and turn my back on her. My eyes sting. There's no reason to cry, but I'm crying. What is wrong with me? I can't let her see my face. She'll think it means something that it doesn't mean or that it *does* mean and then everything will fall apart. "Charlie basically attacked me," I say. "What if he raped me? It felt rapey. Was it rapey?"

She laughs. "He did NOT rape you. You were so drunk.

124

You were being so strange, for real. He says you came on to him and then started freaking out and then you puked all over his leg. Poor guy."

"Poor guy?" I repeat. Is she right? Could my memory be wrong? It's blurry and dark when I examine it. I'm not sure. But I remember Seth. And the feeling of panic when Charlie was on me and I didn't want him to be. There's no mistaking that. I knew it wasn't what I wanted. I told him to stop.

"I . . ."

"Yeah?" she says.

"Did you know that within a couple of years, there's not going to be ice in the Arctic anymore?" I say.

"Oh!" she says. "That reminds me. You may want to rewind the tape on that camera. I think Fatty was filming you and Charlie down on the log."

"Why would he do that?" I ask, my blood running cold.

"Well, you were really going at it, for one thing." She raises one eyebrow at me. "You were all over him. He probably forgot that it was your camera and you weren't likely to post it to Snapchat or anything."

"Charlie was all over *me*, you mean," I say. "Soup saved me. Charlie was an octopus with his stupid man-tentacles and strength. Did you know that octopuses don't have a brain but they can solve puzzles and play games? They're really cool. Unlike Charlie."

"Isn't it octopi?"

"No, octopuses."

"Yeah, well, you didn't start screaming for help until it went *prettttty* far," she says.

"Are you kidding me? I told him right away to stop!"

She taps the camera. "Watch the footage," she says. "The camera doesn't lie."

"Well, it adds ten pounds," I joke weakly.

"If there's no ice and the sea levels rise, I guess everything we have will be underwater. Like Atlantis. If that's really going to happen and not just, you know, media or whatever, then we should leave artifacts for future divers to find. A time capsule."

"The world is such a mess," I say. "And it's true that it is. Why would anyone make that up? Nothing matters. There won't be anyone to find it. Everything will be extinct. Do you ever think about how humans are basically animals in captivity? But we do it voluntarily. Like we live in houses, which are basically cages, and we perform acts of going to work and whatever, but we're not exactly living in the wild. Did you know there are only forty red wolves left in the wild but thousands in captivity? It's messed up."

"Wow," she says. "You're like young David Attenborough or something. Surely you can cash in on your weird fixation with THE END OF TIMES." She leans her head over mine, her hair falling like a curtain in front of my face. "Should I call existential 911 on the emo phone?"

"Ha ha," I say. "I'm not. I shouldn't have brought it up. Forget it."

Piper imaginary dials her phone. "Yes, hello, existential operator? We're having a crisis here over on Holly Point Drive? Come quick! Send pizza. And alcohol."

I laugh, even though it's not really funny. "Give me that!" I say. "Who did you really call?"

"No one, you nut," she says. "I was only playing. But don't you want to know more? About me and Soup? Forget about the apocalypse for, like, five minutes."

I sigh. "Fine," I say. "I hope you used a condom."

"Are you my mother? Duh. The last thing I want is little Soups. Souplets. Cup-a-Soups. That would wreck everything."

"Truth," I say. I get up and turn the fan on and we both watch for a second as the curtains lift and billow like Halloween ghosts.

"Okay," she says. "It was like this . . ."

I wait. "Come on," I say. "You wanted to tell, so tell."

"Sloane?" she says. "The thing is . . ."

"WHAT?" I say. "You're driving me nuts. Spill it. Dreamy, et cetera. Remember?"

"I *can't* remember," she whispers. "I drank too much and I

can't remember anything between us taking our clothes off and him chucking the condom into the nettles."

"Into the nettles!" I repeat, horrified. "That's so gross! Mr. Aberley is going to find that thing!"

She makes a face.

"And you said it was dreamy! You said it was ethereal!" I throw a pillow at her. "Liar!"

"It might have been!" she says, laughing harder. "I didn't want to commemorate for all time the fact that I can't remember it! And anyway, stop, I'm going to wet my pants! When you do it the first time, you have to be sober! For both of us!"

"Don't pee on my bed!" I say, clutching my side, which is cramping from laughing so hard. I pull the curtain open and we're blinded by the sunlight, which pours in everywhere, hard and bright. The camera falls off the bed and onto a pile of laundry and I don't pick it up. "Ethereal!" she shouts, and we're laughing like we'll never ever stop.

NOW

THE POLICE HAVE QUESTIONS. I HAVE
questions. Everyone has questions.

I hate these cops. I hate Piper. I hate everyone. I don't know
where it's coming from: the hate is leaking out of me. Hissing.
Can the police hear it? I'm not someone who hates. My heart
skips a beat and mumbles.

I want to break something. I look at my thin wrists and
think about how easy it would be. I press my thumbnail into
one of the blue veins. It leaves a little valley in my skin, a
crescent moon.

Focus.

The police (who are now in the kitchen) have *questions*.
Some. A few.

The police, who are looking around at the cherrywood floors and new cabinets and stainless steel appliances and granite countertops, have very important questions.

The police, who think this is a "nice place," have some/a few/very important questions.

I'm someone who can answer their questions.

Am I?

I'm a minor. They can't ask me questions without a parent present. Where are my present parents? If Peter Piper picked a peck of pickled peppers, how many present parents did Peter Piper pick?

I'm wearing a bikini.

My bikini is bright pink. A bright pink bikini does not seem to be the right thing to be wearing to answer questions or to wait to answer questions, as the case may be. My eyes are impossibly dry. My tongue is stuck to the roof of my mouth. The air conditioner is pulling goose bumps out of my skin by the millions. All of that is happening.

Oh, and also, *Piper is dead.*

It's all jumbled up.

It doesn't make sense.

It's about Soup.

It can't be about Soup when Piper is dead.

Can it?

"Soup," I whisper. "Call me, call me, call me."

He can't help me now, in the kitchen, with these cops, shifting and breathing and making noises and interrupting the calm air in here with their importance and radios that blast short bursts of static.

I love you, Piper says. *What is supposed to happen next?*

I'm imagining that. I must be.

I'm crying.

I'm not crying.

I'm asleep.

This is a dream.

A nightmare.

The waiting questioners' eyes skate over my body, slipping and sliding. They are men, after all. Adult Charlies, reducing me to a sum of my female parts. The uniform doesn't change that. I cover my skin with my hands. Too much skin. Not enough hands. The men stare at my too-small hands and what they are hiding.

They have tiny notebooks.

They have big pens. Ready.

Time is hiccuping. Too fast, too slow.

It was always about you, Piper says. *Anteeksi.*

* * *

131

"I'd die without you," Piper said.

I was twelve.

I was lying in a hospital bed. That was the year the migraines started. The headaches so bad that I could barely open my eyes. I couldn't eat or sleep or move. Mom and Dad thought it was a tumor. I'd lie awake and hear them talking late at night in hushed voices that somehow I could hear like the volume had been turned up, bathed in static. I thought I was going to die.

But the MRI showed my brain was clear of flaws, the gray matter folding neatly like stacked towels. There was nothing wrong with it. "It's a perfect brain," the neurosurgeon said.

There was everything wrong with it, but what was wrong with it didn't show up on the scan.

Now that I'm seventeen, I think I understand that the migraines were the way that my anxiety looked when I was younger. A panic attack was a headache. A headache was what I feared. So I was scared all the time, of the headache that meant I was scared.

I was so scared.

Piper was the only one who I could tell. She always got me. She was always with me, my parents bringing her to the hospital the way the girl in the next bed's mom brought her a huge green teddy bear.

The walls of the room were a terrible mint green and my gown was a terrible mint green and the sheets were the same terrible mint green and now even the sight of mint green makes me queasy. I was drowning in mint green. I was dying. The pain in my head was a huge, blossoming flower that grew and grew and grew until I thought my skull would burst.

Piper lay beside me on those green sheets with her orange Chucks on, her head on my shoulder. I wanted to go climb inside my headache and curl up in it. In my mind, the headache was a cramped room with a fire that burned too hot.

"Dying," I'd burbled.

"You won't," she said. "I'll die before you, anyway." She grinned. "The good die young."

"You'll live forever," I said. I tried to say something funny, but all that came out was, "Singing funeral."

"Ha ha," she said. "If you die, I *am* totes going to sing at your funeral. Something fierce, maybe Beyoncé"—she paused—"or Justin Bieber."

"NO!" I managed. "I'm going to haunt you so hard."

"Deal," she said, and then we both laughed and my head hurt in a different way and the bed spun around on the ceiling and made patterns with light that scrolled across my line of vision and then my parents came in and then the doctor.

Within a few days I was fine again and now I'm in the kitchen and she's going to have a funeral because she did it, she died first.

"Two zero seven Adam," the radio interrupts. "Please respond."

The kitchen chair squeaks on the floor.

I am you, Piper says.

The feeling I get before a migraine floats onto my skull and settles there like a cat, delicately kneading with his claws pulled in.

BEFORE

PIPER IS SITTING ON THE EDGE OF HER
bathtub, her hair pulled into a ponytail. My iPhone is playing
top European dance music. We're trying to get used to it, to
enjoy it. We want to like it so that when we're in Europe, we
can say, "Oh, I love this song," which right now is a lie. The
music makes me think of veins, squeezing blood through
extremities, under high pressure.

I'm sitting on the counter, the camera pointing at Piper.
I'm trying not to laugh, trying to let the music be the only
sound. She snips the scissors in the air three times and they
make a swift scything sound.

Then she reaches behind her with the shears and I can feel
as much as hear the sharpened blades slicing through it; I can

see her head lift up suddenly like it's floating, untethered, a balloon. I gasp, which I'll have to edit out. Her ponytail falls into the tub with a sad thump. She grins. "And . . . cut," she says. "See what I did there?"

I stop recording. "Ha ha," I say. I feel light-headed. I look in the mirror to make sure my own hair is still there.

Piper stands next to me. Her hair falls jaggedly to her chin. "It's cute, right?" She sounds doubtful, and she should.

I nod. "Maybe lighter blond," I suggest. "It would look more intentional."

"Yeah," she agrees. She reaches up and touches her hair. She lifts it and drops it. I touch it, too. Then we are both touching it, mussing it, messing it up. She's laughing, but suddenly, she's also crying. "I'm a woman now!" she shouts. She shakes her head vigorously, an animal, a wild thing.

I laugh and start filming again, the twirl of her hair against the light, me beside her, my hair still to my waist; it looks like gold. *I'm the pretty one now*, I think, and then the familiar surge of self-loathing sweeps over me like a curling wave. Later, when I watch the video, I'll see the moment that my facial expression changed, which will make it seem worse somehow.

The thing with the hair—our hair—is that it's so easy to hide behind. You don't have to worry so much what your face looks like, or your body for that matter, when your hair is long and blond, a gleaming golden curtain. Behind that, you can be anything. You can be anyone. Piper looks naked now. Her neck is long and skinny, like a plant that hasn't been exposed to the right amount of light. The battery light on my camera flashes.

"It's dead," I say.

"Hair?" she says.

"Well, that, too, I think," I say. "But I meant the camera."

"Oh, man," she says. "That sucks. I wanted to say why I did it, on film."

"But people will see it!" I laugh.

"I think people should know," she says. "Why is it always a secret? It's not shameful. I've had sex!" She looks at her face in the mirror, leans way in until her nose is practically touching the glass. "I'VE HAD SEX!" she shouts, and her breath makes a cloud on the glass. She stands up straight. "So there," she adds.

"It's kind of crooked," I say. "Want me to straighten it?"

She scratches at her skull. "Nope," she says. "It still feels way too long. I think I'm going to shave it."

"Shave it?" I repeat.

"It's just not *enough* like this," she says. "I still look like a little girl. And I'm a woman now."

I laugh. "Do you even hear yourself?" I drop my voice and mimic, "*I'm a woman now.* You don't even remember it!"

She gives me a hard stare. "Sure, but I'm different. Fundamentally. I should look different. I should look as different as I feel."

I shrug. "If you say so," I say. "I'm a dumb virgin. What do I know?"

She frowns. "We really have to fix that," she says. "It's time." She pulls her remaining hair back from her face and looks closely at her nose in the mirror. "My pores are gross." She reaches for a washcloth, soaks it in hot water. Then she carefully lies down in the empty tub, and lays the cloth over her face. "Om . . . ," she says.

I sit down on the toilet and balance my feet on the edge of the tub. "I don't *like* anyone right now," I say. "I don't want to sleep with someone for the sake of it. What are the options? Anyway, the boys at school are basically different versions of Charlie. They want to grope a boob and tell everyone about it."

"They aren't," she says, her voice muffled and her face hidden by the cloth. "You're so hard on people. You know Soup and Charlie had a huge fight about you? They aren't even talking anymore. Besides, who says you have to like the first guy you sleep with? If you choose him, if you choose *it*, then it's empowering. It's not like how most girls lose it, drunk and accidentally. It's *purposeful*." For a minute, she sounds like her old self. Her pre-boyfriend self. Her powerful self.

I nod. "I guess."

"It's not like he—whoever he is—won't want to do it. Boys want to do it. They're pretty much at the mercy of how much they want it. But think about it. Your choice, you're sober, you'll really know what sex itself feels like without being too drunk to remember or too caught up in feelings." She sits up straight and the washcloth falls off her face, which is now bright red, and onto her lap. "It's feminism, if you think about it. It's taking charge, before everything gets confused by love. I'm messed up by love. Look at me! But I think it's the sex that made the difference, and it would have even if I didn't love Soup. I feel *unlocked*."

"Unlocked!" I repeat. "Well, why didn't you say so?" I pull out my phone and fake dial a number. "Hello? Yes? Will you please come over and unlock me? I will shave my head! And be transformed!" I start to laugh but she's not laughing along with me. "Come on," I say. "Hey, remember those Hare Krishna people from the airport? I bet they've been . . . UNLOCKED."

"Shut up!" She glares at me. "I'm serious. Oh!" She reaches up to the back of the toilet and grabs her phone. It has a big crack across the middle. Her phones are always broken and she never gets them fixed. She starts typing frantically.

"What are you doing?" I say. "That's rude."

"I totally had to tell Soup that I'd done it," she says, biting her lip. I fight the urge to throw a bottle of shampoo at her. "Selfie!" She tilts her head to the side and makes a kissy face.

"Stage one. That's what I'm telling him. This is just the first step. God, he's cute. Don't you think he's cute?"

I shrug. "He's *fine*."

"Yeah, he is." She raises one eyebrow. "You think so."

"I don't *like* your boyfriend," I say, blushing. I can see it in the mirror. I know she can see it, too. I hate her for being able to tell, for knowing. "Stop trying to make it sound like that's what I'm saying!"

"I'm not!" she protests. "But I have an idea. A terrible, wonderful idea. Let's go to a movie tonight."

"Wow," I say. "That's thinking out of the box. What a wild idea."

She throws the wet washcloth at me. "I'm serious!" she says.

"For the air-conditioning?"

"Yeah, totally," she says. "For the *air-conditioning*. Now pass me the clipper things. Go big or go home, right?"

"Sure," I say, passing her the clippers. "Go big or go home."

NOW

ONCE, IN THIRD GRADE, I THREW UP ON my desk. The teacher had been reading *Old Yeller* out loud. No one should read a book about a dog dying to children. I kept swallowing the sadness but it found a way to get out.

The puke pooled and then started its slow slide toward my lap. Piper got up and took me by the hand. Other kids were screaming. There was basically a riot whenever someone threw up in the room. Piper took me to the bathroom, like a mom would. She held a wet paper towel to my forehead while I puked and puked and puked until I was nearly inside out. She held my hair out of the way. She told me, "I've got this. I've got you."

I threw up again on her shoe, something purple that I drank at lunch.

"The dog shouldn't die!" I kept saying. "The dog isn't ever supposed to die!"

The next day, when she threw up at recess, I wasn't there to help her. I don't know how it was contagious, but it was. I'd thought it was sadness, not norovirus, but I was wrong. It was the timing that made it seem like it was the dog's fault.

When Piper puked, I was at home on the couch crunching on ice nuggets, my feet on Dad's lap, cartoons playing on the TV that hung on the wall.

When I got back to school, everyone seemed to have forgotten that I'd started the barf sickness, and the nickname Piper Puker had stuck to her. Luckily, it didn't live through the summer and re-stick in fourth grade. But still, every once in a while at a party, she'll drink too much and someone (usually Fatty or one of his idiot clan) will bring it up. "Uh-oh," he'll shout, "look out for Puker!"

Jerk.

I hate everyone.

No one will ever call her that again.

Because now she's dead.

Piper is dead.

The fact of her death scrolls over everything in the room,

like a ticker tape. There's the coffeemaker, half full of cold coffee from this morning, and Piper is dead. There's the sink, shining in the sunlight, and Piper is dead. There is a plate of cinnamon buns covered with plastic wrap, the icing flattened and sticky against the cellophane, and Piper is dead. There are my fingernails, painted blue for the party last night, now chipped, resting on the table, and Piper is dead. There are two cops with pens and notebooks and Piper is dead dead dead dead dead

dead.

You're going to have to get used to the idea, she says.

"I can't," I mutter, teeth clenched.

It was supposed to be you, she says.

"It was supposed to be me," I echo.

"Are you okay?" one of the cops says, trying to sound sympathetic.

I shiver. "No," I say. The migraine gives me a tiny preview, fireworks that burst across my field of vision like sparklers.

He averts his eyes.

"Sorry," he says.

We wait.

And Piper is still dead.

Well, duh.

* * *

I'm glad that I'm not the dead one.

This makes me a bad person.

Right?

I guess that I'm guaranteed a longer life because *only the good die young.*

Answer the questions.

Well, I would if someone asked one.

Question: If you're comfortable, just answer this one thing. Do you know . . . ?

Answer: WHAT HAPPENED? TELL ME WHAT HAPPENED?

Statement: PIPER.

The word "Piper" is not a question. Piper is not a question. Or an answer. *Piper* is a fact. The fact is that Piper is dead.

I look for a question on the floor, near my feet. The hardwood lies there solidly and does not bother to answer.

If I died, the floor would keep existing. I'm simply not in the floor's future for as long as the floor will have one.

Unless the house burns down, I guess.

My skin is hot.

I could burst into flames.

And then what?

All of our futures are the same anyway.

Dead.

Everyone Dies at the End, a documentary by Sloane Whittaker.

Remember: the best way to stave off a panic attack is to find something to see, something to feel, something to hear, something to touch.

I touch the table.

I feel the table: crumbs, something sticky.

I feel dizzy.

I feel sick.

I hear nothing.

I hear static.

The Internet lies.

I hear the sound of men who I don't know breathing in the air of the kitchen that belongs to my parents, not to them.

I hear a vacuum cleaner.

I see two men.

I see the table.

I see the window.

I see the sky, which is the blue of Slurpees that stain my teeth, and I want to get up and close the blinds but I'm trapped on a kitchen chair, the backs of my bare thighs stuck to it. I'm still in my pink bikini and this is all wrong and the panic isn't subsiding and I sort of wish I could have a drink.

The Slurpees I've been drinking lately have been heavily spiked with vodka from Piper's mom's endless supply, which she keeps in the freezer so that it's always tooth-achingly cold. Those Slurpees taste like something inside me is loosening its grip.

I need something inside me to loosen its grip right now.

Its grip is ice cold.

I shiver.

I'll never drink again if you make her not dead, I bargain with God. *I'll quit. I swear.*

God laughs.

The Slurpee I haven't drunk seeps around my heart and freezes.

It's like that.

Did I invite these policemen into the house? Did they ring the doorbell? Did I open it and say "Yes?" Did I say "Come in?"

The migraine is like the tide, inevitable and all-powerful.

That seems impossible. Another impossible thing on a long list of impossible things that seem to be happening, that are happening, that have already happened.

"*Uxolo*," I mumble.

"Sorry?" says one of the cops. "What did you say?"

"Sorry."

"What?" he says again.

On the wall over the table there is a photograph that my dad took of me and Piper on the beach at sunset. We are maybe eleven in the photo. We were kids. The two of us are silhouettes, facing each other, the wind lifting our ponytails symmetrically, perfectly. We look like mirrors of each other, our ponytails floating upward as though just outside the shot, a giant UFO is about to pull us up and away from all this.

Right after that photo was taken, I tripped and sprained my ankle. Piper carried me up the beach in a wobbly piggyback. She kept nearly but not quite falling, and I was scared but also laughing and I held on and the gravel came closer and receded and eventually we got to the car, stunned by how funny everything was even when it wasn't.

Did I ever look after her?

Well, no.

The policeman clears his throat. He looks worried. Well, he should. I'm worried, too. My migraine starts to hum, increasing in volume.

The two men are too big for this space, for this table. They make everything look wrong: Too bright. Too shiny. Too new. Too expensive.

These two men in police uniforms—dark blue shirts, pants, black belts, guns—are sitting at the kitchen table, where Mom and Dad would be if Mom and Dad were home. There is a newspaper open on the table and a bowl of half-eaten yogurt and three empty coffee cups and a spray bottle of SPF 60. There is a pile of drying-up orange peel and an AA battery and a handwritten note that reads, "Dentist @ 11, don't forget to FLOSS." There is a single red sock.

"Can I go upstairs and get dressed?" I ask. My voice is too thin to penetrate the thick air.

One of the men clicks his pen. *Click, click, click.* I can feel that click in my teeth. *Please don't click*, I want to say. I might say it out loud. I don't know. Something is happening between the voice in my head and my actual voice. I don't know which is which. There's a weird prickling feeling over my entire scalp, like my head has gone to sleep. He doesn't stop.

I have to lie down.

I need a pill.

I need my mom.

I need Soup.

* * *

I get mixed up.

Everything swirls: The past. The present. The future.

The migraine is a flickering light show and everything I'm seeing is melting against it, smearing at the edges.

I feel sick.

Mom is home.

There is hushed conversation.

There is louder conversation.

She nods at me. I have to say what I know.

I tell them what I know, which is my name. I know my name. My name is Sloane. Piper-and-Sloane. Sloane-and-Piper. Slo-and-Pipes. Pipes-and-Slo. "Sloane Campbell Whittaker." And my age. "Seventeen." And yes, I did know Piper Sullivan. I totally know Piper Sullivan. Yes, Piper Sullivan is my best friend. Is, was, will always be, never was, I don't know.

Mom answers their questions.

I answer their questions.

There was a party.

I don't know.

I don't know.

She was mad.

I kissed her boyfriend.

I don't know! I don't know!

I don't know who that is.

(I do.)

Well, maybe he's a bit familiar.

(Oh my God, not him.)

No, he isn't.

(He is.)

Who is he?

(I know who he is.)

He did what?

Why can't I know?

Mom?

My ears are full of sand and broken glass. I'm cold. I need to get dressed. I keep thinking about seaweed. I don't know why. I can't stop it. My brain is seaweed. The chair is stuck to my legs.

Mom is saying that it is enough.

One of the men is not talking and one of them is talking but his voice is getting mixed up with the ringing in my ears.

She floated in on the current from somewhere. Where?

The island, the island.

He was sleeping on the island.

My island.

Our island.

Mr. Aberley's island.

I can feel the seaweed on my skin, flat and clammy like a hand.

A woman comes into the room. Who is she? Now there

are two cruisers in the driveway. The woman is not in a uniform but the way she moves gives away her police-ness. It's the square, rigid way she holds her shoulders. The way her mouth has settled into a flat line. Her no-nonsense ponytail pulled so tight that her roots are showing. She says to the men, like I'm not even here, "What have you got?"

Maybe I'm not here.

Maybe I'm upstairs getting dressed.

Maybe I'm asleep on the cold, silky sand.

Mom strokes my forehead and my hair. I'm leaning on Mom. She's pulled a chair close to me. It seems strange to have the chairs like that, close enough to touch. I can see the makeup settling into the pores of her nose. Sometimes migraines turn my eyes into magnifying lenses. Sometimes they are fun-house mirrors. Images ripple and bend. Nothing is quite real.

Something cool slips over my skin.

I'm in the water and the cold hands of the seaweed are not letting me reach the surface. I breathe harder and harder.

"Mom," I say.

Someone has put a blanket over my shoulders. The blanket is cashmere. It is as soft as a baby goat. The blanket smells luxuriously clean. I pull it over my nose and breathe it in, like the expensiveness of it will erase what is happening.

Mom says, "Enough."

The men and one woman glance at one another in ten

different ways. Messages zing back and forth between them that are unspoken but are about me in my pink bikini and the way that Piper died.

"He does look sort of familiar," I say.

The eddy of the lie pulls me down, far and fast, and the surface is so far away and the water is like velvet and it closes over me.

I knew him.

I did something.

I made him angry.

If no one knows, it didn't happen.

It was meant to be me.

BEFORE

PIPER SHOWS UP AT THE MOVIE WITH her hair cut in a perfect pixie, dyed platinum, truly silver. It looks as soft as feathers. There is nothing about it that suggests she shaved it with clippers. I reach out and touch it. "You did that?" I ask doubtfully. "It's so soft!"

She laughs. "Mom FREAKED out when she saw my butchery. She took me to her guy. Do you like it?" She points her chin down and makes a duck face at me, which looks way cuter than it should.

I sigh. "It looks amazing," I admit.

"See?" she says. "I feel so different. Between my hair and the sex, I'm a completely different person."

"Don't go nuts," I say. "You look good, but you're still you."

"Don't be so sure. Maybe you don't know me at all." She laughs, draping her arm around me, grabbing my hand. "Come on, let's get tickets."

"What are we seeing, anyway?" I say, squinting at the billboard. The choices are pretty limited. Big Action or Cheesy Romance or Animated Kids' Film. None of them really appeals.

"Oh, who cares?" she says. "Not the point. There's someone"—she winks at me, hard, like her contact is falling out—"who I want you to meet."

"Who?" I say, suddenly uncomfortable. "Are you setting me up?"

"No! Nothing like that! Well, *sort of* like that. But not exactly like that. Come and meet him. Then you'll see what I mean."

We buy tickets for the film that starts the soonest, the Big Action. At least it's air-conditioned inside; our usual reason for going to movies is to escape the heat (her) and to see the newest documentary (me). There are no documentaries playing, but the sidewalk outside is shimmering with heat, making everything seem surreal, a mirage.

That heat does something strange to my eyes, to the way I see Piper. For a minute, she looks like someone I don't even know.

Piper drags me through the lobby, our footsteps muted by

the thick and filthy crimson-colored carpeting. It is all pop-corn smells and kids running around, crying for a candy bar, sticky hands clutching at their parents. "Kids these days," I murmur to Piper, and she rolls her eyes.

"Okay, Grandma," she says. "I'll get them off your lawn." She's joking, but still, my heart drops because Grandma isn't doing well. I heard Mom and Dad talking last night. They think she had a stroke. I haven't said it out loud yet because I don't want it to be true. Grandma is too young to die. Grandma is not too young to die. I feel a wave of sad nausea clutch my throat and gently squeeze. I have to go see her, but I can't.

Piper lets go of my hand. "Okay, look pretty."

Automatically, I flip my hair, the only thing about me that really IS pretty.

"Look," she says, pointing, and there, behind the counter, wearing a stupid hat, is Soup.

"What?" I frown, not getting it. "Since when does Soup work here?"

She laughs. "He doesn't!" she says. "Look closer."

I squint. I need a new prescription or new contacts or both. Everything has been slightly blurry lately. Closer, I can tell this boy isn't Soup—he's older, taller, skinnier—but also he looks so much like him that my brain keeps superimposing Soup over Not Soup. I shake my head a little. "Weird," I whisper. "They could be twins."

We move up in the line.

"Flirt," she murmurs. Then, louder, "Two Diet Cokes, please. Large. Size matters." She winks and does that *thing* with her tongue. Automatically, I take a step back, bristling.

The boy who is Not Soup looks slowly from her to me and back again. She reaches up and touches the short hair above her ear. I don't know how she knows how to do that, how to make everything look like sex.

"Popcorn?" he drawls.

She laughs, like he's the funniest person in the world. "Have to watch our girlish figures, you know," she says, quoting Mr. Aberley. "I'm kidding," she adds. "Yes, popcorn. Extra butter. I love butter, don't you?" She lets her hand rest on his for a beat too long. He stares at her hand. I stare at her hand. We all stare at her hand.

Afterward, in our seats, I burst out laughing. "What was *that*?" I say. "What were you doing? You were like a sexxxxxx kitten. 'I *love* butter.'" I make a purring noise. I pretend to lick my paw.

She looks at me calmly. "Don't be childish," she says. "I did it for you. He's interested now. But you have to take over. Make this about you, not me. He's yours. He's going to be your first."

"Um, no," I say. "No. God. Are you kidding? Are you out of your mind? No thanks! I don't need you to—"

"Hey." A man kicks the back of my chair. "Do you mind? Shut up."

"Sorry," I say. I slouch down so he doesn't get annoyed with me for being too tall.

He leans forward. "Your disgusting hair is in my drink."

"Jeez," says Piper. "Stand down. Jerk." She gestures, and we both move over a few seats. "Loser!" she throws back over her shoulder. I put my curtain of hair between me and the man so I can't see him.

If I can't see him, he can't see me. Isn't that how it works?

The movie is so loud. A crash makes me look up at the screen. I let myself get pulled into it, the stupid loud noisiness and bright action. I put it out of my head, the whole thing with Piper and the popcorn boy, and her whole idea about that.

BEFORE

PIPER IS LYING BACK IN THE STERN OF
Mr. Aberley's boat, her face tipped up to the sun, her legs hanging over the edge. We went to ask if we could borrow it and we found him on a chaise on the front porch, sound asleep, his mouth open, his fat white Persian cat next to his feet, squinting at us with suspicious eyes.

It was the same as asking, but without waking him up.

I feel guilty. There's already a small crack in the repaired hull, and a puddle of seawater lifts the paint off the bottom in skinlike sheaths. I hope we don't sink.

Piper takes a photo of herself with her phone. She looks like a model in a catalog, like a natural Instagram filter follows her around, making her skin glow. But to get the shot, she has to hold her arms incredibly awkwardly.

"That looks really uncomfortable," I observe.

She looks at me over the top of her aviators. "Nope," she says. "It's good." She tilts her head back again.

I dip an oar in, splash her sort of on purpose.

"Hey!" she says. "It's cold. I hate the water. You know I hate the water."

"My bad," I say, grinning. Nothing feels more like me and Piper, Piper and me, than taking the boat out to the island, just the two of us, no boys, no parties, no nothing but us, some huge blue Slurpees (spiked), towels and sunscreen and magazines. Piper reaches up and snaps another selfie, then starts texting.

I turn around in the seat so I can start rowing instead of letting us drift out on the tide. Watching her text Soup is infuriating, and I'm infuriated with myself for feeling infuriated, so basically I'm a trifecta of infuriation, which I know isn't a word. At least, I don't think it is. "Is 'infuriation' a word?" I say.

"Duh, yes," she says. "Also a great name for a rock group. The Infuriation. Think about it." She looks at me. "Soup's coming tonight, okay?"

"Sure," I say. "Of course! I'd hate to do anything without Soup. Soup, Soup, Soup. Why would I want to spend time alone with my best friend when I can spend my time being a third wheel?"

She frowns. "Okay, whatever. I get it. I'll tell him."

"No, he can come, I don't care. I was being snarky."

"Big shock," she mumbles. I pretend that I don't hear her and I pull harder on the oars, leaning so far that my back touches her leg. The boat cuts through the light chop easily. It's a heavy old thing, made to be stable. Mr. Aberley himself taught us to row in it when we were in second grade. It was huge then. It's shrunk, like Mr. Aberley, the island, and everything else.

"Safe as a bathtub," he promised Mom and Dad. "Not going to flip for anything, this old girl." He patted it adoringly.

"What are we doing tonight, anyway?"

She doesn't answer, but she's still typing. I row faster. Mr. A taught us to think of the water as a solid, to think of dropping our blade into concrete and then pulling against it, the water pinning the oar in place as a pivot that we moved against. It works.

"Whoa," Piper says. "You in a race?"

"Getting a workout," I say.

"Are you still trying to lose weight? You're crazy," she says. "You're too thin. Are you going 'rexic on me?"

"Lame," I say. "You know me better than that. Duh."

"I don't know," she says. "Listen, I'm scrolling through your last twenty texts."

"Why?"

"Are you listening? Here they are: 'Going to yoga with Mom, later!' 'Going to the gym.' 'On the treadmill, phew!' 'Running!' 'Yoga tonight!' 'Got to work out!' 'See you after gym tonite?' 'Yoga, yoga, yoga, am so stretched out am like rubber band, floomp.' 'Sweat is pretty, right?' 'At the gym!' Do you see a pattern? Do we need to talk, Ms. Thing?"

"WTF?" I say. "I run when I'm anxious. Maybe I'm more anxious lately. You know, the last summer and all that."

"The last supper," she intones. "I didn't know you were religious."

"SUMMER, not supper, and I'm not."

"I know! Don't try to change the subject. Maybe you're doing this overexercising thing because you miss me and you're trying to get my attention."

"God, Piper, what are you now, my therapist? Lay off! I like working out. Is that a crime? Besides, I only ever see Mom at yoga. She's so busy at work. And after this summer, we'll be gone. I like my mom. Just because you hate your mom doesn't mean we all do."

She whistles. "Low blow."

"Sorry," I manage between breaths. The boat gets heavy

quickly when you're rowing this fast. I stop pulling the oars and let it glide.

"Anyway, slow down, you're going to hurt a seal or something."

"Unlikely," I say. I bend over, taking deep breaths.

"Well, tell me when I need to worry," she says finally. "I don't want you to say later, 'Oh, you only care about Soup and you don't notice me.'"

"Don't be dumb," I say. "I'd never be like that."

"So how come you never ask me about him?"

We are drifting toward the far side of the island. I dip my hand in the water and grab a piece of kelp, long brown seaweed with its own built-in round float. I pop the round part in my hand. Inside the bulb, there's a liquid slime. I chuck it back into the water. We've come out and around so we can use the secret cove, which you can't see from the mainland at all. The sudden silence and calm of the protected water is disconcerting. A seagull caws from the rocks somewhere. My breathing is still ragged.

"I don't know," I say. "I guess I figure if there's something you want to tell me, you will."

"Well, there is," she says.

"What is it?" I say. "Tell me." She doesn't answer. "Come on, Pipes. I really do want to know. I'm sorry I've been kind of mean about it. I am seriously very interested. I've never been more interested in anything. Not ever. If I had my camera—"

"Okay, enough," she says.

I swivel around on the bench so I can see her at the same time as the boat bumps the shoreline. She is already halfway out, pulling the rope, tying it casually around the end of the log we call Seth, which has been there for as long as I can remember. "Look after the boat, Seth," she says.

"Seth has seen too much," I say. "I can't make eye contact with Seth anymore."

"Seth will never tell your secrets," she says. "Don't worry."

I grab our stuff and follow her along the short path through the nettles to our favorite spot, a sandy stretch about seven feet long, surrounded on all sides by huge rocks. The sky is clear and blue and still. A light, hot wind blows through the purple flowers that grow between cracks in the rocks.

"Are you going to tell me?" I ask when we're finally settled. A wasp flies close to my ear and she flicks it away with her hand.

"I don't know how to say it," she says. "It's not something I want to tell you, not really. Just . . . I guess I can't figure out if you're jealous or what."

"Jealous?" I snort and laugh at the same time, choking on my melted Slurpee. Then, firmly, "Not even a little." I relent,

"Maybe I feel a bit weird because, you know, it's always been you and me, and now it's you and Soup." I add quickly, "But it's no big deal. Growing pains, I guess. It was going to happen sooner or later. That one of us met someone and, you know."

"So you *are* jealous?" She grins, leaning into me. I can feel her hot skin, the sweat making us stick together like decals. We peel off each other.

"Ouch," I say. "I swear, I'm not jealous!"

"Maybe a little?" she wheedles, and then I realize that she wants me to be. Badly.

"Sure, fine, a little," I give her, like a gift. I make a face. "Now tell me everything."

"Okay." She smiles at me in the way that she has, where you feel like a spotlight has been shone on you and like you're the only person who ever matters to her and ever will.

I lie back on the hot sand and float in and out of listening. A plane cuts through the sheet of blue, carving a solid white line upward from the horizon. An eagle, far overhead, soars silently, focused on a distant point. "He does this thing when he's kissing me," she says. "Where he holds the back of my head, like he's carrying an egg."

"An egg?" I laugh. "Wow, that's romantic. I wasn't jealous before, but now I'm seething with it. What kind of egg? Robin's egg? Crow's egg? Ostrich's egg? Those are huge. Kind of head-sized, I guess."

"It is romantic!" she protests. "I'm probably not describing it right. It's like he's cupping my whole being, you know?"

I roll my eyes behind my sunglasses. "Uh-huh. That's . . . well, it's something."

She leans up on her elbows, her shadow stretching over me, long and cool. "I can't explain it," she says. "I know I sound like an idiot. I don't even believe in love, right? I believe in science. It's dopamine. A rush of chemicals against receptors. I get it, but at the same time, it sure feels good." She pauses. "That's probably true of heroin, too."

"Sure, except heroin is a narcotic that eventually kills you after robbing you of everything you've ever had and cared about."

"Yeah, exactly," she says. "I knew you'd get it."

"Ha ha," I scoff. "I don't, but I do. You're in love. If love wasn't a thing that people got all goo-goo about, then Hallmark wouldn't exist. Or even if they did, no one would be buying their stupid heart-carrying teddy bears."

"Truth," she says. "Should I buy him a teddy bear?"

I laugh. "I get the feeling he's not a teddy bear guy," I say, in case she wasn't kidding.

"Duh," she says. "It was a joke! I am anti–teddy bear. I am going to start an organization of People Against Teddies. I will devote my life to ridding the world of button-eyed bears in bow ties."

I take one last gulp of my drink, which is now a warmish sweetish mess. "This is terrible," I say. "Why do we drink this? We need to drink something better. Champagne. Or a nice brandy."

"Brandy is worse," she says. "Champagne, for sure. It could be our signature drink."

"Yes! Vodka and blue Slurpee is definitely not it." I burp. I tip the dregs out onto the sand and it disappears into the ground, leaving a blue circle.

"That's going to attract bees," she complains. "Why did you do that?"

"Ohhh, bees, scary," I mutter. "It's okay when you do it, though."

She flips over onto her back and sprays sunscreen all over her front. A cloud of it billows into my face. I cough. "Hypocrite."

"Because I don't want skin cancer?"

"Because you smoke!" I say. "You're already doomed to be one of those old people pulling around an oxygen tank, barking like a seal."

"So are you," she says flatly.

"At least we'll be together," I offer. "They'll have cured cancer by then. We'll have synthetic lungs or pigs' lungs or we'll regrow our own lungs from stem cells or something."

"Well, as long as you've thought it through," she says. "I'm going to quit smoking. Soup says it's like kissing an ashtray."

"Is that before or after he cups your egg head?" I say with a deadpan face.

She flips me off.

I get up and take the few steps to the water. I dip my foot in. It's so much colder out here than at the beach in front of my house. I can't figure out how that's possible. It's all the same water. Piper would probably know—some complicated explanation of thermodynamics or perceived temperature—but I don't really feel like hearing it. I wade in up to my knees.

"Watch for jellyfish!" she says. "I'm absolutely not going to pee on you when they sting you, you know."

"I am," I say. "I know. I'll pee on myself. Don't worry about it."

I scan the surface of the water, but it's bottle green today and uninterrupted by the fleshy red mass of a lion's mane. They float up to the top when they die, wash up on the beach, lie there flattened and powerless. But when they aren't dead, they can lurk below the surface, surprising your bare legs with their sticky long stingers, wrapping your skin with welts.

"It's cold!" I call to Piper, but she's busy typing on her phone.

"Uh-huh." She doesn't look up.

I take a few more steps. I need to pee and it's not like the island has a bathroom, so I have to swim whether I want to or not. The last step before soaking my bathing suit is the worst;

I can see my legs through the water turning white from the shock of the chill. I take a deep breath, tip my hair back so far that it gets wet, then I dive, suddenly, surprising myself, into the water. I can feel my chest tighten and my lungs constrict from the shock of the frigid water. I swim fast and hard out about twenty strokes. I'm a decent enough swimmer, but not good enough to go very far. I tread water for a few minutes, looking back toward Piper, still hunched over her iPhone. Her shoulders shake with laughter. "What?" I call, but she doesn't answer. I float on my back, look up at the blue sky. So much blue. Why is the sky blue? I don't know that either.

Piper would know.

Piper knows everything.

She's so smart. Or she was. Now I'm not so sure. She seems to be slowly reinventing herself as dumb Piper. Take-my-breath-away Piper.

I've let the current take me a little too far. When I turn back over and start to swim, I have about two hundred yards to cover. It doesn't sound like much, but I have to swim hard out of the rip, sideways, another hundred yards out of my way. A seal pops out of the water and stares at me, nearly scaring me to death. "Shoo," I tell it. Its eyes are as black and liquid as oil. It drops below the surface. I swear I feel it brush by my leg. I swim harder. I swim as hard as I can.

I'm entirely winded when I get back.

"Hey, I almost drowned!" My chest is heaving. "I got stuck in that stupid current. Thanks for noticing." I'm furious, even though I wasn't scared, not really, when I was out there. It's true that I didn't call out to her. She could have saved me with the boat. She would have come for me if I'd called her.

"Huh?" she says. "Oh, sorry." The casual way she says it means that she's not sorry.

"You don't even know what I'm talking about!" I say. "You weren't even watching! What if I'd been pulled under? What if there was a jellyfish?"

"God, Sloane, calm down. You didn't even yell!" she says witheringly, putting her phone into her bag. "I don't think you were dying. Look, let's go in. I have to pee, anyway."

"Go in the water," I say, through gritted teeth.

She laughs meanly. "Um, no thanks. I'm not six."

"Whatever that means."

"Listen," she says. "Tonight, don't bring up the thing that happened with you and Charlie. I think Soup misses Charlie, but he's sticking to his guns and not talking to him. You know, because of you."

"Because of *me*? You mean because Charlie wouldn't take no for an answer? So because of *Charlie*, that's what you mean, right?"

She frowns. "Yeah, Soup's really mad at Charlie. But the

thing is that before you started saying no, you weren't exactly saying no, you know?"

My heart skitters in my chest in a way that absurdly makes me think of parrots rising in a flock, against a background of dark green jungle leaves.

"I don't know, no," I say. "I remember. I said no."

"You said no, but you didn't *start* saying no. I mean, there was a lot of hair flipping and sideways looks and you kept licking your lips."

"I do not do that. God. That's the most annoying thing in the world. *You* do that. I am not the lip licker here."

She stares out to sea, away from me. "I thought you should know, Sloane. Soup and Charlie have been friends for as long as we have and now they aren't talking and I wonder if you're—"

"Shut up," I interrupt her. "Just shut up." I close my eyes. I imagine myself hitting delete on the video, erasing what she's trying to say. "Seriously, shut up."

"I've already shut up," she says quietly. "I'm not saying anything."

"Great," I say. "Let's go. I can't come tonight, I forgot. I promised Mr. Aberley I'd play Scrabble with him." I stand up so fast that I'm dizzy, the world loosening its grip on me and spinning me in place. I grab my stuff and cram it into my bag. "I thought you had to pee."

"I do," she says. "Sloane, I'm sorry. Don't be mad."

"I'm not mad," I lie. "We have to get the boat back."

"Fine." She shrugs, dumping her blue Slurpee into the sand. "That's just fine with me. I hope you and Mr. Aberley have a great date night."

"Hilarious," I say.

I shove the boat into the water, not wanting to look back at the island, not wanting to remember how Charlie and I leaned on Seth, how he kissed me and I let him, how I don't know if I said no too late or if I said it at all, how Soup appeared like a knight on a horse and saved me: Charlie falling into the surf, the look on Charlie's face.

Did I say no so that Soup would save me?

"If no one knows, it didn't happen," I mutter.

Piper gives me a sharp look. "What?" she says.

"Nothing," I say. "I didn't say anything. Forget it. Less talking, more rowing, okay?"

"Fine," she says. "Fine by me."

NOW

"IF NO ONE KNOWS, IT DIDN'T HAPPEN."
That was Piper's mantra.

It started with the chickens.

The class chickens.

In sixth grade, we had a plot of land beside the track that we spent days digging up and weeding and planting with zucchini seeds. We fertilized and watered. It was better than sitting inside at a desk, better than gym class, better even than art, which was my favorite.

Then they gave us eggs.

And the eggs hatched into baby chicks.

Everyone took turns taking the chicks home on the weekend. They don't stay chicks for long. By the time it was Piper's turn, they were really chickens. Small chickens, but definitely not little yellow fluffy chicks. I didn't like the skin around their eyes, the way it wrinkled like thin paper. The smell of them. They were the only animals that I've ever met that I didn't like. Piper didn't like them either.

We squealed a lot and the chickens scattered, as far away from us as possible. One of them stole a sandwich from my hand and I ran the other way. At night, I had a dream that the chickens were pecking the flesh off my bones and I woke up crying. I still have that dream sometimes. I still wake up terrified.

That weekend, her mom used her passes to fly us to Cleveland. She was a flight attendant; sometimes she got extra passes for these random weekend trips. I can't remember anything about Cleveland except the swimming pool in the basement of the hotel and the vending machine that was entirely empty except for one row of Cokes, tantalizingly available, but the machine refused to accept coins. We stood in front of it, dropping quarters and nickels and dimes, over and over again, as though if we changed the angle of the drop, we could make the Coke appear.

The bottom of the pool was gritty, and when we got out, our feet were raw, nearly bleeding. We stayed up all night, whispering and giggling, watching movies on the pay-per-view TV in our own bedroom, bouncing on the beds like littler kids than we were. Outside it poured rain, and in the morning, we ran up and down the street and bought matching T-shirts that said CLEVELAND ROCKS!, gummy candies, and weird, faceless Amish dolls.

When we got home, a raccoon had gotten into the big crate we were using as a chicken house and three of the chickens were dead, nothing but a smear of blood and a pile of feathers. In our sleepy state, it felt like a dream. Her mom drove us around all evening, out in farm country, until we found a farmer willing to sell us three chickens. They were a different kind, but the same color. Maybe everyone just thought that the chickens had grown and changed again, but I think the teacher knew.

"If no one knows, it didn't happen," her mom said.

We never told.

Piper bought into it, that mantra. She said it all the time. Every time something happened, something terrible, even: *If no one knows, it didn't happen.*

I whisper it in the dark now, in my room, the blackout curtains closed. I'm not cold but I'm still shivering in layers of clothes, under the blankets. From far away, I can hear the rise and fall of Mom's voice and the cops' voices and the sound of outside trying to come in: a crow cawing, a distant car alarm.

"No one knows, Pipes, so it didn't happen," I say. "Right?"

I wait for her to answer, but there's nothing but silence.

Then she says, *Why didn't you tell them?*

I close my eyes and let the medication gently pull me into a long tunnel of sleep, cushioning me from what I know and what I didn't tell.

"Telling wouldn't make you not dead," I say.

"I'm sorry," I say.

"I'll tell," I say. "But not yet."

"Being pretty is the most boring thing about us," Piper once said.

I'm not pretty now.

Neither is she.

I am in bed with my lie, which is as cold and real as a corpse, and everything is sweaty and freezing at the same time and she is dead.

She was murdered.

He was at the party.

He took her to the island.

Our island.

Did they talk first? Did she think it was something else? Did she reach up and tuck her hair behind her ear, give him that crooked smile, touch the tip of her tongue to her top lip accidentally (on purpose)?

He was never supposed to matter.

He wasn't supposed to be part of our lives, after. That's why she picked him.

For *me*.

That's why I agreed.

For *her*.

So why was he there?

The patches of sand at the beach are so cold and silky. Sometimes, when I run handfuls of it through my fingers, I find smooth white stones. Wishing stones.

Every time I've found one, I've rubbed it between my thumb and finger and then I've thrown it as far as I can into the waves. I always wish for the same thing.

I wish for everything.

My room is too bright and my head is hollow. That's how it is when a migraine lifts, like my brain is saving room for it, in case it wants to come back.

A crow caws and caws and caws. The sky outside stays beautifully and obscenely blue.

At one point, Piper was going to make a time machine.

She got these ideas sometimes.

"Manic," Mom said. But Piper wasn't, not really. She didn't

take medication or anything. It wasn't like that. But she got overly enthusiastic about certain ideas. Sometimes she'd stay up for days, reorganizing her room, alphabetizing her books. This time, she made a box.

Inside the box was a jumble of circuits and old keyboards she'd bought at the computer recycling place. There was no way it would have worked or done anything, but when she turned it on, it did hum. It felt peculiarly alive, like it was trying to take you somewhere but couldn't quite lift off.

It vibrated.

Then it smelled like wires, burning.

Then it quit working altogether, and like everything else she did, she abandoned it before it was complete. It's probably still in her mom's basement somewhere.

She really believed she could go back in time and save her dad, a butterfly flapping its wings and changing history. But what if it misfired? Her dad saved, but the rest of humanity suddenly being extinguished, all at once?

To me, it's always seemed like a mistake to mess with things, especially things that are bigger than you, like death and birth.

"I'm sorry, Piper," I say. "I'd totally bring you back now if I could make it work."

You have to tell, she says. *God, you're so frustrating sometimes.*

"I will," I lie.

I stepped sideways, she says. *The edge of the boat was there and then it wasn't.*

I'm crying really hard. "Please stop talking to me," I say. "Please go away."

I can't, she says.

"You have to. Go away go away go away."

I'd forgotten about Time Machine Piper. I'd let her become Soup's Girlfriend Piper. I'd started to hate her.

"If no one knows, it didn't happen," I say out loud, and my voice interrupts the silence in my empty room. The curtains lift slightly in the breeze. The window must be open on the other side of them. A bird flies by and the shadow of its wings silhouettes like art against the backlight from the sun.

It's eerie how much seagulls' calls sound like human laughter.

Or maybe she's really here, hiding in the curtains, stifling a laugh. The hair on my arms prickles upright—a porcupine, a hedgehog, me.

"Piper?" I say. The silence is so vast. It rustles and sighs. My room is disguised as a ghost.

"I can't do this," I mutter. "Not this time."

I take an extra pill. It's the only thing that I can do. I close my eyes and the pill tastes as blue as a Slurpee and I can feel myself separating from me, vodka-filtered, Instagram-bright.

I get my phone out and scroll through my stuff. I like a photo of a balloon. I don't even like it. I'm losing my grip. I've let go.

And I'm so cold.

She was probably cold, too, when she died.

So cold, she agrees.

"Shut up," I say.

I open my messaging app, and before I can change my mind, I type, "Call me." Then, "Please."

I press send.

BEFORE

ON THE DAY BEFORE I LOSE MY
virginity to James Robert Wilson, I ask Mom if I can come to
her yoga class with her. She's in the kitchen. I feel nervous, like
she might say no. I imagine saying, *Today is the last day that I
will do yoga as a virgin.* I want to know what she'd say.

Dad brushes by me on his way out the door. "Bye, lovely
ladies!" he says. He kisses me on the head and I want to cry. *I'm
not a little girl anymore*, I want to say to him. *Dad, everything's
about to change.*

I don't say anything.

"Bye, love of my life!" Mom calls after him. Then, to me,
"Of course you can come. You're coming with me a lot. Not

that I mind! I don't mind. But is there something you want to talk about?"

"I like yoga," I say. "Sorry. God. I won't come." I push my stool back from the counter and stand up.

"Sloaney." She puts down her cup of organic mint tea on the counter. "I like it when you come. It's just that I haven't spent this much time with you since . . . oh, I don't know, was it fourth grade when you started to sleep over at Piper's almost every weekend? Where's she been lately? I haven't seen her around."

I shrug. "Busy, I guess."

She gives me a funny look. "If you think about it," I say, "mint tea is potentially pretty gross. I saw a raccoon in the garden last night. What if he peed on that mint? Technically, that could be raccoon pee tea. I always think that when I drink Mr. Aberley's nettle concoction. What if?"

"I washed it!" She sniffs her drink. "Well, it does smell different. Anyway, I'm sure Mr. Aberley sterilizes those leaves. He's ninety-something! He'd be dead a long time ago if he drank pee tea."

"Pee tea?" I giggle. "Pee tea!"

She laughs. "You make a good point, though," she says, wrinkling her nose.

"What are you talking about?" Dad comes back into the kitchen. "I forgot my keys!" I smell sweat and cigarettes, which is probably me, not him. I can't imagine Dad smoking. I can't picture him making any bad choices, not ever. He wraps his arm around my neck and gives me a hug. "Do you have my keys, young lady?"

"Don't!" I push him off. "I have no keys." I hold up my empty hands and show him.

"I don't understand how you two do hot yoga when it's this hot," he says, finding his keys in the cutlery drawer. "Is the air-conditioning broken? It's a sauna in here."

"We're going out!" Mom says. "It doesn't need to be on when no one is here. Besides, we're acclimating for hot yoga."

"You two are both peculiar," says Dad. "Lucky for you, I love you. What are you doing here, anyway?" he asks me. "No Piper today?"

"Oh my God," I say. "Give me a break! I'm sorry to be home with my family! I'll go get ready for yoga, Mom."

I storm out of the room and stomp up the stairs hard, each step vibrating the banister under my hand.

"What is with her?" I hear Dad say. "She doesn't seem like herself."

"Piper has a boyfriend," Mom says in a low voice.

I slam my bedroom door before I can hear any more.

I throw myself onto my bed and pick my phone up from the bedside table, where it's been charging. Sixteen texts from Piper. I delete them all without reading them.

My hand is shaking. I open the app on my phone that measures my heartbeat and put my finger over the bright light. I watch as the line weaves up and down: 89, 120, 97, 137. How fast is too fast? I'm breathing fast now, too. If I slow it down, I might stop, so I can't. If I think about breathing, I can't do it. I stand up. I sit down.

I lie down on the floor and start doing crunches. Faster and faster, my abs burning in protest. More and more. A hundred. I lose count. The ceiling spins above me. But I don't stop. If I stop, I might die. That's how it feels. Like death is right there, on the other side of my door, waiting to come crashing through, to take me to where I'm not ready to go.

"I haven't even barely started," I say, between crunches. "I haven't done anything yet! Not yet, not yet, not yet."

I keep going. I go until I feel like throwing up, until my back is drenching the carpet with sweat. I only stop when Mom knocks. "Are you coming, Sloaney?"

"Yes," I call. I'm already gasping for breath. I go out to join her, trying to pretend that hot yoga is a totally normal thing for me to do on a Saturday afternoon, in the last summer holiday of high school, on a day when everyone else is on a beach, Frisbees flying, music playing, the ocean lapping at the tide line, pushing the dead onto the land, a graveyard of jellyfish corpses shining under the light of the relentless summer sun.

*　*　*

Piper appears the next day. Sunday. Like I knew she would.

Mom and Dad are spending the day with Grandma. It's her birthday. I made up a lie about why I couldn't go, I just couldn't. Grandma used to run a business empire. Now when she leans forward, sometimes a string of drool hangs from her lip and she doesn't notice. She never wipes it away. I know Mom and Dad wanted me to go but I also knew they wouldn't make me; it wouldn't fit their "cool and understanding parents" shtick they have going on. I'm not proud of it, but I used that to my advantage.

They left.

I waited.

The house has been empty with only me in it, vibrating with anticipation. I showered and dried my hair. I straightened it with the straightening iron, but then it looked too serious, so I dampened it and curled it. I redid it until my arms ached.

Since then, I've been waiting.

I'm relieved when Piper comes right in through the French doors off the living room. I'm lying on the couch, about to put dark blue polish on my toenails.

"You don't knock?" I say, faking a mad voice, and she laughs in a way that says that she forgives me. The line between who is mad at who is so blurry that I can't even see it. I don't even always know. But I do know that it goes away.

It always does.

"Are you going to chicken out?" she asks. She makes a chicken noise. "Here, let me do that." She puts down the drink tray holding two huge iced mochas and takes the polish out of my hand. Then she goes over and turns up the air-conditioning. "Too hot." Her short hair is spiked up with sweat or product, I can't tell which. "I'm so tired of being hot. Sweaty is not my best look."

"You need to use those blotting paper things. Matte is the new black," I say.

"That doesn't even make sense," she says. "Racially? Is that a commentary on the state of the nation?"

"No," I say. "A commentary on shiny skin." I lean my head back on the leather armrest. I lift my foot up and balance it on the coffee table so she can reach my nails from where she's sitting on the floor. "Am I really going to do this? What if he doesn't want to? I mean, this is *our* plan, nothing to do with him. Maybe it will just be like, hi, let's get to know each other. Maybe he won't even want to do it with me. What am I supposed to do, jump on him?"

"He'll want to," she says. "Of course he'll want to. Look at you. You're all long blond hair and a bikini. And soon-to-be-stellar toenails. What's not to want? Your hair looks amazing, by the way."

"I want to be more than hair and a bathing suit."

"You are! That's the point! But you're more than hair and a bathing suit to the first guy who matters. James doesn't matter. That's why he's in the picture. Because for him you *are* a body, some hair, and a bathing suit. For the next guy, you'll be *you*. You'll be the Sloane who I know and love."

"I love you, too," I say. "Even when you're mad at me."

"I'm sick of being mad at you. It's boring." She stretches out luxuriantly. "I miss you when you're being moody. God, air-conditioning is the best. I have to come over more often."

"You're always at work! And the mall is air-conditioned."

"Not today," she says. "Today, I'm here for you. To be your witness."

"You can't *watch*," I say. "That would be creepy."

"I won't," she says, winking.

"Pipes, seriously. Don't invite Soup over and have both of you gawking. That's beyond creepy. I think it's illegal, actually."

She makes a face. "Soup's at work. I won't watch. But I want to be here for you. In case he turns out to be a psycho." She rolls her eyes, takes a long sip of her drink. "I wonder how much sugar is in these things? They're really disgusting, but also delicious. How can something be both disgusting and delicious?"

"Proof," I say, raising my cup and gulping. She's right: both disgusting and delicious. I inspect my feet. My big toe is already smudged. I check the time on my phone. One o'clock.

"I can't do this," I say. "Not for real. How well do you know this guy? Really?"

"What? Of course you can. I know him well enough. Sometimes he comes in and pretends to be a customer. He's funny in a sarcastic, dry way. He takes a while to get used to. Anyway, I brought the clippers. We'll get your hair cut right afterward."

I blink. "Do you try clothes on for him? Do you twirl?"

"What? No! We talk. He's an interesting guy. He's from Texas. Or maybe Arizona. I forget now. One of the states that have cactuses. Do they have cactuses in New Mexico?"

"So you're really close, then?" I say sarcastically. "So this isn't like you're setting me up with a total stranger? What if he has syphilis?"

"For one thing, no one has syphilis anymore, that's from Ye Olden Tymes. For another thing, even if he did, it's not like that would have come up while he was telling me about the time his dog ate a rattlesnake. Or a rattlesnake ate his dog. I forget. But no matter, he's cute and seems like a no-strings-attached person who is perfect for this. That's the main thing."

"Is it? Because seriously, Piper, I'm not sure I remember

what the main thing is anymore or why I'm doing this. This is crazy. I can't do this."

"Are you joking or serious?"

"Both?" I start hyperventilating.

"Are you hyperventilating?"

I nod, waving my hand toward the kitchen. She pulls herself up and goes to the drawer and gets a paper bag. "This is so funny!" she calls. "I didn't know you still hyperventilated!"

"I do," I gasp. "Sorry. Is not funny. When it's. You."

She passes me the bag. I put it over my nose and take deep breaths; the papery smell of it makes me feel safe. I keep breathing into it for a few breaths beyond what I need, the crumpling loud sound of it filling the space.

"Come on," she says. "Keep it together. Remember who we used to be? Go big or go home!"

"Yep," I manage. "I know. But you love Soup. So it's different."

"Doesn't matter." She shakes her head impatiently. "Remember when you started your period and I got mine the next day? We are in sync. We have to stay in sync." She seems agitated. "We're the same, Sloaney. We have to be the same. When we're not, everything is wrong, don't you see? We've been *off*, this whole summer, you and me. It's not working. Because we're out of sync." She looks like she's going to cry. "You have to do this."

I lie back on the couch and close my eyes. I think about everything that I know about sex, the technicalities of sex. "What does it mean, anyway?" I say. "I probably don't even have a hymen or whatever to break."

"Right," she says. "It's just bodies. But you'll see. It's more than that."

"How do you know? You don't even remember! And you haven't done it with him again. Why haven't you?"

"I can't! I'm waiting for you to catch up!"

"That doesn't make sense!"

"I know, right? But it also does, because we're us!"

"We're us," I agree. "I know. I'm sorry. I'm freaking out. I don't even know him!"

"It doesn't matter," she says. "*I* know him. I have a feeling about him. A good feeling. Like he's the right one for this. He's meant to be connected to us somehow. We have to intellectualize this. We have to be the smart girls we used to be before I fell in love like a dummy. And we know that sex is nothing more than a physical connection, a click, just . . . friction."

"Friction?" I say dubiously.

"Well, meaningful friction."

"Like rubbing a magic lamp!" I laugh. "Do I get to make a wish?"

"Basically," she says.

"So if I do this with James, are you going to start doing it with Soup again?" I can't make eye contact while I wait for her answer. Instead I watch the gardener, who is trimming the hedges. The hedge trimmer is loud and almost drowns out her answer.

"Oh," she says airily, "I'm thinking of breaking up with him now."

And just like that, the air is sucked out of the room, out of my lungs, out of the house, out of the world. My vision goes gray, like I'm going to faint. I drop my head between my knees.

"What?" I say. "I'm going to faint, don't mind me."

"You're not," she says. "I totally love him, but really, we're too young to fall in love."

"I'm . . . ," I say. "What happened to 'He takes my breath away'?"

She laughs. "He does. But I don't want him to be the only one who does."

"Oh," I say. "I—"

The doorbell rings.

The doorbell rings, and the air in the room starts to shake.

The doorbell rings, and I start to shake.

The doorbell rings, and everything in the world starts to shake, an earthquake that cleaves the island in two, that cleaves us in two, that cleaves everything in two—who I am and who I'm going to be.

Piper jumps up and hugs me, hard. Tight.

"I love you," she says. "Remember."

Piper disappears up the stairs and I walk slowly to the door and open it, and there is a boy I barely know, James (not Jimmy, never Jim, according to Piper), smiling crookedly, holding a six-pack of beer and one of those furry blankets that I've seen on Amazon with a wolf on it, its mouth grinning, half open, tongue hanging out.

"Hey," I say, trying not to sound as terrified as I feel. I run my hands through my hair. His eyes drift down from my face to my body to my bright pink bikini.

"Hey," he says.

He leers. So he's definitely the kind of boy who leers. I shiver.

His skin is covered with pockmarks that look like divots in the ground, the kind made by clams and geoducks at the beach.

"It's so great to meet you," I lie. My voice sounds like someone else's voice. "Want to go to the beach?"

He smiles wolfishly.

He nods.

I reach out and take his hand.

I close the door gently behind me.

We head down the beach trail.

NOW

MOM KNOCKS AND THEN COMES IN without waiting for me to answer. She puts a cloth on my forehead. The cloth is wet and ice-cold water seeps into my hair. I'm already too cold but I don't know how to tell her. My mouth isn't making the right words.

"Mom," I start, and then I'm crying and crying and choking and crying. I'm strangling on sadness. "I don't know what happened," I say around the impossible lump that's in my throat. "Tell me what happened to her."

She shakes her head; she strokes my cold, damp head.

"I'm sorry, Slo," she says. "I'm so, so sorry. It's the worst thing. It's an awful thing."

"Tell me," I choke.

She gets up and opens my curtains. My eyes slam shut. It's too bright. So much sun. How can there be sun when Piper is dead? Mom sits back down, and she strokes my hair like she used to when I was little. A crow lands on my balcony and starts to caw. I feel like he's telling me something. His feathers gleam in the sunlight.

"He's trying to tell me," I say.

"Honey, it's a crow," she says. "It's only a crow."

But what if it isn't? I think but don't say, *What if it's Piper?*

It's not, says Piper. *God.*

"Mom, Piper is dead."

"I know, shhhh."

The crow caws again.

"Shut up," I say ferociously. "Shut up, shut up, shut up." I am clawing at my ears and I hear the crow and Piper and I can't make them stop, either of them, and Mom is pulling my hands away.

"Stop," she says. "You're scratching yourself! Honey, no."

The crow stops suddenly, like a slamming on of brakes. The silence is hard and huge. There is my breathing and Mom's and the breeze rustling the curtain and the sound of my heart lolloping crookedly. On my bedside table, the battery light on my camera is flashing. I swallow bile. The crow stretches his wings. I can hear the *tock-tock-tock* of his feathers separating from one another, and my heart is pounding so wrong and so faintly that I think for sure I'm going to die, too.

I want to.

I can't do this without Piper.

I need her.

Come with me, Piper says. She twirls in the water, making it look pretty. My mouth tastes like salt.

"Leave me alone! You aren't real."

So why don't you know what I'm going to say before I say it? I'm real.

"I don't believe in you."

You don't? I know. I mean, I knew. I knew you didn't. You didn't even like me anymore.

"Mom," I struggle to say. "Help me."

But what comes out is not that. What comes out is a scream. The scream starts somewhere in my core and I can't stop it and it splits me in half and I'm turning inside out and I want to know what happened and I don't want to know what happened and I'm thinking terrible things, all of the terrible things that could have happened and I'm maybe saying out loud, or maybe not, what happened what happened what happened.

"Shhhhh," Mom says. She sits next to me, her back perfectly straight, like the dancer she used to be. Her hand is calm and cool and everything I'm not. Her calm, cool hand strokes and the cloth is cold and sinking into my forehead, which is melting and cold at the same time. My brain is frozen and numb and no one can shiver like this and survive.

It's going to be okay. Don't get hysterical.

"Please don't be dead."

I can't help what I am. It's not so bad.

"It is. It is so bad."

No one saw, so it didn't happen.

"That's not how it works! It's not!"

Shhhh, calm down. Hold my hand.

"Shhhh, calm down. Hold my hand," says Mom.

I'm either holding my breath or not, I can't tell, and I'm with her and I'm underwater and we're drowning, we keep seeing sky and knowing we can't reach it, is that you, Piper, I say or think or dream. It's us, it's us. We are. We aren't.

We aren't any longer.

We aren't anything.

The water, the water.

I'm dreaming.

I'm not dreaming.

Mom holds my hand.

Piper holds my hand.

We're dancing.

We're drowning.

The crow caws.

Dad comes into the room. I can smell his cologne, his crisp cotton shirt, the Dad-pressed smell of him. He talks to Mom in a quiet way that I can't decode. Everything is a different language.

Anteeksi, I think.

There is rattling, gentle hands, a pill dropped under my tongue.

Let it dissolve, they say, and I do, particles of me seeping into the blue of the sky and into the dust and into the bed and into the water and into the crow and into everything.

Blood dissolves, she says.

We dissolve.

I trip and crash into sleep by accident, headfirst, my skull crumbling. I dream of oceans and waves covering me, water all around me, in my mouth, and then it is blood and a dancer in a red silk dress that fades to the palest of pinks, twirling and twirling, and look at me and the dress is empty and falling from the hanger to the floor in a wisp of air and I choke and wake up and dream again and the whole time Mom's hands are there, stroking my forehead, erasing, erasing, erasing me and what we did.

"Sloane," she says. "Shhhhh. Sloane, you're going to be okay."

But she's wrong; I won't be.

The crow rises up suddenly and flies so hard into the glass that it cracks.

The crow falls.

The crow dies.

Piper dies.

We die.

Everyone dies at the end.

BEFORE

AFTERWARD, I FEEL COMPLETELY DIFFERENT
and no different at the same time.

It's not necessarily a good thing.

I feel like a balloon that someone has accidentally released,
floating toward a bad fate.

I also hurt in places I didn't expect to hurt.

Why didn't I expect it?

Dumb.

I feel violated.

I thought about telling him to stop.

There was a point when he looked angry.

I was scared.

Is that a lie?

I said yes.

I want to erase it all: the wolf blanket, how cold the water was, how I thought about screaming so that Piper would save me.

Did I need saving?

Why couldn't she tell that I did?

I hate her.

I hate myself.

In the mirror, my face is exactly the same. I have a pimple on my chin. The sun exposure has made my freckles flare.

"Do freckles come and go, or do they only darken in the sun?" I ask Piper.

"I don't know," she says. "I think they are always there. I had a mole removed, remember? In sixth grade. Anyway, the doctor showed it to me afterward and it had a root."

"A root? Seriously? So freckles have roots?"

She frowns. "I don't know. I don't know if they're the same or not. Anyway, your freckles are cute."

"I hate the word 'cute,' " I say.

She slowly opens and closes the scissors. "I love that sound," she says.

I nod. "Me, too."

"Are we doing this?"

I look at her in the mirror, pixie-blond and gorgeous. I try to imagine my face without hair to shade it from everyone, from everything. I can't do it. But I want to be ugly. That's my impulse. If I'm ugly, then I'm safe. I want to grab the scissors from her hand, make my face ugly with the blades. The impulse is so strong, it scares me.

"I didn't like it," I say.

"So you've said," she says. "Doesn't matter; it's done now."

"Gee, thanks."

"I don't mean that it doesn't matter." She hangs her arm over my shoulders. "I only meant that you were brave to do it and now we're the same again and thank you, thank you, thank you, I appreciate it more than you know, and I love you."

"It still doesn't make sense," I say. There's an aching in my vagina that's not quite a pain. The feeling of it reminds me of what I did. What I chose to do. I want to unchoose. *Sorry*, I want to say. *I made a mistake. I meant no.*

"Be brave," she says.

"I'm not brave," I mutter.

"But you did it!" she protests. "You were brave. Now you're going to be brave about the hair." She touches her tongue to her lips, forgetting that I'm not a boy and I'm not going to go crazy for that. I want to slap her. That's a strong impulse, too.

What I really want is to tell my mom.

I want my mom to make it okay.

But I can't tell. I can't ever tell.

"That's not bravery," I say. "It was terrible."

She shrugs. "So it can only get better from here. Think about it. You don't have to explain to the love of your life why you're a virgin, and you'll have such good sex the next time you have it."

"Again, that makes no sense," I say. "It was really uncomfortable. I don't think I'll want to do it anytime soon. It was like"—I think about it for a second—"it was like being stabbed by a pencil."

Her eyes meet mine in the mirror. "Stabbed by a pencil!" she repeats. Then we're both laughing and laughing and laughing and I'm crying and crying and then she stops laughing because I'm crying.

"You are completely wrong," I manage to say. "It would have made all the difference if I loved him."

She looks away from me. I can't make her eyes meet mine in the mirror. I grab her arm. "You tricked me," I say.

"I did not!" she says. "You wanted to do it." She puts her face right next to mine, fiercely hugging me to her. "We're the same. Remember?"

"But it wasn't the same." It comes out fiercer, sharper than I intend. "It was like I was an actor in a crappy porno. I wasn't involved with it. It *did* matter. I don't know why I did it! Now I'm not a virgin and it hurts and I lost something. I lost something that I can't get back. Not ever."

"Don't be so dramatic," she snaps. "It's friction."

"It's more than that and you know it," I say quietly. "You knew it."

She shrugs. "Think what you want."

"Well, that's what I think. That you wanted it to suck for me and be awesome for you. I just don't know why."

"You sound crazy." She rolls her eyes. "I love you. I just wanted you to feel what it was like."

"Yeah," I say. "Now I know."

I grab the scissors from her. Before I can change my own mind, I pull my hair into one handful and I slice. The scissors don't cut through cleanly, but I saw away at it until it's gone. My hair feels so soft, falling down, falling to the bathroom floor in drifts like blond leaves being shed from a tree in the fall, golden leaves, leaving me winter-bare and pale, eyes wide in the mirror, surprised at what I'm capable of doing, at how brave I really am.

While the bleach simmers on my scalp, we sit on my bed. Between us, the camera is plugged into the wall. Charging. I have in my hand the cord that will connect it to the computer, that will upload the files.

"I didn't know you filmed it," I say. "That's sick. I want you to delete it. I don't want to see it. Why did you do it?"

She shrugs. "Documentaries are merciless," she says. "Remember? Nothing is off-limits. What did that guy who you like so much say?"

"Werner Herzog?" I ask. "He said lots of things. He said that being filmed could destroy a person."

"He did not," she says. "You're just saying it."

"He did so," I say. "Seriously, I think watching this could destroy me. I can't see myself like that. I don't want to. I don't even want to upload these. Can you delete it right on the camera?"

"No! We'll lose the good stuff, too. Besides, you might not be ready yet, but you should see it." She pauses. "You looked really beautiful."

"*Beautiful?* Are you serious? I don't care about being beautiful!"

"You do so," she forges on, even though she can tell I'm about to cry. "Everyone does. Being beautiful has been wrecked because men want to consume beautiful girls. But if there weren't men, we'd still want to be beautiful."

I stare at her. "You're a terrible feminist," I say finally.

"No, I'm not," she says. "I'm right."

She grabs the camera and hits the play button.

I can't see it but I also can't not see it. It starts with Charlie.

I'm smiling.

I'm laughing.

I don't remember smiling or laughing but I'm watching myself smiling and laughing.

I can't be smiling and laughing.

Can I?

"Turn it off," I say woodenly, but I don't reach for the camera. The angle changes, like the camera itself has been dropped in the sand. Then I can see myself pushing him off, but I'm still laughing, and he looks confused. What does laughing and pushing mean? Yes, no, no, yes, what?

And then there is Soup, his knees, his feet, I recognize his sneakers. Then the fight unfolds blurrily in the distance and then it stops. My heart is beating fast, like I've been caught. "What?" I ask irritably.

She shrugs. "Nothing," she says. "Camera never lies, right?"

"Sometimes it does," I say.

The camera keeps playing. There's Piper, cutting her own hair. There's some footage I took sitting at the beach, the waves going in and out. The splash of the oar going into and out of the water. A tree, bending in the wind. A crow, who stared into the camera long enough that I started to laugh; the camera shakes.

"That crow is creepy," I say.

"I love crows," she says. "Did you know that crows are really smart? You can teach them to mimic. Like parrots."

"Maybe I should get one as a pet," I say. "It's probably the closest thing to a pet that my parents wouldn't know about. Do you think I could tame one on the balcony? It could be like a homely parrot."

"Sure," she says. "I don't like parrots. They're too colorful. They're offensive to the eyes."

"Weirdo. But *crows* are beautiful?"

She shrugs. "They are," she says. "They're *sleek*."

"*You* should get one as a pet," I say.

"Maybe I will," she says.

"A whole murder of them," I say.

"Funny," she says. "But one would be plenty."

The screen goes blurry for a minute, then I see Piper's foot. She's sitting on my chair on the deck upstairs. She films the island, a long sweeping view of the beach.

Then there we are.

Me and James.

The terrible, ugly blanket that smelled like dust and something worse, something masculine and animal.

I can't stop looking at myself. I don't look like me. Am I really that thin? We both are. We look like catalog models. I look like I'm trying too hard. Showing off.

It looks sped up and then slow motion. Piper isn't very good with a camera. It jiggles and jumps. "Very *Blair Witch*," I say.

I close my eyes, but I can't stop seeing it.

I can see the moment where I should have stopped it.

I can see the moment where I wanted to stop it.

I can see the moment where Piper must have known I wanted her to help me, to call out, to save me.

I hate her, I think.

I hate him, I think.

I hate *him*.

"I hate him," I say out loud.

"He didn't really do anything," she says. "He did what you wanted him to do."

"What *you* wanted him to do," I spit.

"You didn't say no."

"I should have," I say. "You've got to stop saying that. Anyway, not saying no isn't the same as specifically saying yes."

"True," she agrees. "But you specifically said yes, in this case."

We both watch, me on my back on that ugly blanket, my long hair spread around my head like a halo, my eyes closed against the sun, against James, against this thing that I was doing that I didn't want to do.

"Too late," we both say, together. We sit there for a long time on my bed, heads on each other's shoulders, the smell of bleach burning in our noses, stinging our eyes, both of us crying, but I don't know really why.

* * *

The texts start coming the next day.

James: "Hey, want to meet up?"

James: "Thinking about you. Guess why?"

James: "Want to hang out?"

James: "I'm off at 9, meet me."

James: "Do you have me blocked?"

James: "I'm not going to give up."

James: "Sloane?"

James: "Are you kidding me with this?"

James: "WTF?"

It goes on and on. I turn my phone off. I go to the gym. Piper is at work, but I don't stop in to see her. I feel like I have to run. I have to run so hard and so fast that I don't hear the beep of my phone.

I get on the treadmill.

I run.

I run.

I run.

I can outrun myself.

Can't I?

"You stink," says Piper. "Why don't you shower at the gym like a normal person?"

"I don't know." I shrug. "I don't like people seeing me naked."

"Weirdo," she says. "No one is looking. It's a gym. You can't be in here smelling like that. You'll scare people away."

"Fine," I say, "I'll leave."

"No, stay. I'm bored out of my mind."

"I'll sit downwind." I move to the other side of the blowing fan. "Better?"

She wrinkles her nose. "Not really, but I'll take it." She grabs a box cutter and slices open a brown box of new merchandise. "This is hideous." She holds up a fringed top.

"Seventies," I say. "Boho chic."

"Ugly," she says. "I'm going to put it on. Don't move."

I hold my hands up. "Not moving. Too sore to move."

While she's changing, I take out my phone. Forty-two texts, six missed calls. James. What is wrong with him? "James keeps messaging me," I call. "What should I do?"

"Call him back?" she says.

"No way," I say. "He's not going to suddenly show up here, is he?"

"Nah, he only works in the evenings. Actually, he hasn't come around since you did it with him. That's weird, no?"

She emerges from behind the curtain in the terrible top. It's the shade of green that can only be called bile, tie-dyed with red. She looks like the insides of an organ. She looks like something that's been opened and flayed. But she still looks good.

"You look good in that, you cow," I say. "How is that possible?"

She shrugs, goes to the mirror. Twirls. "It's kind of cute," she concedes. "I'm going to wear it, see how many I can sell today."

"All of them, probably," I say. "Do you get a commission?"

"No," she says. "Just something to do. So why don't you call him back?"

"No! I thought you understood. I never want to see him again. Like, never never. I want him to . . . well, not *die* exactly, but not exist either. I want him to stop existing."

She makes a hand gesture. "Like puff away in a cloud of smoke?"

"Exactly!" I say.

"I get it," she says. "I kind of want Soup to do that, too. He likes me too much, you know? It's weird. It's enough. But what am I supposed to say to James when he comes in here? You've kind of put me in an awkward position."

"Golly," I say. "Sorry for you."

"Don't be like that," she says. "I'm on your side, remember?"

"A cloud of smoke would be perfect. Anyway. Should I block him?"

"Nah," she says. "He'll stop. I'll tell him you have herpes or something. I'll tell him you decided to go gay or get back together with your ex or . . . something. I'll make something up. Don't freak out. I swear, he's really a cool guy."

My phone buzzes on the floor beside me. We both look at it.

"What if he isn't?" I say.

The bell chimes to indicate someone has come into the store. "Shhhh!" she whisper-yells.

I put my finger to my lips to indicate that I won't say anything. "I'm invisible!" I whisper.

"Oh, hey," she says in her normal voice.

"Hey, yourself," says Soup. His voice is so familiar to me, I feel like I recognize it on a level that's below sound. It's something inside me. My spleen, my heart. That doesn't make sense, I tell myself. That's dumb.

But I can feel every part of me tuning in to what he's saying, listening, needing to hear. I look at my phone. My headphones are in my bag. I need to put them on. I need to listen to something else. A podcast, anything. There's one that I was listening to on the treadmill about someone who was obsessed with stalking a celebrity, only to find out how tall he was. That's all he was interested in: the man's height. It was both scary and funny. I want to hear the end. How tall *is* Jake Gyllenhaal?

But I don't reach for my bag.

I listen.

I can hear the sound of them kissing. For a second, I want to die or hide or both. Then I'm angry. I'm not allowed to even exist in the store, but she can kiss him in full view of the whole mall?

"Want to do something tonight?" he asks when they finally break it off. "I feel like I don't see you anymore."

"Your work hours have been messed up," she points out. "But sure. I mean, I promised Sloane I'd help her with something, though."

I laugh silently at the lie.

"Yeah?" he says. "What? Maybe I can help, too."

"Maybe. The thing is, she slept with this guy and now he won't stop calling her and I think she should get to know him better before she decides that we need to off him with a hit man or something."

I can't believe she said that.

I can't believe I heard that.

I can't believe she told him.

And now he knows.

What must he think of me?

I want to stand up and storm out so badly that my legs feel like they're going to start straightening of their own volition. My voice is in my throat, ready to yell. My ears are ringing so loudly, I can't even hear what she's saying anymore.

You told him, I want to scream. *You promised you wouldn't tell him.*

You monster, I want to hiss. I want to hurt her.

I want to kill her, if I'm being honest.

I close my eyes and I picture her dead.

I'm that angry, my pulse roaring in my ears like wind pushing the waves onto the shore, my breath coming so hard and fast that I'm beyond hyperventilating, I'm so far past the part where a paper bag might help, I'm gasping, I'm gasping, I'm . . .

When I come to, Soup and Piper are both crouched down next to me.

"Are you okay?" Soup says, at the same time Piper is helpfully explaining, "You fainted!" She smiles sweetly, looking largely unconcerned. I squint at her through the fog in my head. Nothing comes out of my mouth.

"Don't talk," says Soup. "Take a few seconds and breathe normally." He's holding my wrist in his hand, his fingers pressed against my pulse point. I can feel my heart speeding up.

"Soup," I whisper.

"Anyway," says Piper. "Dramatic, much?"

I don't think I've ever hated her more intensely than I hate her in this moment. *She doesn't even like you anymore!* I want to say to Soup. *She's going to dump you! She's a terrible person!* My vision goes cloudy again.

"Hey, whoa," says Soup. "Head between your knees."

"I'm fine," I say. "It's passed." I pull my wrist out of his hands. "I'm totally okay, I swear. It happens sometimes. It's no big deal."

"It's totally a big deal," he says. "Are you sure you shouldn't go to the clinic? The hospital? Maybe you have that thing that athletes sometimes die of suddenly, long QT syndrome."

"Yes," I say shortly. I don't know what else to say. The awkward silence is broken when the store bell goes. "I'm sure. I don't have long QT," I add. "I was tested for it already."

"Someone's here!" says Piper. "Stay invisible."

Soup slides down next to me. "I spend a lot of time here," he whispers. "The floor in this shop is so lovely, don't you think?"

"Oh, absolutely," I whisper back. "We should bring pillows. Make it a real home."

He leans against me just enough that I feel like he's holding me up. I'm aware of the warmth of his skin, the smell of him, the strange tinny taste I get in my mouth after I faint. I close my mouth so he can't smell it.

"Are you fainting?"

"Nope, being invisible." I cover my mouth with my hand so he doesn't breathe me in.

"I'll take these things to a changing room for you," I hear Piper say in a stagy loud voice. She means that we're being too loud. I'm so close to Soup's face that I could kiss him. I want to kiss him.

If Piper is bad, I'm worse.

I'm so much worse than her.

I pick up my phone off the floor and tilt the screen so Soup can't see it. I methodically delete James's messages and then delete them from my deleted folder for good measure.

"That looks amazing on you," Piper says. "You look so incredible in that. Not everyone can pull that kind of look off, but it looks like it was made for you."

"It's too tight," the girl says. "I look fat."

"You look amazing," says Piper. "You look like sex on a stick."

"Is that a compliment?" says the girl.

"Totally," Piper coos.

When James kissed me, it felt too wet and too loose. His kisses made me think of spawning salmon, slapping the surface wetly in the shallow river. I feel almost bad for him. Poor spitty salmon James. He'll be fine. He'll recover from this terrible rejection. And besides, we only met once. How can he be so hung up on me? I don't owe him anything!

I don't owe anyone anything.

"Are you okay?" says Soup again. "Your face looks weird."

"I was thinking about something," I say. "Someone. Sorry."

"You don't have to be sorry, I just didn't want you to faint on me again," he says. "You say sorry a lot."

I laugh quietly. "Habit."

"Which part? The fainting or the apologizing?"

"Apologizing, obvi," I say.

"You faint a lot, too," he observes. "Swooning. Very Victorian."

"The first time I didn't faint!" I protest. "Anyway, those Victorian shows are all the rage now on Netflix. I'm just trying to keep up with the trends."

"My mom watches those," he says. "I think those shows are targeted at moms. Not trendy, per se."

"Trendy, for the olds, what's the difference?"

He laughs.

"Hey, stop flirting with my boyfriend!" Piper is back, reaching her hand down to help Soup up. He ignores it and stands by himself. I find myself secretly cheering for him. "I can't believe that girl didn't buy that shirt. It looked awful on her."

"Maybe that's why?" I say. "And I'm not flirting with anyone. I have to go."

"No!" she says. "I've been thinking about it, and I think you need to give James another chance. Did you know that his dad was in jail for something terrible? I forget what, but it was something clean, like embezzling money or maybe murder."

"Murder isn't clean," I say.

"Well, it was a business deal gone wrong. Or maybe it was stolen jewelry. I forget. Or a DUI."

"Do you ever listen when anyone talks?" I say. "You've listed basically every crime known to man."

"It wasn't something terrifying, I'd remember that," she says. "Like cannibalism or a mass-murdering clown."

"Gee, that's reassuring," I say. "I'm going to block him. I'm *definitely* not going out with him again."

She shrugs. "He knows where you live," she points out. "Maybe I will suggest that he try to woo you. I think you're woo-able. You think he's cute, right? So why not?"

"Are you not *listening*?" I say. "Do you not care what I think? I don't like him! I don't want to see him again! Ever! I don't want you to tell him anything at all! He'll figure it out when I don't answer for a while. I'm sure he's been ghosted before. He'll deal with it."

"Okaaaaay," she says, in a way that makes me feel embarrassed. "Well, me and Soup have a date tonight, then."

"A date?" I say, hitting the word "date" hard. "Are you guys my parents? They do date night, too."

"Basically," Piper says. "Old married couple!" She laughs and presses her head into his chest. He's been quiet this whole time, smiling a funny half smile and staring at me.

"I've got to go," I manage, my throat starting to close up with panic. "Later, gator hater."

She doesn't even say it. She doesn't say anything. "While, vile 'dile," I mumble for her, to ward off bad luck. I can hear the sounds of lips on lips behind me. I'd run, but my legs are shaky from the faint, so instead I walk as quickly as I can, willing them to keep me upright, keeping my eyes down, not wanting to look at anyone, not wanting to see anyone.

I'm almost at the mall exit when I hear a voice that my body recognizes before I do. Goose bumps jump up on my skin before I turn around.

"Your phone broken or what," he says flatly, a statement, not a question.

"James," I croak. "Yeah, it is. Broken. My phone. Why?"

"It is?" His eyebrows shoot up; a smile plays on his lips. "Because I thought maybe you were ignoring my texts and calls." He has a mean smile. A cruel smile. A stingy smile that doesn't reach his eyes.

"Oh, yeah, no," I lie. "It fell in the water. It's been in a bag of rice for, like, three days."

"Really," he says, deadpan, like he knows that I'm lying.

"Really," I say, trying to sound convincing. "I'm late, I've got to . . ."

"Let's make plans. You cut your hair. You and Piper, you got to be the same all the time?"

"Oh, um, plans?" I say. "I don't have my calendar and I . . ."

"It's summer. You don't work. How busy is your schedule?"

I stop, stung. "I'm busy," I say frostily. "I see friends and . . . stuff. I do stuff."

"So you are avoiding me. I get it. Was the sex that bad?" His voice is too loud. An elderly woman leaning on a walker stops in her tracks and slowly turns around to look at us. Her eyes have a sag underneath them that shows pink. It makes it look like she's weeping.

"My grandma is ill," I say coolly. "I've been spending time with her." It's half true, half a lie. Grandma *is* ill, if having had a stroke is "ill." She's dying. Grandma is dying. I haven't been to see her once. I can't. I just can't. My hand is shaking. I stuff it into my pocket so he can't see it.

"I'm sorry," he says.

"Me, too. Thanks." He's just a boy, I remind myself. He's just a person.

"I'm sorry," I add, without saying exactly what for.

"No big deal. Anyway." He draws it out long. His body is slightly too close to mine.

"Anyway," I repeat, taking a step back. "I really do have to go."

"Yeah," he says, "I get it." He takes a step toward me and I freeze. He's going to kiss me. I don't want to be kissed. The no is stuck in my throat. I try to say it, but I cough instead. He reaches up and taps my nose. His black eyes are assessing

218

me, measuring me, searching me. I don't want him to see me. *It's not you!* I want to scream. *You aren't my One!*

He's smiling bigger now and there's something stuck between his two front teeth. His hair looks slightly dirty. A wave of revulsion sweeps over me.

"Bye," I mutter, pushing through the heavy doors, making my escape.

"Sloane?" Elvis calls. "Someone's here to see you!"

I know it's not Piper. Piper would just come upstairs. Besides, she's at work today. Today is a terrible day. Today is the worst day of my life, so far.

Grandma died this morning.

Grandma, who smoked cigarettes through an elephant's tusk.

Grandma, who once made a man in a suit cry in the middle of a meeting.

Grandma, who sat silently in the home, staring out the window at things that weren't there, talking to people who died a long time ago.

Grandma, who always said that boys didn't matter.

I love her.

I loved her.

I try saying it out loud. "Grandma died this morning." But it doesn't feel true. It can't be true because I haven't gone to see her.

"Sloane!" Elvis calls again.

I click pause on the movie that I'm watching on Netflix. It's one from my favorite documentary series, where they made a bunch of films, the first one with a group of seven-year-olds. And the next seven years later. And another seven years later. It's lives sped up. Some of them don't go as well as others. I frown.

I know who it is. I think of Piper, her tongue on her lip, saying, "Give him a chance!"

I think of Soup, nodding.

Smiling.

He doesn't like me.

I was wrong about everything.

I was definitely wrong about him.

"Coming," I yell.

I glance at myself in the mirror, quickly change into a clean tank top. Hot pink. Our power color. We reclaimed pink. We made pink cool and tough, not girly and weak. Pink is strength. Pink is strong.

"Right, Piper?" I say.

I flex my bicep and smile at myself in the mirror. Too toothy. I try again. Better.

There's a trick I read about that said that if you smile when you aren't happy, you can fool yourself into being happy. I eye my bed, the rumpled blankets. I could get back in. I could tell Elvis that I'm sick. I could say that I'm on my way out somewhere else.

"Sloane?"

"COMING," I yell again.

I open my door and I head downstairs. He's just a boy who likes me. He's not a monster. He's someone who wants to be with me. Not with Piper, with *me*.

Is that so terrible?

Maybe I can get used to him.

Maybe if I get to know him, I'll like him.

Maybe I could try.

Poor guy, his dog was eaten by a rattlesnake in a state that has cactuses.

How bad can he be?

My mouth feels dry and there is a buzzing in my head that is a feeling that is a sound that is a feeling that is a sound, and I feel like a film that's jumped the reel somehow and who am I, anyway, to tell this James that he's not good enough for me, that no one is good enough for me except for Soup Sanchez who is my best friend's boyfriend, *I'm* the monster and I'm not worthy and I'm not anyone or anything and I don't deserve any better than this boy and his loose tongue and his grappling crab hands. I hear a voice come out of my own mouth, which is my voice, but also not my voice, and I reach up and touch my ugly hair and I say, "I figured you'd show up. Want to go somewhere with me?"

I drag Mr. Aberley's boat to the shoreline. "Are you sure this is okay?" says James. "We should ask. This belongs to your neighbor?" He has a slow way of speaking, a drawl, which makes everything he says sound like it might or might not be a joke. He smiles slow. He talks slow. He squints slow. He reaches for the boat to help me, slow slow slow. If I were to film him, I'd do it in slow motion, his hand reaching slowly to his hair, his lips parting slowly in a smile. I take my camera out of my bag and I point it at him.

"Hey," he says, slow like that. Backlit by the sun, maybe he's cute. I'm not sure, I'm not sure, I'm not sure.

"Mr. A doesn't mind," I say, lowering the camera, answering his question. "He's napping. He always naps between two and four. It's a thing."

"Is he your grandpa or something?"

"Friend," I say.

"Rich friend," he says, eyeing Mr. A's house.

"I guess." I shrug. "He's an old man."

"Uh-huh," he says. "Bet he has lots of cash."

I laugh even though it's not funny. "What are you going to do, rob him?"

"Maybe," he drawls; then he winks. "I'm joking. You look so serious."

I shrug. "I don't know you very well," I say. "I can't tell when you're joking."

"You'll get to know me," he says. "And you know me well enough to know what makes me—"

"Stop," I say. "I don't want to talk about it."

"Uh-huh," he says; the drawl again. "Okay, girl."

"Don't call me girl." If I weren't mad at Piper, I wouldn't be doing this. And I don't know why I'm mad. I don't know why I'm doing this. I feel like someone who's been broken, the sun bifurcating into two separate versions of me.

Me, Before.

Me, After.

I'm rowing now; he's leaning back in the stern of the boat, dragging his hand through the water. He reaches into my bag, casually, so casually. He takes out the camera. I stare at him. No one touches my camera, no one but me and Piper. He presses record. "Tell us how you feel about James Robert Wilson," he says. "Tell the world."

"I don't know yet," I lie quietly. I do know. Don't I? I hate him.

He lowers the camera. "What are you, some kind of film-maker?"

"Kind of," I say. "I want to be."

"What kind of films?" He raises his eyebrows. "I know what you'd be good at."

"Stop it," I say. "Are you trying to be funny? That's not funny."

"I was going to say comedy," he says. "You're funny. You're a spitfire, that's what my dad would say. Like what's-her-name from that show, *I Love Lucy*."

"Lucy?" I say.

"Nah," he says. "The other one. The friend. What did you think I was going to say?"

"I don't know," I say. "Forget it. I want to make documentaries. About people. About animals. Not comedies."

"Like cute cats, stuff like that? You want to go 'viral on the Internet'?" He makes air quotes with his fingers.

"No, like global warming," I retort. "Like animal extinctions caused by human activities. Did you know that by 2020, two-thirds of animal species will be extinct?"

He laughs. "Oh," he says. "You're one of *those*."

"One of what?"

"One of those superior girls who think they know so much, they're so much better."

"That doesn't make any sense."

"I know girls like you," he says. "You're white girls with tons of money, dripping with privilege."

"That's offensive," I say.

"Exactly," he says. "That's what a girl like you would say."

I keep rowing without talking. My brain feels like a broken clock, ticking over, not quite ever getting to the next minute. "Look," I say. "I shouldn't have done that with you."

"You can't say you were drunk, because you weren't. You wanted to." He looks uncomfortable. "Is this a trap? Are you going to call rape?"

"No! It's not like that. For me, that's all. For me, it was a mistake. No offense."

"Huh," he says. He scoops up a handful of water and flings it at me. It stings my eyes. I drop the oars. "That's offensive."

"Hey!" I say, blinking.

"How did you think I was going to react to that?"

"Well, it's not like I thought you thought it was a big deal for *you*," I say. "It wasn't even really a date."

"Felt like a date to me," he says. "In the South, we call that a date."

"I doubt it," I say. "Unless you're a time traveler from 1950 or something."

He shrugs. "You ever film animals?" he says. "Those snow leopards or whatever that are on the brink of going extinct?

Or do you just take selfies with you and your bestie, looking sexy?"

"You're really aggressive," I say. "I'm not sure why you're being such a jerk. I thought you liked me."

"*I thought you liked me*," he mimics. He laughs, a deep unexpectedly rich laugh. He puts his hand on my knee. "I'm just kidding around. I do like you. Thing is, I thought *you* liked me. But no, you used me for my body."

"I didn't," I say. "It's only that I don't *know* you." My heart is beating too fast, too hard. Everything about this was a terrible idea. I can't remember why I thought it wouldn't end badly. Of course it will. He isn't a normal boy. He's older. He's off. He's *different*. I row harder, then I let the boat skim. It makes a hissing sound over the calm water. A tiny wake chases us. "I *do* film animals. Sometimes. When I can find them. I've been filming the jellyfish a lot."

"The dead ones?" he says.

"Mostly," I admit.

"So it's basically a snuff film," he says.

"Not actually. They're already dead. But I'm going to edit it together with a bunch of other stuff about climate change and then interweave it with . . . you're not interested in this." I don't know why I'm telling him except that I want him to see me as something other than a body in a pink bikini. I want him to know that I'm smart. I'm powerful. I'm not just a girl. I'm stronger than that.

"Not really," he says. "Sounds boring. It would go viral if you made a catapult and splatted the corpses against a target. Hitting seals with jellyfish! Something out of the box."

I roll my eyes. "Well, at least you're honest. I'm not really into catapulting corpses for page hits, though."

"Sounds like you're trying pretty hard to be something you're not."

"Jeez, what are you, a therapist? I didn't ask you to analyze me."

"I'm just sayin'. What's wrong with being you? Everything doesn't have to be about the apocalypse. Like it doesn't make you more important to only talk about Big Important Problems."

"We're all going to die," I say doggedly.

"Yeah, I know," he says.

"My grandma died this morning," I say.

"Seriously?" he says. "Huh. Kind of thought you were lying about her being sick."

"I wasn't. And it's pretty normal at this point to say something like, I'm sorry."

"I'm not sorry, though," he says. "She was probably old.

Everyone dies, you said so yourself. Why should I be sorry? I didn't know her."

"Whatever," I say. "Stop talking." A wave of vertigo sweeps over me. I feel my phone buzz in my pocket. Piper, probably.

"So an island, huh. Sounds private."

"It's my favorite place."

"So why are you taking me there?" he says. "So we can be *alone*?"

"Look." I stop rowing. My heart is still topsy-turvy in my chest. My breathing is all wrong. I can't remember what my mom said about holding my breath or breathing out through my nose or in through my mouth. Nothing makes sense. "I'm not going to have sex with you. But I thought we should know each other. Piper said that I should . . . *I* think we should . . ."

"Oh, I get it," he says, sitting up. "You're freaking out that you had sex with me because you're not that kind of girl and now you want to turn this into a 'relationship.'" He makes air quotes with his fingers again. "Cool, I guess."

I row a few more strokes. "I think there's something wrong with me," I say. "I'm not feeling good. I feel weird."

"We all feel weird," he says. "Who feels like themselves? Who can really say that? We're always trying on new versions of ourselves all the time. Next up, I'm going to be Jack the Ripper."

"It's been done." I shiver. I hate him. I want to go home. "How about just being a better version of yourself?"

"Don't think so," he murmurs. He opens up his backpack, takes out a can of beer. "You want?"

I shake my head. "We should just go back," I say. "I have to go back, actually. I don't know what I was thinking. Piper said . . . Anyway, we should go back." I feel the panic starting to prickle at my skin, in each of my cells. My lungs constrict. I tell myself I can't hyperventilate. Not here. Not now. "This was a bad idea."

"No," he says. "It was a good idea. We should keep going."

He reaches forward and gently takes the oars out of my hands. He starts to row, like he knew where he was going all along, like this was his plan, not mine. Like there's nothing he wants more than to get me alone. I swallow a scream. It isn't rational. There is no reason to be afraid.

But I am afraid.

"I have to get the boat back by four," I whisper.

He nods. "No worries," he says as the boat bumps the shore of the island.

We climb to the peak of the island, a hill covered entirely with bracken that scratches our legs. On the way, he walks right through the nettle patch and doesn't seem bothered by the stings. *Maybe he's an alien*, I think. *Nothing makes sense. Maybe he's not human.* I reach down and grab a leaf. My skin tightens and stings.

I could get into the boat, I tell myself. I could row away.

But I don't. I follow him.

Piper texts: "Work done. Going to Soup's to Netflix and chill. Come over!"

Then: "By chill, I mean actually chill not Do It, FYI."

And: "Don't be weird. Get over u."

Finally: "B that way. I still<3 u. C U tmrw?"

I text back: "OK." She can take that as an answer to whichever one she wants. I think about taking a selfie with James, texting it to her. *Look at me! I'm having fun! With a boy! Like you wanted!*

Am I doing this for her?

Because she wants me to have a boyfriend?

It would make it so much easier for her.

Maybe she'd even be jealous.

He takes my breath away, I imagine saying to her. *When we touch, it's electric, you know?*

But I'm not having fun and he's more man than boy. In the sharp, unforgiving sunlight, I can see the beginnings of creases around his eyes. How old is he? Twenty-five? Thirty? I don't even know. My parents would be so angry if they knew I was here with this boy-man who I barely know, but they are at the funeral home with Grandma, who is not a hunter of elephants but who is dead anyway and the elephants would bury her and I am here with a boy-man who I don't trust and a migraine is starting to slowly, faintly stretch across my skull. I squat down.

James is pulling out bracken by the roots.

"Clearing a spot," he says when I seem startled or confused, or both. A seagull perched on the shore looks up at us and tilts his head. A second and third land beside him, all staring up at us, like they know better than I do what is happening here.

"Help," I whisper to them.

I take out the camera. James stops pulling the plants. "Don't you ever ask first?" he says. A dark shadow on his face, like the black wings of a crow. I put the camera away. "Not everyone loves cameras."

"I don't know you," I say. "I mean, I didn't know you didn't like it."

"Now you know," he says, smiling slow. His facial expressions never quite match his words, so conversing with him feels like I'm constantly decoding something without the help of a cereal box decoder. He sits down in the cleared spot and pats the rock next to him. I go over to him. I sit.

I am not someone who sits when they are told to sit.

Am I?

The rock is covered with a fine layer of dust and dirt, stirred up by the torn-out roots of the plants.

"This is nice," he says. "Pretty." He waves his arm, indicates the expanse of the ocean in front of us. The sun flirts with the waves and scatters a blinding field of light. The sky sighs with frustration at its own blueness. I wish I had a spiked Slurpee. I need something.

"Beer," I say. "Please."

"Good manners." He tosses me a can. I crack it open, watch the bubbles fizz and pool in the rim. "I liked your hair better long. Piper looks good, but you just look exposed."

I scowl at him and take a long drink. "Does negging work for you a lot?" I ask. "Because girls hate it, FYI." I gulp the beer down, half a can in a few swallows.

"Whoa." He laughs. "We could poke a hole in the bottom and you could funnel it if you're that desperate."

"I'm thirsty," I say. "Rehydrating." The beer hits me quickly. I didn't eat lunch. Or breakfast. There was the phone call about Grandma, the way Mom folded in half and Dad caught her, the hushed voices and the crying, and their gentle grieving that made me want to smash my face through the glass of the door. Mom and Dad held hands. They murmured. I wanted to scream and break things. I folded up my anger into an origami dove and it flew away. I can't possibly be drunk. I hiccup.

"Are you drunk on half a beer? Lightweight."

"I'm not," I say. "Tell me your life story or something."

He puts his hand on my leg. I take it off again. "Life story," I repeat.

"So you can see if I'm good enough for you?" he says.

"Something like that," I say.

"Okay, well, fine. I grew up in a house with a mom and a dad and two sisters and a dog. I miss my dog the most," he says. "That pretty much sums it up."

"What happened to the dog?" I say.

"It died," he says. "Everything dies."

"What was it named? I always wanted a dog."

"Fluffy," he says.

"Fluffy!" I laugh. "I was picturing something like Spike or Killer."

He doesn't laugh. "Nope."

"Rattlesnake?" I ask.

"What is it with you and stereotypes?" he says, his face darkening. "House fire."

"Oh."

"Change the subject." His voice is low. If it were music, it would definitely be off-key. I don't like it.

"Okay, well, tell me about your tattoos, then." I try to keep my voice normal. "Every tattoo has a story, right? I watched this really cool documentary where they—"

"Mine don't," he interrupts. "My buddy is a tattoo artist. I let him practice on me."

"Oh." I take my phone out of my pocket and look at it. The screen seems too small and far away. Fleetingly, I wonder if he roofied my beer. But I feel fine enough. I'm okay.

"My grandma owned a hotel," I say. "A bunch of hotels. She sold them to Hyatt when she retired."

"Is that why you guys are rich?" he says.

I shrug. "I guess. My parents both work." I've forgotten what I was going to say about Grandma now. I frown. The cigarette holder. Elephant tusks. Zombies. I take it out of my bag and look at it. I want to throw it into the sea, but it doesn't want to leave my hand. I want to plunge it into his eye. I don't know what I want. He stares, unblinking. If I knew him better, I'd say something like *Take a picture, it lasts longer!* I'd make a joke, elbow him, laugh it off. But I don't know him. Everything about him feels ominous but I'm being stupid because this isn't about him, it's about me and Piper, and what she talked me into doing, and what I did.

He was just there.

He isn't the monster.

Piper is.

I rub my eyes and blink. "Sun in my eyes," I say, even though he didn't ask.

He takes a long slow gulp of beer and belches into his hand. "Do you have grandparents?" I say. "I mean, living ones." He shrugs. "Dead."

His hand is on my leg again. We both stare at it. He slides it up my thigh. His skin is slightly cold, slightly sticky from the beer. "I—" I start.

"Holy!" he says. "Look!" Then he's standing up, shielding his eyes from the sun. "Look!"

I pull myself up to my feet, knocking over my half-drunk can of beer. The liquid glugs out of the opening, pouring down the slope into the roots of the remaining dry shrubbery. I look where James is pointing, out into the strait. There, in the distance, the distinct black fin of an orca. Then another. Then another. I can hear them blowing. I can hear one breaching and landing hard in the water. It echoes around us like a slap.

"Wow," he says, sounding awed in a way that makes me like him, maybe a little. Or at least makes him seem different. Harmless. Like a kid. "Oh my lord, this is amazing. Come on." He grabs my hand and half walks, half runs down the slope to the shore. When we get there, he starts shedding his clothes.

"What are you doing? Why are you doing that? Stop!"

He doesn't answer, instead chucks his clothes into the boat, dives into the ice-cold water like it's nothing. He's stark naked. He starts to swim.

"What are you *doing*?" I repeat, half laughing, half not. "There's a current!"

The whales are moving closer. Above them, a flock of seabirds. There must be herring. One orca slaps its tail against the water. Two larger ones blow spray simultaneously. There must be ten, fifteen, twenty. They swim closer and closer.

James is still swimming out toward them strongly, a certain stroke, a sure pace, a straight line.

"Come back!" I yell. "It's illegal to swim with orcas! It's interfering with the whales!"

He starts treading water, flicking the wetness from his hair. He yells something I can't hear. Sound only really travels in one direction over water.

The whales are putting on an amazing show. I see them pretty often, but each time it's magical all over again. I'd rather be sharing this moment with anyone but James. He's now a dot in the distance. Maybe he'll keep going. I can pretend he never existed. *James?* I'll say. *Never heard of him.*

When his body washes up, I'll say, *Oh, that's so sad! I wonder who he was.*

He's too close to the whales now. Way too close. They must be thinking, *Stay away.* They must be thinking, *What is wrong with you? Can't you see that we're huge and predatory? Don't you know better?*

An orca has never killed a swimmer in the wild.

I take out my camera. He's too distant to see through the lens.

I crouch down onto my haunches. One of my favorite documentaries is called *Blackfish*. It's about orcas, both captive and wild. It's about how they belong out there, where they are. For a second, I feel a surge of something like love for this boy, this James, the way he swam out there. But then I start feeling irritated. He's been drinking, for one thing. What if he drowns? What if the whales decide to come closer? What if he gets hurt?

I stop filming and I wave at him, a huge beckoning. "Come back," I yell, so loudly that he must be able to hear me.

He raises one hand in a salute, or maybe he's flipping me the bird, I can't tell. I stand up on Seth so I can see him better. He's really close to the place where the current starts to flow. *I used to love this island*, I think. *And now I don't know if I do.*

Everything is changing.

Everyone is changing.

Even me.

Especially me.

I close my eyes. Eventually I can hear the rhythmic splash of James swimming back to shore, the regularity of it, like a pulse. Like my pulse. Slow, steady. Slow. Slower.

I open my eyes and use my hand to shield the sun. He's lying on his back in the water, floating. "Are you dead?" I call. "Did they bite your legs off?"

He doesn't answer

"Oh, for God's sake," I say. I wade out to my knees. The water is ice cold, cloudy with seaweed and wood chips that must have come off a passing barge. "James?"

Suddenly, he sprays water from his mouth in a huge arc. He's laughing. "I'm fine," he says. "That was amazing. Come and swim."

"No," I say. "It's too cold." I go back to where I was sitting, lean on sun-warmed Seth, and wait. He emerges a few seconds later. "Put your clothes on!"

"You've seen me before," he says. "Want to see closer?"

"No," I say, keeping my eyes focused on a boat on the horizon. "Get dressed. You're making me uncomfortable."

"*You're making me uncomfortable,*" he mimics. Then he laughs, his slow-rolling drawling laugh. "I'm going to get the rest of the beer."

He shakes like a dog, water spraying everywhere.

"Hey!" I shriek. "That's cold!"

"Not too cold," he says. "It felt good."

"Woof," I say.

"You're a strange one," he says. "I'll give you that. You're different."

"Gee, thanks," I say flatly. "You know, it's almost four; I've got to get the boat back."

"I'm going to have another drink," he says. "Come up."

"No thanks," I say.

"Aight," he says. "Back in a flash." Before I realize what's happening, he's leaning over me, he's launching his tongue into my mouth, he's pushing me against the log, and he's Charlie, and Soup isn't here and I don't know whether to fight or give in and what would Piper do? Can a no follow a yes?

I put my hand on his chest and he grabs it and puts it on his crotch and I feel a faint sneaking up on me, I'm going to faint, and everything is gray, and then just like that, he's gone. I can hear him crashing through the dry shrubbery, heading back up to where his bag is, where the beer is, and without thinking about it very much, I stand up woozily and use my full weight to heave Mr. A's boat back into the sea and then I'm in the middle seat and the oars are in my hands and I'm dropping the blades into the water and I'm pulling with my back and I'm focused and the water is concrete and I pull against it and I row and I row and I row like I'm some kind of athlete, my muscles are a symphony of strength and power and the boat is cutting so fast through the water that I'm leaving a wake. I think I can hear James shouting, but it's only a flock of circling gulls who have found a feast in the water—a flock of herring, dead jellyfish, someone's trash—shouting about their good luck to anyone and everyone who will listen.

When I get home, I delete him from my camera. I go on a deleting rampage. I delete Charlie. I delete James. I delete and delete and delete. I delete the whales and the seagulls and the sun on the sea. I delete all of it. I delete everything.

I delete Piper.

I delete myself.

Mom shakes me awake in the morning. "You slept in your clothes?" she says, making it a question. "Anyway, honey, I know you're really upset about Grandma, but I was wondering if you could go see Mr. Aberley. Just let him know that Grandma is gone and see if he'd like to come to the service with us. They weren't exactly close, but I know he sometimes brought her that strange tea."

I groan, rolling over. "Headache," I mumble.

"Oh no." She sighs. "Migraine?" Her voice cracks, like she's going to cry, and I feel guilty, so I say, "No, no, I'm okay. I'll go. It's fine."

"Thanks," she says. "We want to get everything organized because the funeral is going to be the day after tomorrow. I want to make it really nice. Grandma always liked things to be a certain way." She starts to cry again for real. "What if no one comes?"

"I'm sorry, Mom," I say helplessly. "I'm sorry. People will come. We'll be there, right?"

"I know," she manages. "It's so hard."

"I know," I echo.

When she finally leaves, I get up and shower. I get dressed. I look out my window at the island. What if he drowned? Did I really do that?

I feel panic curling around the edges of my vision, a migraine that isn't a migraine. "James who?" I say out loud.

I have to go out there. I have to go get him.

Don't I?

"Going now, Mom!" I shout, running through the kitchen.

"Whoa, slow down!" says Dad, nearly crashing into me by the patio doors.

"I have to go to Mr. Aberley's," I call back over my shoulder. "I told Mom that I would!"

"It's not a race!" he calls after me. "The service isn't until tomorrow!" but I'm already jumping over tree roots on the gnarled path to Mr. A's front door. I'm already feet-crunching-gravel sprinting to his porch.

I burst through his door without knocking. "Mr. A!" I shout.

"Kitchen!" he calls. He's sitting at the table when I burst through the door.

"Oh, great. Mom wants to know if you want a ride to Grandma's funeral. She died."

"Is that what they call 'breaking news gently'?" he says,

chortling. "I'm sorry, it's rude of me to laugh. Sit." He pats the seat next to him. He smells like expensive cologne and freshly ironed clothes.

"I'm sorry," I say. "I *really* have to use your boat. It's basically an emergency,"

Mr. A looks at me with his bright blue eyes. They aren't smiling. "Mr. A?" I say.

"Would this have anything to do with a certain naked young man who seems to have stolen the gardener's overalls from my shed?" he says. "And perhaps these?" He nods slightly and indicates a pile of neatly folded clothes.

James's clothes.

"Oh," I say, sinking into the chair. My legs are shaking. "I can explain."

"Can you?" he says. "It's funny how I have a feeling that your story won't make sense." He pours a cup of tea for me, his hand shaking slightly, his eyes fixed to my face. "I'm sorry about your grandma." He stares out the window and rubs his throat. "She was very accomplished but not terribly easy to get along with."

"She just didn't like men that much," I say. "She probably really liked you and your weird tea, she just couldn't let on." I think about it. "She didn't let many people get close to her."

"Like you," he says.

"Like me," I agree.

I gulp the tea, which is too hot. A bit of a leaf gets stuck in my throat. I cough. *Pee tea*, I think, and I want to laugh but I don't. "You can't tell anyone," I croak, choking on it. "You have to promise."

"Cross my heart," he says. "Cross my heart and hope to die. Now talk."

PART TWO

SOUP

I AM STILL ALIVE AND PIPER IS STILL
dead. Those are the two things I know for sure.

Two is an even number—good luck. But there is nothing
lucky about any of this.

I'm not going to school, I'm not doing art, I'm not doing
anything but replaying all of it in my head, the stuff I know.
The stuff I can't know, but I can guess.

I was watching the news when they brought him to the bail
hearing. The reporters were all asking questions, shouting
things at him as he ducked through the crowd, surrounded by
lawyers. He was ignoring them, but then someone shouted,
"Why did you do it?"

And he stopped in his tracks.

He turned to stare right at the camera. "Why not?" he drawled.

That's the fact that erases the other facts and stands out, like ugly paint applied to a clean blank wall.

That's what they keep replaying on TV: his sly grin—that's totally what it was, *sly*—and the shout, "Why'd you do it?" Then him freezing, standing still, and the quietness, like something he chose, like he waited for it, and into the silence he lobbed those two words: "Why not?"

His mouth looked soft, like a girl's.

He *smirked*.

I want to know if Sloane saw it. If she knows he said that. I want to know what she thinks.

Who is he?

I want to know what she knows.

She won't answer me. Not now. Not ever, probably.

She's busy going back in time to stop my parents from screwing without a condom, which is funny because I don't have a dad and Mom says he did use a condom but it must have broken because here I am.

He doesn't know.

She says she didn't know how to find him but she told me his name.

So I know who he is.

I follow him on Facebook.

The only connection I have with my own biological father is on social media.

I'm one of 4,566 people who follow him on Facebook. Even. Good luck.

But I'm the only one who is his son.

If I hadn't kissed Sloane, Piper wouldn't have run.

Piper loved equations, so here's an equation: Me + Sloane = Piper.

It's my fault, even though I didn't do it.

The guy who murdered Piper has a name: James Robert Wilson.

I wonder if he is a James, or a Jim, or a Jimmy.

He worked at the movie theater, selling tickets, cleaning up after movies. When they asked him if he knew her, he just shrugged. "Might have seen her around the mall, I guess," he said. Like me, he has tattoos that sneak upward from the collar of his shirt. Like me, he looks a little bit Mexican, a little bit who-knows-what-else.

Like me, he killed Piper Sullivan.

We killed her together, me and James Robert Wilson. I gave him the time to do what he did. I gave him the opportunity.

I want them to arrest me. Charge me with something. But

the lead detective in the case, Detective Marcus, won't take my confession as anything.

He says, "Son, you need someone else to talk to." But he doesn't say who that is. I'd talk to God but I don't think he's listening to me, not now, maybe not ever. I can't talk to Mom because she needs so bad for me to be okay even when I'm not, I'm definitely not. I could message my dad on Facebook, but what would I say? "Hi, I'm your son. My girlfriend was murdered when I kissed her best friend. Well, talk to you later! Philip."

Not likely.

I look at James Robert Wilson's photo, zoom in tight to his face on my screen. He has dark eyes. Pockmarked skin.

He's twenty-six years old.

Eight years older than me.

There's something about him that's familiar.

Maybe it's that his face looks like the After picture of mine. His mouth is frozen in an almost smile, a happiness that pisses me off. I want to punch that smile right off his face, feel my knuckle crunching into his jaw. He's wearing a plaid shirt, open a few buttons too far. He's got pecs. He looks like he smells damp, musty, like he never lets his clothes dry the whole way, like he regularly lies on the driveway, underneath the body of an old car from the seventies that he's fixing.

He doesn't look like a guy who kills people for no reason, but who does?

My non-condom-wearing dad has a shaved head and a piercing through his nose like a bull's ring. I guess he's never killed anyone, but he looks like he could.

James Robert Wilson did.

He killed Piper Sullivan.

His mouth looks wet. He lived in a suite in the basement of his uncle's house. His entire family died in a fire when he was eleven, dog and all. He tried to save the dog.

Everyone says he was a nice guy. He had no record. He did a year of art college and dropped out.

He could be me.

I could be him.

I stare at his face and I think about killing him, about how that would feel: my hands around his throat. A blade separating his skin from his muscles and bones. His eyes begging and me smiling into them and telling him "Why not?" even while

I'm divesting him of his soul, cutting him free of the cancer in him that made it okay for him to kill her like that.

Piper could talk anyone into (or out of) anything.

How could she not have talked him out of this?

I don't get it. I don't get how it could have happened. I don't get *why*.

I look at his photo and the way his eyes are squinting and his hair, which is the long, soft straggly-looking hair of a guy who is trying too hard to look a certain way.

When I rub my hand over my own head, it's like touching a man's stubbly face. I told Piper that touching stubble made me think of the father I never knew, and she laughed. She laughed until she was bent double, and I think I know that it's possible to hate Piper Sullivan. I hate myself for wondering but I wonder what she did or said to James Robert Wilson. I hate myself for wondering if she laughed at him so hard that she had to hold on to something to stop from falling down.

Because is that like saying she was asking for it?

No one asks for that.

But mostly I hate him and I want to smash my laptop screen and I want her to text me something, anything. I want her not to be dead so bad that my skin hurts from it. Everything hurts from it and I'm inside out from hurting like this.

I kissed Sloane. Piper ran out, alone.

Piper was almost never alone.

It's my fault. Mine and Sloane's.

We did this.

I look at my phone, at all the texts from Sloane that I'm not answering.

"Please," the last one says.

I shut the phone off.

The room is full of silence and of me. The shadows don't want me here. I have to go to school but I can't. I can't stay here, but I can't go anywhere. I don't think Jim Bob—that's what I call him in my head now—knew what the body count was going to be. I feel like he killed me, too.

I bet he wouldn't care, if he knew. I bet he'd do that now-famous crooked half smile and drawl, "Well, so what?"

Mom is at the dining room table, working. She's working from home "for a while," which means until I don't need her here. But I don't need her here. And I do need her here because I keep forgetting that Piper is dead. When I wake up in the morning, it takes me a few moments to realize what's wrong. Then I hear my mom. Mom is home because Piper is dead.

Even just sitting on the couch, the smooth fabric of it cool underneath me, I can feel the rush of tears wanting to come out. I'm eighteen years old. I'm a tough kid, everyone says so. I'm not someone who cries.

Mom looks up. "You okay?"

I nod a lie in her direction. All I want is to unkiss Sloane, and I want for Piper to not be dead.

I close my eyes. I let it just sweep over me.

I let it pull me under.

Outside, I'm perfectly still, but inside, I'm screaming.

"Why not?" he says, grinning slyly, over and over again.

Nothing about him is real.

He's an actor playing a killer, when everyone knows the real killers are me and Sloane. The only thing is that no one is going to be sending us to jail, no matter how much we deserve it.

He strangled her with her own shoelace. He raped her. He sliced her skin with blades. He stole a boat and rowed out as deep as he dared and pushed her body over the side. Was she still alive? Did she jump off? Was she trying to escape?

Her blood was in the boat. Her blood was on the beach. It's like he didn't even try to hide it. He didn't bother.

They found him on the top of the island, not even trying to hide or run.

I'm hollowed out, but I'm still here, on the couch. I stink. I can smell my sweat. Mom yawns and types something on her computer, leaning close to the screen. Squinting. Sometimes she hugs me so hard, it's like she's forgiving me for something I didn't do.

When she's done with her work for the day, we sit in the living room and watch TV side by side. Sometimes Mom cries, even when the show isn't sad. Last night, during *Anchorman*, the guy said, "I love lamp," which is the best line, the funniest in our favorite funny movie, and she burst into tears. I got up and stormed out of the room, slamming doors hard behind me to cover up the fact that her crying made me cry, too. "Soup!" she called after me. "Philip, come back!"

I ignored her. I put my headphones on. I filled my ears with music. Anything to not hear *that* tone in her voice.

She didn't even like Piper that much. She'd make this clucking sound with her tongue when Piper threw herself onto the couch like she owned the place. She'd shake her head sadly when Piper would jump into the pool and then come up screaming swear words because the water was so cold. She never liked the way Piper wore her body like a loosely buttoned shirt, always something showing that shouldn't be shown.

"MOM," I yelled when she knocked. "LEAVE ME ALONE."

But today, I'm not going to take it out on her. Today I'm not going to be so angry.

The phone beeps and Mom answers it, talking work talk, her voice small and singsongy, her professional voice, and I can't stand it. I punch my fist into the palm of my hand, bruising my knuckles.

There's something wrong with me. I have to get out of here but I can't leave. I have nowhere to go because I can't get away from myself. I really want to see Sloane and I also want to never see her again and the only person who I want to talk to about this is my dad, who I know only on Facebook, who exclusively posts jokes and gig schedules.

He's a musician.

Everything I know about my dad can be summed up in the following:

He plays the drums.

He likes jokes with punch lines you have to think about. Intellectual jokes.

He's playing at the Fall Fair with his band in three weeks. Piper and I were going to go to his show. She'd talked me into agreeing to introduce myself.

And now we're not going. Because Piper is dead. Because I kissed Sloane.

Simple, right?

I didn't kill Piper, but I'm guilty of Sloane, that's for sure.

* * *

"Mom, are you ready?" My voice cracks.

Mom looks down at what she's wearing, which is a black dress, black stockings, black shoes, like she's surprised to find herself in that kind of outfit on this kind of day. Outside, it's sunny. The weather has been so perfect, it's like an insult to everything I feel. The skies should be weeping for Piper, for me, for all of us. It should be winter. There should be ice.

"Ready as I ever will be," she says, squaring her shoulders.

She hasn't been sleeping. Under her eyes, there are black shadows. Her skin looks dry and pale. I pour her a glass of water, add ice cubes. I slice up a lemon, the blade slipping and nicking my thumb. The juice runs into it and stings so bad that tears are in my eyes. I squeeze some lemon in her water, make her sit down, make her drink it until she feels more like herself.

"You're so sweet," she says, and I shake my head because she's wrong.

The funeral is in an hour. Sometime between now and then, we have to get to the car, drive to the church, pretend that everyone isn't staring at me. Thinking about what they know: me making out with Sloane while Piper was dying.

"The lawn's dead," I say. "I'm sorry about the lawn, Mom."

Mom says, "Never mind, it's not a big deal."

I go, "It is to me."

"It's just grass," she says. "I don't care."

Piper, Sloane, and I were lying on that grass only a couple of weeks ago and it was green and soft, like a different planet from this one, where the lawn is dead and so is Piper. Piper was giving Sloane a bad time about some guy she apparently hooked up with. The whole thing was hard for me to imagine. It seemed nothing like what I'd think Sloane would do. But Piper wouldn't lay off her about him. "Go out with him again. Give him a chance. Don't be such a prude," she said.

"Leave it," Sloane said. "It's none of your business."

That's how they talked to each other. Like they hated each other.

But they didn't.

"I love you, but shut up," Sloane added.

We'd made cold drinks. We'd spread huge towels on the grass and lain down, reading books or pretending to, or listening to music, or just sleeping in the sun, the gentle softness of the green, alive lawn holding us up and cooling our skin. Sloane took her drink and poured it over Piper's head. Piper pushed Sloane into the pool. The whole time, they were laughing. Like the jokes that my dad posts, it took me a while to figure out what was funny. I'm still not sure I know.

Anyway, if you lie down on that lawn now, it would be like lying on sticks, prickly and unforgiving.

I pull out a chair and sit down next to Mom and drink a glass of water of my own, with four ice cubes, an even number for good luck.

There's something about Piper being dead that makes everything I do seem exaggerated, like a performance. *He raises the glass to his lips. He sips the water slowly. He remembers the lawn and the fun time they had there, together, which was neither happy nor sad, just time spent.* My inner narrator has an accent, a serious tone, a heaviness that clunks along in a boring monotone that I can't shut off.

Maybe Sloane can make a movie about that.

I'm going to see Sloane today.

I'm going to talk to Sloane.

I have to talk to Sloane.

I take a deep, slow breath and practice not crying. I'm not going to cry at the funeral. I'm not going to be the one everyone is staring at.

Mom smells like she's freshly showered. Her hair is neat and crisp, just like she is. I pick up my water and put it down again. I make four perfect drink rings on the table and then wipe them away with the sleeve of my black wool suit. I only have a black wool suit because of Halloween last year. I'm wearing a *Halloween costume* to my girlfriend's funeral.

Here's something I'd never admit out loud: I think Piper knew that Sloane and I had a connection that she and I didn't have. That she was playing with us, both of us, and the way we kept catching each other's eye like kids in some dumb movie, thinking no one noticed.

Turns out, I have a lot of reasons to say sorry to Piper. Is that what funerals are for? People call them the last goodbye, but maybe they should be called the last apology. *I'm so freaking sorry, Piper.*

I am every bit as guilty as the murderer.

Right?

I wore this suit to a Halloween party in someone's backyard. A bonfire that got too big. The fire department had to come and put it out. Drinks in red cups. Everything always spinning slightly out of control. Piper and Sloane laughing in the firelight, sparks landing in their hair. Piper and Sloane before I really knew them. Piper and Sloane before I ruined everything by asking the wrong girl out in the first place.

I've had a crush on Sloane since fourth grade, but when I saw Piper at the art show and she was crying because she said my art made her feel so much, I don't know what happened. I mean, that kind of thing is a pretty hard thing to not fall for, when someone likes you enough to cry about your paintings.

I thought she got me.

She never got me.

Not really.

Mom stands up. She goes and looks through the gap in the closed curtains, her high heels clip-clopping on the über-clean floors. "Hot day," she says. "Too hot. Global warming." She sighs. Even in heels, she looks little, like a kid playing dress-up.

Let's skip it. Let's stay home and watch TV, I want to say. I want to protect her. Or me. I don't want to do this thing but we have to do this thing. *I* have to do this thing.

"We could get a sprinkler put in," Mom says.

"No," I say. "I can water it. I'll do it after. I'll start doing it again. I'm sorry about the lawn."

She shrugs.

I actually *love* taking care of the lawn, which makes me sound like a middle-aged man, but I've always been my own dad. I was proud of that stupid lawn. It was the best one on the block. It died so fast; I can't believe how fast. Only a couple of weeks of sunshine and neglect and it browned up and crisped, dried out and gave up, and even though the weather is cooling, it's showing no signs of coming back to life.

Like Piper.

I squeeze my eyes shut tight. In my mind, the evening when she died replays itself.

Right before I kissed Sloane and everything fell apart, I broke up with Piper Sullivan.

"It's not working," I remember saying to her. "I think we should break up."

"Are you kidding me?" she said. Then she threw her drink in my face. My eyelashes were dripping with it, blue and sweet. I licked it off my lips, wiped my eyes with my hands.

"Grow up," I said.

Then I walked away. I left her there, crying.

I drank more.

I drank and I drank.

Then Sloane found me.

Everyone knows what happened after that. Our feet dancing on the sticky floor, our bodies pressed together like we were going to do it, right then and there.

I'm an idiot.

It's my fault.

Is there a difference between the truth and a lie if everyone believes the lie? I wasn't Piper's boyfriend. I was Piper's ex-boyfriend.

I get up from my chair and shove open the screen door and step outside. It's like a wave of heat that wants to push me back in, but I don't let it. I take a few steps, grass crunchy under my feet. The air is hot as dust. I cough.

I go inside.

Mom goes, "Ready?"

"In a minute," I say, sitting down, sipping from my sweating glass of water, wearing my slightly too small, slightly itchy black wool suit. "I'll be ready in one more minute."

I will never be ready, though. That's the truth.

My dad's band is called the Asteroids. They play locally. They once went on tour with Aerosmith as the opening act. I think that was the pinnacle of their success. It was downhill after that.

On the telephone pole beside the meter where we park—the lot is full already—there's a poster, tattered and half covered by a missing-cat ad, for a gig he did two months ago. I watch Mom and see if she pauses on it, but her eyes don't land there at all.

I want to shake her.

Come on, Mom! TELL me!

I have a right to know!

But she doesn't. Maybe she won't ever.

I'm at my girlfriend's funeral.

My dad should be here, shouldn't he?

Why am I making Piper's death about my dad?

The two things are locked together in my head and I can't snap them apart.

The sidewalk is so hot, you could fry an egg on it. Our feet distort in the shimmering heat like we're wading in the sea.

People are slowly streaming in the doors of the church. The kids from school look awkward in their grown-up suits, in high heels and black dresses. Everyone looks like they are performing in a movie, but not quite getting it right. It's either too sincere or not sincere enough or I don't know what, but it's weird. It makes my skin crawl. Everything is wrong.

Car doors slam. Someone's alarm goes off. From the green-turning-gold maple tree that shades the entrance, a flock of crows lifts off and scatters up into the sky like noisy black confetti.

I follow Mom into the church, my head down, looking at nothing but the back of her heels in her high shoes, the steady way that they strike the floor.

The funeral is crowded, a party that isn't fun. Everyone is here, looking like they spent a bunch of time doing their hair and makeup, the phonies. I hate them. Funerals should be ugly and bare. There are piles of bouquets and stuffed toys out front, actual stacks. Piper would have laughed about that. What do people think is going to happen to those? All that plastic wrapping would have made her go nuts. And the teddy bears and dolls are flat-out creepy.

The pew is uncomfortable. People are squeezed too tight. My legs are too long. I can't look beside me because I don't want to know who is there.

I see the back of Charlie's head. He hasn't called me even once since Piper died. That jerk. I want to jump over the backs of the pews between me and him. I want to yell things at him. I want to beat him up. Again.

Without Piper, I'm pretty sure I don't have any friends left. Only Sloane. And are we even real friends?

I see Piper's mom, her face covered with a black veil. Her head is bent forward like the effort of keeping it up is too much. I don't blame her. It is too much.

Charlie turns around but I can't tell if he's looking at me or not. He's wearing aviator sunglasses, like a movie star. I wish I'd done that. I wish I'd brought something to hide behind.

Then I see her.

Sloane.

Her white-blond hair shimmers silvery in the light. It's not lying flat or straight; it looks more like she washed it and left it to dry its own way, bits sticking up and out, as though maybe she just woke up and found herself here.

Maybe she did.

She looks kind of high or maybe drunk.

She is swaying slightly. I know the feeling. Her hands keep going up to her hair and touching, touching.

She can't keep still, can't sit there, but can't leave either.

I get it. I want so bad to squeeze out of this seat, to climb over everyone like I'm crowd-surfing at a concert, hands reaching up to pass me toward her. When I got to her, I'd say, *Me too*, but I don't. I can't.

I will.

When this is over.

The priest starts talking, his voice a low hum, like my inner narrator, soothing and grating at the same time. Around me, I hear people crying, full-on sobbing, coughing on their own phlegmy pain. It's contagious because pretty soon even Mom is doing it on one side of me, the school's shop teacher on the other. I'm not crying. I'm swallowing and swallowing and swallowing all the blood and bile inside me that threatens to come out.

Amen, says the priest. *Amen, amen, amen*, everyone murmurs, waves of *Amen* all around me.

If she were here, she'd be rolling her eyes. If she were here, she'd be giggling inappropriately.

If she were here, we wouldn't be here.

If she were here, this wouldn't be happening.

An old lady starts to make her way up to the front, to say a few words about Piper. Her voice is as thin as a glass breaking. "I met Piper when she was merely a wisp of a girl," she starts. "She'd come to my door like a stray cat, seeking cookies, the kind with icing. She liked the pink the best, even though they were really the same flavor . . ."

In my head, I'm replaying the party. The fight. The breakup. The look on Piper's face when she saw me and Sloane. Sloane. Oh God, Sloane.

The lady finishes, and someone else goes up. A man. Then someone else. And another. A girl who Piper hated. Fatty.

"She was one of the good ones," he intones. "Piper will always live in our, um, hearts." He smirks. I want to punch him so bad. I want to punch everyone.

Ms. Featherstone, who teaches physics, approaches the microphone. "She had a brilliant mind. There was something about Piper Sullivan that was special. She was able to . . ." She stops. "She could . . ." She starts crying, blubbering. There's a silence. It's taking everything in me to not burst out into heaving, little-kid sobs. "I'm sorry. I just can't."

Sloane's dad starts to tell a story in his strong, confident voice, about Sloane and Piper in ballet class when they were six. I can't listen. I won't listen. The Piper who is dead is not the Piper dressed up as a lamb for a recital. The Piper who is dead is *my* Piper. They didn't know her as well as they think they did. Piper hadn't been a *lamb* for a long time.

Who knew so many people had so much to say about Piper?

I swallow and swallow. The lump in my throat is strangling me.

The priest asks if anyone else has anything to say. People are restless. The place smells like body odor and wet wool. The funeral has gone on too long, a party that should have ended an hour ago. Eyes swivel and look at me.

I shake my head. Not me. No.

I bet people are disappointed, but I won't give them the pleasure of hearing my voice crack, watching me fall crying to the floor, needing to be helped up. No way.

There are four screens at the front of the room, which start showing a slideshow of photos of Piper. Baby Piper. Toddler Piper. Piper and Sloane. Sloane and Piper. A song plays through big speakers, a shot of feedback making everyone gasp.

Then it's over.

There are six people carrying her coffin. Even. Why didn't they ask me? I'm the boyfriend! The ex-boyfriend.

I'm no one. Forget it.

I manage to not cry, which is actually kind of a miracle.

People start to file out, stopping to hug one another.

No one hugs me.

The no ones who are hugging me make me look extra visible. Everyone is hugging! Even my mom is hugging people.

I am unhuggable.

I'd hug myself, but that would look stupid. Now is not the time for jokes.

I try not to notice them staring at me, all of them, judging me, keeping away from me as far as they can, like they might catch what I have, which is a dead girlfriend.

It's not contagious, I want to say. I want to raise my hands and show them that there is no blood. *It wasn't me, it wasn't me, it wasn't me.*

Anyway, we'd broken up.

Mom stops to talk to Piper's mom. They hug, cheeks against each other's. I can't. I can't say anything. I can't do anything. I look at Piper's mom's shoes, shiny and black, high and pointed.

Then, suddenly, I feel Sloane beside me. She's put on sunglasses and I can't see her eyes and I want to see them so bad. I want to touch her arm. I want to grab her and hold on so tight. But her dad is next to her, holding her up. Through her sleeve and my sleeve, I can feel her arm shaking, a tiny tremor that I recognize. I want to say something. I want to. But I can't.

I want to hug her.

Hug me, I will her silently.

She doesn't. But I can tell she wants me to hug her.

But I can't.

It's weird, both of us like we're holding our breath.

What did we do?

Then I grab her hand and then we're walking.

We're walking fast, shimmying around people who are like immovable objects that make me think of chess pieces or topiary. We dart through the crowd, shiny as fish.

Me and Sloane.

We get outside and I stop. She goes, "Keep going," so we

run for real, even though no one is chasing us. Fact is that I'm not a good runner. I hardly ever exercise or anything. Exercise is for the Charlies of the world, not the Soups. That's how I've felt ever since I was a little kid.

I'm skinny, but that doesn't mean I'm in good shape, which is pretty apparent by the way my chest is heaving.

Sloane is hardly even panting.

"Don't stop," she calls over her shoulder. She's way ahead of me now, her shoes in her hand, and so I start trying to run again, even though the pain in my side is killing me.

Well, not really *killing* me.

And the whole time we are doing this, Piper's body is lying in that box, dead. And my breath is coming hard and fast and I'm exhaling the last of her from my lungs outside into the shimmering heat of the day. And even while everyone is listening to a Beatles song and hugging one another and Piper's face is watching the crowd that is now missing me and Sloane, she's still dead.

She's trapped there in a loop on the screen, indifferent to everything happening in the present, in the now, in this tiny moment balanced on the line between the past and the future that she doesn't have.

I start running hard again, I pass Sloane, I'm flying now, my feet hardly even touching the sidewalk, barely making any contact with the ground.

SLOANE

I DON'T ASK HIM WHERE WE ARE GOING.
It's enough that we're going away from *Piper is dead*.

No, I hear her say.

Then, *Stop*.

"Piper?" I whisper.

I'm on the front steps of Soup's house. There are a bunch of flyers and some mail sticking out of the mailbox. YOU MIGHT HAVE ALREADY WON $1,000,000!, the writing on a yellow envelope reads.

Soup goes into his house through the open kitchen window. I don't watch because he falls the first time he tries to hoist himself up. I don't want him to feel as awkward as he looks, finally going in face-first, his legs wiggling for a second like something funny. I laugh. I forget that nothing is funny.

Not now.

Maybe not ever again.

I don't deserve funny.

I swallow it down.

Soup comes out with keys in his hand. His car looks like it might disintegrate on contact. There is rust on the doors and around the wheels. One door is a flat pink color, even though the rest of the car is painted matte green, like camouflage.

Inside, the seats are vinyl. It smells like cigarettes and plastic and fast food and peppermint gum. I take a piece from the packet that's sitting in the drink holder. It's spicy and soft from the heat. It's so hot in here. It's hard to breathe. I crank the window down with a handle that turns.

"It's okay," he says, even though nothing is okay. I don't know what he is talking about specifically, but I nod.

Piper is dead.

Stop, she says. *Stop saying it.*

It takes a few tries for the car to start, the engine trying to catch. It coughs like Grandma used to, thick and spluttering.

I put my bare feet up on the dashboard and then take them down. The black plastic is hot, but also, I can picture Piper sitting here, doing that.

This is Piper's seat.

You have no idea what's important, she says.

I sit up straighter, put on my seat belt. I scratch my ear, like I can get the sound of her voice to leave, which I know I can't. A bus goes by. Through the windows, I can see people looking at their phones, wearing headphones. *PIPER IS DEAD!* I want to scream at them. But they don't know her. They are having an ordinary day in their ordinary lives. They aren't in their dead best friend's boyfriend's car, having run away from her funeral before the end.

They aren't terrible.

The engine finally catches and Soup exhales and that's when I realize he'd been holding his breath. Sweat is trickling down his forehead and he wipes it on the sleeve of his suit, then contorts to get the suit jacket off. His shirt is soaked through with sweat. That should be gross, but it isn't. I take a lungful of the smell of him in, pretend that I'm yawning.

The silence is huge. It fills up the car. It spills out the windows and onto the street.

"Does your radio work?" I go.

He shakes his head. Then, "Sorry."

"Doesn't matter," I say.

But it does matter, because it's too quiet. I wait a beat too long to say anything else and then it feels like what I say next should be something important, but I can't think of what that could be, so I don't say anything. I'm really tired. This is the most I've been out of bed in a week since she died. I lean my head back on the seat. It's a bench seat, like in the front of a truck, so I can't recline my seat.

I stare at him. His jaw is grinding. He looks younger in his dress shirt, like a kid who is dressing up. It's too big around the neck. His ear stretchers look like they don't belong on the ears of someone who is wearing a blue dress shirt that is soaked through with sweat.

He keeps his eyes fixed on the road.

I want to ask him where we are going, but I don't really care.

I put my feet up on the dash.

Piper isn't here now. Just me.

And Soup.

My toenails are dark blue and chipped.

Piper painted them.

I painted hers.

She died with dark blue toenails.

My feet are on the dash.

My toes are the same as her toes.

I close my eyes.

It's the only thing that I can do. It's all I can think of to do. I'm so tired of the heat and the blue sky and the crows, which seem to be in all the trees that we pass, lining the telephone wires, screaming into the sun.

* * *

When I open my eyes, Soup is holding my hand. I freeze. I stare at our hands, locked together on the bench. We're on a highway. I don't know where we are.

We're holding hands.

I want to smoke.

I want to take a long drink of a cold blue Slurpee that is cough-medicine thick with vodka.

I want to scratch my face, which is suddenly so itchy.

"What?" he says.

"Nothing," I say. My hand feels weird, like a piece of meat that is only slightly something to do with me, lying on the hot vinyl of the seat. I feel like I'm holding it too still, like it's dead, or at least in a coma.

"I can't hold hands with you!" I burst out, and I snatch it back.

"What?" he says again.

"Come on, Soup," I say. "Come *on*."

"I hate having vague conversations," he says quietly. "I hate not knowing what you're thinking. I hate not knowing how to talk to you."

"It's my fault that she's dead," I say flatly. "So we don't get to do this; I don't ever get to be happy again. I have to pay, don't you get it? I have to pay." Until I say it out loud, I don't

275

realize how true it is. Soup swerves to miss the body of an animal in the road, a flattened rat or a squirrel, a flash of fur and blood.

"I don't know what that means! We can't talk? We can't hold hands? We can't know each other? It's vague! That's so annoying, Sloane."

"Yeah, well, sorry to be so *annoying*." I curl my legs up under me, hiding my toenails from view.

"Give me a break," he says. "You know what I mean. This is crazy enough without—"

"Without what? Without me being *annoying*?"

He sighs. "Sorry I said that. Look, what do you want me to say?"

"Nothing," I lie. "I want you to say nothing."

"Fine. Whatever." He wipes his face again on his sleeve.

"Air-conditioning is a thing," I say. "Or are you crying?"

"Yeah, well, I can't exactly afford it," he says, ignoring the question. "This is my car, not my mom's. I'm saving for stuff. A stereo. Air conditioner. All that."

I shrug. "Well, I'm hot. I'm sorry."

"I know this is weird," he says. "Right?"

"It's not only that it's weird! It's that she's dead! She's dead! If we hadn't—"

"You can't do that," he interrupts. "You can't think like that."

"It's impossible not to! We were drunk. It was the last thing she saw. She died mad. It's a big deal!"

"We'd broken up," he says, so quietly I can't really hear him.

"What?" I say.

"Right before that, when we were upstairs. We broke up."

"It doesn't make any difference," I decide. "We still did it."

"We didn't do anything wrong."

"Are you insane? We totally did! She's my best friend."

"But there isn't a rule that says that people can't, like, fall in LOVE."

Soup's shouting and then he stops, and the silence in the car is unbearable. I can't believe he said it, that he put that word out there, in here, with us.

I don't answer.

I can't.

Not for a few minutes, anyway. Then I do. "This isn't love, you idiot," I say. "It was alcohol."

I don't believe myself; how can he?

It's love, I want to say to him. *It is.*

This is it.

You are the One.

But I'm mute. I'm silent.

His face caves in, exactly like hers did when she saw us.

His face *crumples*.

It's me.

I'm a crumpler of faces.

I sit up straighter. "I really need a drink or a cigarette or something. Can we stop somewhere? Anywhere?"

"Yeah," he says. "Sure."

Both of Soup's hands are on the wheel now. None of him is touching any of me. My body wants to lean into his, but it can't. This can't happen now. I have to tell him. I have to say it. I have to say it out loud. *I know James Robert Wilson. I did something. This is about me.*

It's the hardest thing I've ever had to say. Because once I say it, I'll have to tell the police. I'll have to tell everyone. One day, I'll be on the stand and I'll have to say it. And the media will make me out to be a slut.

I totally don't care about that.

But if I'm a slut, then so is she. And they'll end up trying *her* and not him.

Mom's a lawyer. She works these kinds of cases more often than anyone would believe. Not murder, but rape. Rape where the victim is tried for having had sex. Rape where the victim is shamed for wearing a tank top with no bra.

Like Piper was.

I had sex with the man who murdered my best friend. What does that make me?

I'm shaking all over. Soup either doesn't notice or doesn't say anything.

He pulls into the parking lot of a 7-Eleven. I go inside. The cold air smells like refrigeration and some kind of industrial cleaner. I buy cigarettes. Suddenly, I'm starving. I buy candy and chips. Gummies and nachos. I get the biggest Slurpee cup that I can find and I fill it with the familiar blue.

I take it back to the car.

"Picnic?" It's a peace offering.

Soup shrugs. "I'm not hungry."

"Where are we going, anyway?"

"Nowhere," he says, but I know he's lying. He had a place in mind. "Home."

"Liar," I say. "Take me wherever we were going."

"I don't feel like it now," he says.

"Screw you," I say.

"Sloane, I can't. I don't know how to do this. I don't even know how to talk to you! You're so—"

"So *what*?" I say.

"I don't know," he says. "Ferocious?"

"I am not," I protest.

He pulls out onto the highway going back the way we came. I'm not hungry anymore, but I start eating. The food tastes like plastic, like something unreal. I crunch and chew and swallow and smoke and the whole time, he doesn't look at me. He doesn't eat anything. He stares straight ahead and what we don't say to each other is the clouds that are filling up all the blue, blurring out the sharp edges of the sun, of everything, of us.

He drops me off at the bottom of my driveway.

"See you at school," he says.

"Yeah," I say, "see you."

He pulls out in a squeal of tires. The cloud of dust rising up behind his car gets in my eyes and I'm crying.

Maybe I'll be crying forever now.

Piper is still dead.

"Eff you, Soup Sanchez," I shout. "I don't need you."

The gravel hurts under my bare feet but I left my shoes in his car. I'm still holding my Slurpee cup. It has no vodka in it but needs vodka and I hope Mom and Dad aren't home yet so I can top it up.

I start walking. The gravel chips at my nail polish.

I have to tell him.

Don't make it matter more than it does, Piper says. *We're too young for love. Anyway, it's a construct, remember? Chemicals. Lies. Friction.*

"But I love *you*," I say.

Liar, she says.

I step off the gravel and walk on the lawn, which is soft under my feet and cool. The sprinklers have left it damp. When we were little, we'd run through those sprinklers in our clothes, soaking wet. We'd turn cartwheels in the rainbow mist. We'd sleep out there in sleeping bags and shiver under the stars and stay up all night, scared, but brave.

I'm not brave anymore.

I don't know when it stopped.

I don't know how to get it back.

SOUP

I MAKE A PORTRAIT OF SLOANE, USING TINY handwritten *Sloane*s, black ink on white paper, her eyes closed, each eyelash its own Sloane, as though if I write her name enough, I can purge her out of me.

It takes the whole weekend, and afterward my wrist is so seized up, I can't bend it.

Sloane and I drove right by the house where my dad lives. It's small and white, but the paint is peeling off in a lot of places. There's a sofa on the front lawn. It looks like a college-kids rental house. I guess playing in the Asteroids doesn't pay well.

I didn't slow down when we passed it. I'd already memorized it anyway, the blue curtains in the front window, the way the chimney looked a bit crooked, the hole in the chain-link fence big enough for a kid to crawl through if he wanted to, big enough for an animal to escape.

One weekend, Piper and I spent a whole day walking the length of the old train track that wound its way through a tunnel that started near the school. I hung out there, a lot, in the tunnel. It was my hideout. My secret place. But I didn't usually go through and out the other side; I stayed in one spot, which became like a room.

It was Piper's idea to go farther. That kind of thing was always her idea.

It was a cardboard-and-gasoline-smelling day that was lined with damp skies and gravel. The tunnel echoed with our voices. We were goofing around. Laughing.

"Hang on," I said when we were at the turn, the place where an open manhole let in light, shining a spot on the wall like an art gallery spotlight. From my pocket, I took a tin of red, a tin of black. Shook them up, the ball bearings clattering as they stirred the paint. I'll never get tired of that sound, the feel of that.

"What are you doing?" Piper whined. "Come on, let's go!"

"Wait," I said. "This is for you, you'll like it."

I sprayed for a few minutes, here and there. I'd practiced

first. It wasn't my first try. Finally, I stepped back. She wasn't watching. She was texting.

"I'm cold," she said, barely looking up.

"For you," I said, gesturing. I tried bowing. I was trying to be charming. I thought I was being the character all the girls would love in a book or a movie. A guy who would spray-paint a rose on the wall of a rat-infested tunnel and deserve to be kissed for it.

"Roses are such a gross symbol of the patriarchy," Piper said finally. "God, Soup, don't you know anything?" I didn't know what to say. I passed her the tin of black and she sprayed over the whole thing, blanking it out. Only then did she laugh and kiss me.

I tried to pretend it didn't hurt my feelings. The way I figure it, at least half of any relationship is faking your way through it. Laughing when you're actually pissed. Not showing that you're mad or sad, even though inside, you're seething. Inside, you know that it's all wrong.

If you go far enough through the Tube, you get to a trestle bridge that crosses over the river gorge that is terrifyingly high. You have to climb over barricades to get onto it and then you wonder why you want to be there at all, the vertigo pushing you back. On the barricades, there are signs that read, DAN-GER, STAY BACK, UNSTABLE BRIDGE.

Even thinking about it makes me spin a little, my knees going noodle-weak.

It was sunny when we emerged from the Tube, a weak, watery kind of sunny. We crossed the barrier to the trestle. Because of the recent rain, the bridge was silvery with moisture. It smelled slick and metallic.

Piper was up over the barrier in two seconds flat. She moved with a gymnast's swiftness. She took a few steps, twirled and bowed, ran farther. Everything she did was a performance. I never knew whether to clap or roll my eyes or what she wanted from me. (Not roses painted on a wall, I got that much.) I wanted to grab her and press her against something, stop her from spinning and moving around. She was going to fall. I knew it. I could exactly picture her body, broken and splayed out, on the ground down below.

"Hey," I yelled at her. "If you fall, there's no way I can catch you."

"Didn't ask you to," she said back, flipping me off.

"Then I won't," I said. I sat down on the barrier, the cold, wet concrete clammy through my jeans.

When she got to the middle, at the scariest point, she turned back to me. Waved. Then one after the other, she turned four cartwheels, her hands on the shiny half-rotten ties, legs flipping through the blueing sky. The sun heated the track, and steam was rising. I couldn't stand to see her, but I couldn't look away either. "Come on," she said. "You chicken!"

"I don't do that," I said. "I can't do cartwheels. It's not a guy thing."

She laughed. "You don't have to cartwheel. Come and walk with me. Unless you're scared."

"No thanks," I said.

She shrugged. "I figured," she said. "I miss Sloane. She'd do it." She pulled her phone out of her pocket, stopped moving while she typed on the screen, then held it up to take a selfie. "Sloane Sloaney. Slooooooooane."

I rolled my eyes. "Sorry for being me," I yelled, louder than I meant to.

"Oh, don't be petulant." Piper hit the word "petulant" hard, her tongue darting out between her lips. Taunting.

I pushed myself off the barrier and forced myself to not look down between the gaps in the rail ties. Ran out to where she was, the distance between me and safety equal in both directions, and both ways were too far. My heart pounded against my bony sternum like someone knocking urgently. *Knock-knock, what are you doing? Knock-knock.* At the last second, my right foot slipped and I tilted sideways, hovering for a second, deciding if I would fall or not. Choosing not, the muscles in my body screaming in protest as I righted myself from an impossible angle. I was panting. The sun behind her had pushed through now with a vengeance; it made her face hard to see. She butted her hip into me. "Hey," I said, trying to sound normal. "You trying to kill me?"

"As if," she said. "You're my favorite."

"Your favorite what?" I went.

"You know," she said. "My favorite boyfriend."

"Yeah, of your dozens of boyfriends," I said.

"You never know," Piper said. "I'm pretty popular." She stuck out her tongue. I laughed, but it wasn't that funny. With Piper, you never knew. I kissed her hard, tasting her tongue, her lip gloss, something stale.

"Ouch," she said, ducking away.

I crouched down, then lay flat, let my head hang over the side, vertigo making the whole world—trees, the creek, the tumbled rocks—cartwheel around me. I smoked a cigarette, pretended the smoke was everything I was scared of and watched it evaporate into the growing blue.

Then with a hard whoomp that actually bruised my ribs, Piper crashed down on me, the end of a round-off that didn't quite work. There I was: pinned between Piper and the sky. Then I was kissing her and kissing her and her shirt was off. She was into it, too. It was good. It was so good. Things with me and Piper, even when they were bad, they were still good.

After the first time—the only time, actually—she always

was into it until the last minute, then she'd stop me cold, abruptly, like I should have known not to cross the invisible, moving line.

Then we fought.

"Why do we always have to stop?" I said. "It's not like you're a virgin." The rail ties were hurting my back, my head resting on the metal track. I hated the height, hated the cold wetness, hated the sun in my eyes, but I wanted her bad. I didn't get why she'd only go so far. We'd already done it once.

"I can't believe you said that to me," she said. "I can't believe you're that much of a misogynist pig."

"I'm sorry!" I said. "It's just that—"

"I'm kidding!" She laughed. "You're so *serious*." She punched me in the arm so hard it hurt. I didn't want to do it anymore, but I did, because she wanted to, and that's how it was, the track grinding into my back, bruising my shoulders, and her face, frowning and intense, saying something I didn't understand.

"Sloane's turn," she said.

She put Sloane in my mind at that exact moment. In a way, it's like she choreographed it. I mean, I'd be lying if I didn't say that I thought about Sloane differently after that. I did.

I totally did.

And the meaner Piper got, the more I liked Sloane.

I think she wanted me to.

I think she chose it.

I think she knew all along that this was how it would go. Not the part where she's dead, not that. But the part where Sloane and I were together.

I think she wanted it.

She needed a reason to hate us both.

It was how she was going to break free.

SLOANE

I'M SOUND ASLEEP WHEN MY ALARM
goes off. I'm dreaming.

I'm driving with Soup. I know it's a dream because it isn't
hot and the radio is on and our hands are intertwined and we're
singing and I'm happy.

I'm not happy now.

I'm awake, my heart thudding in my chest.

School.

Hope comes from somewhere. I don't know where. It's invisible, like a puff of smoke disappearing into the gray sky, but
I feel it. A small lightness. A possibility.

I go downstairs.

* * *

Downstairs looks different than I remember.

Maybe I'm getting a migraine: the rooms look both bigger and smaller than they should; the corners are too close to me but the windows yawn away, bowing toward the sky. But my head isn't hurting. Nothing is hurting.

I stop and look at myself in the huge mirror in the downstairs hallway. Weight has fallen away; I look more like Piper than ever. Bonier than I've ever been. We were always both skinny but she was the skinniest. Her bones resting there so close to her skin.

I touch my hair, which is dark brown, almost black.

I'm not wearing any makeup. It makes me look younger.

It makes me look scared.

I'm not scared.

"Hey, you," I say to my reflection.

Hey, says Piper. *Brown? I like it.*

And for a second, a tiny flash, I think I see her there, right beside me. I swallow my scream and she's gone.

People think they understand what ghosts are until someone they love dies, and then their understanding changes. The ghost is not in a white nightdress, walking down a long corridor, wafting. Her ghost is part of me, looking out through my eyes.

Is she still mad?

Does she hate me?

"I don't know what else I can do, Pipes," I whisper. "I'm leaving him alone. I won't do it. I don't love him. Love is just a dumb rush of chemicals anyway, right?"

The carpet feels thick as mud under my bare feet. Walking the last bit to the kitchen feels hard, like walking in sand, which is always sliding out under my feet.

I wonder if he killed her on the island, on the spot he cleared to look for whales.

I wonder if he knew she wasn't me.

I wonder why she didn't twist free, run, swim for shore.

You don't know that I didn't try, she says. *I tried.*

Dad is sitting at the kitchen table. He's sipping his black coffee from a large white mug. His shirt is impeccably pressed. His tie hangs perfectly. Even his hair looks ready for TV. That's Dad: crisp and clean, like a stock-photo image of a suburban, professional father. In contrast, I feel like I'm encrusted in dirt, something that needs to be scraped away by a sharp, certain instrument.

"Sloane!" he says, trying not to look surprised and failing. "Hi, honey."

"Dad. Hi." I clear my throat because my voice sounds rusty and Piper-esque. Piper always rasped. "I'm—" The rasp is stuck in my voice.

Is that what happened? Is she actually in me now?

Am I crazy?

"Are you getting a sore throat?" Dad asks, concerned.

I shake my head and go to the coffeemaker, three steps to the left, like this is normal and easy, like this isn't the first time I've been downstairs since the funeral last week, since the drive, since Soup. My body feels like one of those creepy marionette dolls that Piper had hanging from her bedroom ceiling when she was little, all pointy elbows and uncooperative legs, tangled string, fake facial expression.

I pour half a cup of coffee into my favorite mug. I bought it last year on the class trip we took to Brazil. It's bright blue and has a faint cobweb cobbling the surface. There isn't anything South American about it, but the web looks so real that it's impossible to not try to wipe it off every time. I bought it at the airport—one for me, one for Piper—the only shop we actually saw on the trip. In the village where we helped build huts, there weren't any shops, only dust and mud and kids playing soccer and staring and a guy with a camera capturing pictures of all of your white-rich-person "goodness." A bunch of high school kids hammering nails. Probably they had to rebuild everything after we left. The whole thing never felt like something real that would ever matter.

I carry the mug to the fridge and top it up with milk, trying to look casual and like myself, Sloane, and not like marionette Piper, dancing on a string. I'm slouching, like she did. I stand up straighter. I'm aware the whole time that Dad is staring at me, flipping through possible things he can say and dismissing all of them. Finally he settles on "Come here, baby."

"Nope," I say. I'm holding the coffee in my hands like I need it to warm me up, even though I don't feel either hot or cold. I feel unreal. "Well, it's a school day. I'm going to school."

"Pardon?" he mutters, distracted by something on his phone.

"Nothing." I sip my coffee and it tastes so good that I gulp it. "I'm going to be late for school."

"Come here." Dad stands and then he's coming toward me and gathering me into his arms, bundling me as though I'm tiny and he's huge and I start blubbering again and get snot on his shirt and I don't know why I've shrunk and he's grown.

"Dad," I say. "Thanks a lot. Now I'm going to be blotchy and red and everyone will know I've been crying."

He shrugs. "You have plenty of reasons to be sad; no one's going to judge you. And don't feel bad about my shirt! I have lots of shirts," he says. "Are you sure you want to go today?"

"I'm going to school," I say. "I'll be fine. I've got to go back sooner or later, right?"

"Well, right," he says. "But it can be later. You can take time."

"Time isn't going to make her not dead, Dad," I say, more angrily than I mean to. "God."

"I know! I know. I . . . obviously. But maybe you're not ready."

"I'm fine," I lie. "Still have to graduate, right?"

"True," he says. "I think that if you feel like it's time, then it's time. But you are allowed to change your mind. It's your call." He rubs the snot spot with a paper towel. "I'll go change this shirt, then I've got to fly." He stands up, stares out the window. "Wow, would you look at that."

Outside, the sun is rising in a band of orange, firelike and vivid, from the sea. We both stare.

"Beautiful sky," he says. "I should take a picture." But he doesn't move. He stares, as though he's frozen in place by the gloriousness of it all.

"Sun's coming up again," I say. "Big surprise, huh." I'm aiming at sarcastic but it comes out wrong. Staring at the sun has left a black hole in the center of my vision. I look around the room and the black hole moves with my eyes. "Fine. I mean, *I'll* be fine. Fly. Me not going to school isn't going to make her alive. I still have to graduate and study. I still have to . . . I mean, people say things like, 'She'd want you to!' but I don't think she'd care. She definitely wouldn't. But I care, I think. I mean, I do. Care." I pour another cup of coffee and drink it down. I'm so thirsty. I pour a third cup. My hand is shaking like something trapped in the wire mesh cover of a fan. I squeeze the cup so Dad doesn't see.

"It's good, sweetheart," he says. "Really. Truly. Take it slow. You can leave whenever you want."

I sit down at the table, my back to the rising sun.

The table is clean. I half expect the red sock will still be there. The note about the dentist.

"I'm okay," I whisper.

Liar, she says.

"Shut up," I mumble. "Leave me alone."

"What?" says Dad. He kisses the top of my head on his way to the stairs. "I like your new hair," he calls over his shoulder.

"Thanks." There were a bunch of different colors under the bathroom sink from last Halloween when Piper and I couldn't decide what, exactly, to be. We went as conjoined twins, our hair (which was long back then) braided together so it looked like we were joined at the head. My neck hurt for a week, but it was worth it. It was amazing.

Everything we did together was amazing.

But now there is no we. There is only me, alone with my

296

awkward shortish hair, which is now dark brown, almost black. I look so ugly. I pulse with self-loathing; then just as quickly, the feeling is gone, like it was an insect that lit on me and then took off again, within the same split second.

Dad comes back, this time in a blue shirt.

"Very corporate," I tell him. "You look like a Best Buy salesman."

"Brings out the blue in my eyes," he grins.

"Your eyes are brown!"

"Nothing gets by you." His eyes twinkle. "Glad you're still paying attention." He grabs his travel coffee mug and fills it up and then he's going.

Then he's gone.

"Bye, Dad," I call, a beat too late, the door already closing behind him, his feet crunching on the gravel path to the garage, the sun now hidden behind the fine veil of gray in the sky.

Dad has left the newspaper on the table, being one of the last holdouts to continue to receive an actual newspaper in the morning, the thwack of it against the door waking the crows every morning so that they caw and wake everyone else up. I take another inadvisable sip of my coffee, the hot liquid in my empty stomach sloshing acidly around. My teeth feel thick and knitted, each one sporting a tooth-warmer of plaque and goo. The coffee rushes up my throat and threatens.

Don't touch the paper, I warn myself. *Do not open up that paper and look at anything. Do not read that newspaper. Stop.*

When Piper first died, the story was full pages in the paper every day, but it's mostly dropped out of the paper now. What else is there left to say? She died. James Robert Wilson is in prison, awaiting a bail hearing. There is no more news. That's all there is.

She's dead.

He killed her.

I'm jittery and itching to smoke a cigarette at the same time as feeling repulsed by the idea of smoking a cigarette. I wonder if I'll ever feel right again, like I fit inside myself properly.

I know that I have to get back to school and make it happen. I grab a brown bag and put a couple of apples in it and a piece of cheese for lunch. A container of yogurt. Some grapes.

From a million miles away, I hear the sound of the shower turning off.

"Mom," I say. I put the bag back down on the counter. My hand is already reaching for the paper and unfolding it and I take yet another sip of coffee like this is just another day and I'm flipping through the paper for the horoscope section, Mom's favorite.

I stare at a recipe for enchiladas and an article about how the algae bloom in the ocean has been found to be the cause for the dead whales, the ocean turning on itself. Seven whales on one single beach up north. They have to burn the carcasses.

Piper was cremated. I don't know where her mom is spreading her ashes.

My mouth turns to ashes.

I need to spit, but I can't.

I gulp coffee. More coffee. My mouth is too dry.

I can't.

I just can't.

But I have to do it.

"Mom," I'll say. "See you after school!"

She'll probably cry and say I'm not ready.

I'll never be ready.

But I have to do it.

"Honey?" Mom calls from upstairs.

"NOTHING," I shout. "I'VE GOT TO GO IN A MINUTE, I'LL BE LATE FOR SCHOOL."

My coffee cup falls on the floor without me even touching it. It's like it jumped off the table by itself.

Piper.

The cup breaks, the blue shattering into crumbs and dust, the webs becoming cracks.

"Sorry, Piper," I whisper. "Sorry," I say, louder this time. "But you have to leave me alone now. You've got to. Sorry." I suddenly can't remember any of the translations. I only have English left.

Sorry, sorry, sorry.

The cup stays on the floor, still broken.

"What happened?" asks Mom, coming into the room, looking fresh and clean in a way that I feel like I'll never be again.

"Nothing," I say. "Careful! Don't step on the broken . . ." I point at the pool of coffee and cup shards.

"Oh no," she says. "Not your favorite cup!" Her eyes instantly fill with tears. Since Grandma's funeral, she's been crying at the drop of a hat. I see her in the kitchen, in the garden, in the car, tears pouring down her cheeks.

"Mom," I say. "Can you . . . It's just a cup. Don't get so worked up. God." The room vibrates with a weird energy, like something is about to happen. She sighs and pours some coffee into her own cup, stepping around the mess.

I exhale and I say, "It looks like you'll be running into a new friend at work today and your lucky numbers are eighteen and two thousand."

"What are you talking about?" She takes a second to catch up. Then, "Well, I'll keep that in mind, I guess. Eighteen and two thousand, huh."

"Yep," I say. "You've got to listen to the stars, Mom. They know."

"They're never wrong." She laughs a little bit, nervously, as though she's worried that I'll break, the worry itself breaking me, almost.

"Proven fact. Gotta go, Mom."

"It's okay if you have to—"

"I KNOW, it's fine," I say. I grab my lunch bag. "Later!"

I make myself do it. I make my legs walk. I make myself keep moving until I get there.

I hold my spine as straight as I can. Shoulders square.

I can do this.

"This is for you, Pipes," I say, and I go through the door.

Which is a lie.

It's for me, of course. It's all for me.

SOUP

EVERYTHING ABOUT THE DAY FEELS
surreal. It's like how I imagine it feels to get glasses when you
hadn't known you'd needed them: things are more sharply in
focus, smaller, crisper. I notice things I've never noticed before, like a crack in the stone wall that separates the school
lawns from the road, the way the iron gate is being held up by
a piece of two-by-four that has vines growing over it as if it
broke ten years ago and no one bothered to fix it, a hole in the
window on the lower part of the boathouse.

I take my phone out of my pocket and check for texts from
Sloane.

Nothing.

I start dialing her number but then I click the phone off before it rings. What will I say?

The sky is tight, holding on to rain that will spill out as soon as it lets its guard down. Soon it will start pouring itself over everything, splattering marks over the pale paved drive.

I push open the doors to the school. I don't know what I'm expecting, but what I get is open, blatant stares. Each one, if I could paint it, would be an orange haze of judgment. Fiery. Hot. I almost step back out again.

Almost.

I make myself go inside. My sneakers squeak on the waxed floors. It smells like everything I remember: wood and dust and cologne and sweat and stale coffee breath and something plasticky.

Charlie.

I make my face go still. I can't look like I expect anything from him. Not now. That would cost me my pride.

He gives me exactly nothing.

I feel like the new kid in a new town except I'm not new and this place isn't new to me.

Screw pride.

I catch Charlie's eye, finally. I raise my hand in a salute. He comes over.

"Yo, Soup," Charlie says after a pause. He doesn't quite look at me, his gaze skating off my face, slipping into the distance.

"Decided to come back, huh," he says, breaking the silence that is hovering like insects around us, practically buzzing. I nod. A couple of other guys make their way over. Charlie punches me in the arm. Hard.

"Yeah," I say. "I'm back. I missed you jerks."

There's a terrible awkward silence.

They don't have to worry. I step off.

I go, "Yeah, I should go figure out where I'm supposed to . . ." I let my voice trail away. They look relieved and I hate them so much, I can feel it in my teeth, which are grinding.

A girl who I don't even know blinks when she registers my face, steps backward, and starts crying. Maybe she was a friend of Piper's, but I doubt it. I don't recognize her and Piper didn't really have friends. Piper hated most of these people. Don't they get it? She *scorned* them.

The bell goes and my heart lurches. I feel like I won't know how to find my locker or remember my combination or where I'm supposed to be. I try to shut off my brain and simply let it happen, see if my body remembers which way to go. I try to keep my breathing steady. I had no idea it was going to be like this.

I don't know what I thought.

I should have known.

But then I look up and there she is.

She's late. She's hurrying.

She looks like I feel: Overwhelmed. Awkward.

Without Piper next to her, she looks nothing like Piper.

She's so utterly and completely *Sloane*. Alone.

The halls are empty now. She has no choice but to come toward me. Then we are simply standing there, actors waiting for our lines. *Are you scared?* I want to ask. *They don't know how to treat us, that's the thing. We're different now. They don't know how to react.* There's so much that I want to say that's waiting to be said, but I don't say it. I stare at her, mute.

"Hey," she says, no eye contact. Why can't anyone look at me? "Philip." My name sounds ironic in her mouth. I look at her lips.

"Mom's the only one who calls me that," I say. I nudge her just to make contact, to feel something.

She steps back slightly, takes her phone out of her pocket, starts looking at it. I don't have to form an expression on my face, which is good because I have no idea what to do with myself. I swallow. My mouth is dry, papery, collapsing. *You know,*

I want to say, *I miss her, too. It doesn't change how I feel about you. You and me.*

But I don't say anything because I'm a coward and I've forgotten how to make my mouth form words and maybe I've had a stroke or this is a hallucination, I don't know.

I breathe her in deep and she smells clean, like toothpaste and coconut and something darker and saltier. My body tilts toward hers, even now. I can't step back.

I have to step back.

I step back before I accidentally lean in too far.

This is *crazy*.

I can't stop staring at her. I can't talk. I want to grab her and hold her. She looks fragile, like she might fall. She's so thin now, she's practically two-dimensional. It's not sexy, but it also is, or maybe it's that *she* is, no matter what. Her hair is so dark, expensive brown, like polished wood. Her face is hollow and bare, washed clean of makeup. You can see her freckles as clear and certain as her new hair and her unblinking eyes. Piper didn't have freckles.

"You look different," I offer.

"Different from her, you mean," she snaps. "Yeah, that's kind of the point."

"I like your hair like that."

She's wearing a men's shirt, open and untucked over a T-shirt, jeans so tight and new and dark that I'd bet when she takes them off, her legs will be as dark blue as blueberries, a permanent tattoo from the indigo dye.

"This is weird," she says finally. "Awkward. It sucks."

"Yeah," I agree. "It's impossible." I spread my hands wide, to show the size of it, the impossibility of everything.

She's scrolling through something on her phone, like there's an answer there.

"I want to leave," she says; it comes out a whisper. "I want to get out of here. Just go, you know?"

"Yeah," I say. "We could get into the car and drive forever or for however long it takes to get somewhere that isn't here."

She looks at me properly for the first time, seeing me. "You know what? I'm late for something. Math, I think."

"Me, too," I say. "Same. We're in all the same classes, remember?"

There are a million things between us, everything is between us, the air alive like it's glittering with all that we aren't saying; I mean, it's practically *shimmering*, can't she see it? But her gaze keeps falling away, onto the floor, away, away, and she says, "Screw this. We get through it. And then it stops feeling like this. Eventually, right? Eventually she'll let us go." She grabs my bare arm, tight, her fingers digging into my arm, nails into my skin. "She'd say that no one saw it, so it didn't happen. So it didn't happen, okay?"

"I don't get it." I try to catch up. Can't. Feel stupid. "What do you mean?" A girl half walks, half runs by, her boots making clopping sounds on the floor like horses' hooves. We both watch her and then Sloane starts walking away, slow at first, then faster and faster, till she's gone, not waiting for me.

I don't want to go to class. I want to leave. I need water. I need something. I make my legs move, make them carry me to the bathroom. I can make it that far, at least.

Someone is coming out as I push the door to go in.

"Hey," I say to Fatty. He blinks at me slowly, like he's suddenly stupider than he is.

How was I ever friends with him? Why? He smells like Axe deodorant body spray. Everything about him is terrible.

I close my eyes and I can see him on the beach clearly, holding Sloane's camera as Charlie pinned Sloane against the log, egging him on. I see him at the party, his face beyond Sloane's shoulder when we were kissing, his tongue making lewd gestures. He's suddenly and unreasonably everything I hate for reasons I don't even know, and I can't take it. I can't stop myself. I shove him, too hard, against the door.

"What the— Dude, what is your problem?"

"You're my problem," I say. My jaw is clenching so tight, it hurts.

"Well, I'm not the one who was groping my girlfriend's bestie while she was getting all hacked up on the beach."

And there it is; it's out there. He's put it out there. He's given me my opening. It's like my hand has ears and a brain of its own because before I can even really understand what he's said, my fist has flown into his nose, his skin exploding under my hand like an egg in a microwave, the hot splatter of it burning my skin, and then I'm on him and someone is howling and I don't know if it's me or him or both of us but my other fist is in the action now and his body is as soft as a pillow, my hands disappearing into him like a faith healer's who is about to pull out the guy's appendix without a scalpel and he is everything that is wrong with the world and I will pull out his beating heart, I swear to God. I'm clawing at him until someone pulls me off, until someone pins my arms, until someone stops me.

Afterward, he's sitting there with an ice pack on his face, making moaning noises. We're on the orange vinyl seats in Mr. Stewart's office and Fatty's writhing around, his pants making farting sounds against the chair. Honestly, I want to pop him again. "Settle down," I mutter to him, and he moans louder. What an idiot.

Then I'm explaining and explaining and explaining and then Mom arrives, and Fatty's mom and dad. Mom's crying and I'm explaining (or trying to explain) and Fatty's parents are staring me down like I'm an animal that needs to be caged up and Mr. Stewart is saying, "We don't want to involve police, we'd prefer to handle these matters internally" like "*these matters*" have ever come up before, like he doesn't simply mean that he's done with the gawking press and needs the school to revert to what it has always been: a fantasy school for rich, entitled kids; a parent's dream tuition payment; not a murdered girl and the two messed-up kids she left behind.

Mr. Stewart keeps clearing his throat, scratching his head, his shoulders covered with the dandruff that his scalp issues in flurries. This is too much for him; you can practically see his eczema flaring under his big white beard. He's a tall guy, over six feet, but somehow he always looks smaller. Inconsequential.

Fatty keeps moaning and his mom keeps rubbing his back and his dad keeps giving me a disgusted look. Scorning me in every way. Like he can't believe I have the nerve to be here, to keep existing. I want to pop him, too. There's a lot of discussion. Talk, talk, talk.

I look up. I look around. I want to crawl out of myself, be someone else, go somewhere else, anything, anything but this.

Then I see Sloane, watching me through the office window, making some kind of gesture with her fist against her chest, then a small smile maybe, I think. Fatty's chair farts again and I look down at my feet, my untied shoes, one of them splattered with what looks like paint but is really Fatty's blood.

When I look up again, Sloane's gone. I can't look at my mom. I can't see her face and what it's doing. Not right now. I keep my eyes down. Fatty's family leaves first. Fatty's hunched over like he's stepped on a mine and his guts have exploded, except he hasn't and they haven't and he's no soldier and he's definitely no hero.

Then it's our turn. Mom shakes Mr. Stewart's hand. He says, "We understand that it's been hard."

Mom says, "You have no idea, Mr. Stewart."

"I do," he says. "I think I do. It's been hard for all of us."

Mom and I walk slowly to her car, through the stares of the kids in the hall, past the trophy case full of things I've never won and never will, through the heavy doors. We trudge silently across the parking lot. Her car is hot on the inside like a greenhouse, the air too heavy to breathe. We roll the windows down, the too-warm air blowing in on us, drying the sweat.

We don't talk. Mom lets the radio play soft rock, which scratches the inside of my skull, and I want to put my fist through the radio but I won't. I'm so angry. I didn't know it was possible to be this angry. It's like everything's come together simultaneously into a hot poker of fury: Piper being dead, Charlie abandoning me, my dad never caring that I exist. A triple whammy of rage connecting the three disconnected things together has turned me into a ball of uncontrollable fury.

Then I'm at home, lying on my bed, the crack in my ceiling the same as it always has been, that crack that I've stared at after every terrible thing, and I wonder when I'm ever going to get out of here and when I'm ever going to never be staring at that crack again, tears leaking down my cheeks like nothing could stop them.

Out the window I can see the willow tree, hanging down over the mostly dead back lawn. The wind makes the branches rustle, lifts the pictures on the shrine, which have all faded in the sun to the point where they just look like white papers, curling at the edges, unsticking from the tape.

I take out some paints from a bag in my closet. I haven't painted since before she died.

I haven't wanted to paint.

I pick up one can, then the next. I decide. I hold the can in my hand, close my eyes, conjure up the painting from the vessels on the backs of my eyelids, from everything I know, from everything I've seen. I shake the cans and feel the ball bearings in there stirring the paint and I still love that sound and that feeling, I can't help it.

I put the paint down and I build a scaffold out of bookshelves, dumping the books onto the floor in big stacks, books I used to read one painful word at a time, like I was decoding what was so easy for everyone else, but I had to read them because they mattered, they had to, or it wouldn't be so hard.

Reading those books made me feel so stupid. Trying to read them, I mean.

I am stupid.

I'm not smart.

Other people decide your life, that's the truth. They decide who you are. They decide what you deserve. Strangers decide. Your friends decide. Your parents decide.

I'm not smart enough to not be in love with my dead girlfriend's best friend.

Just thinking that makes an electrical current surge through my spine, tingling there. *Sloane.*

The top of my desk comes off because it's an old door balanced on a couple of piles of stacked bricks. I move the bookshelves into position and place the door across the top. When it seems stable enough, I climb up awkwardly, wiggling onto the door on my belly. Then I lie on that door and I paint the crack right out of my ceiling. I cover it with everything I can think of, every place where Piper's consciousness might have gone: places we went together—the mall, the tunnel, the island—then places she'd want to go but never did, like Europe, New York City, everywhere. I add wildcats with eyes like jewels peering behind buildings that I can only imagine and a volcano spewing fire and a single glittering diamond and a row of skyscrapers against a night sky, the paint falling down on my face like drops of rain so that at the end of the day (the days) when I look in the mirror, my face is freckled with all the colors that I've used, black and blue and yellow and red, a million tiny bruises, hiding my face behind them.

I look and I look, but I can't see Piper in the picture. I can't find her anywhere.

Because she's gone.

But Sloane is there, peering out from around a tree, her face freckled with dots, her dark hair stark against the sky behind her, a crow perched on her shoulder with shining eyes like Piper's, cawing silently into the stillness of the air.

It's the middle of the night. I can't sleep. I go outside and I lie back on the hard, dead grass. It smells like hay and feels scratchy on my bare arms, the back of my head. Up in the sky, the night is putting on a full show. Tiny stars behind small stars behind bigger stars behind planets behind moons, wisps of clouds threading their way through and between. What must I look like from up there: like nothing. Less than a piece of dust. It would be like if every ant in the anthill stopped to mourn one ant, squashed under the boot of a passerby. All of them, frozen in time. I'm not even an ant.

Half those stars are probably already burned out. We think

they're so pretty, but when they die, the create vortexes. They pull whole galaxies in behind them, extinguishing everything.

A dog barks in the distance.

"Good night, Pipes," I whisper. "I'm sorry."

I was a planet in Piper's galaxy, and when she went, Sloane and I were sucked into the black hole that she left behind.

SLOANE

"YES?" MRS. BEADLE, THE SECRETARY, looks at me over the top of her half-glasses. "What is it, hon? You're late for class. You need a pass?" Mrs. Beadle has a jar full of toffees on her desk and a tiny terrier in a sweater who sits shivering in a basket behind her, even when it's not cold. He yips at me.

"Um," I say. "Well, I'm back. It's my first day back since . . . I thought maybe I should check in?"

She looks at me for a beat too long, then nods once. "You don't have to do anything, hon," she says. "Go ahead and get to class. You know your schedule, right?"

I stand up. "Right. Okay," I say. "Sorry."

I'm not sure what I'm sorry for, not exactly. I don't move,

even though she clears her throat, as though trying to nudge me out the door. I make myself do it. I turn and go.

Math.

I have to get to math. I look down at my feet. My sneakers are mismatched: one is purple, one is blue. I didn't do that on purpose.

Then I practically smack into him, standing there, at the mural. Not moving. A statue.

Soup.

I say something like, "Hey." And I add his name, and so he knows things have changed, I use his real name. "Philip."

He says something. I say something back. I don't know what it is. I can't get my eyes off his lips. If I hadn't kissed him, she'd be alive. Maybe.

We are saying things to each other, but I don't know what they are. My phone buzzes. I look at the screen. It's an unfamiliar number. I press ignore.

"Do you believe in ghosts?" I ask, but there's a girl clip-clopping by so loudly I think maybe he doesn't hear me and I feel too stupid to repeat it. Math is upstairs in the other wing. It must be half over. I should go. I can't stand this close to Soup. I don't want to make a mistake. Another mistake.

A text buzzes through. "Hello, Sloane," it says. I don't recognize the number, but I know who it is. My heart is doing crazy things, like it can't figure out how to get back into a proper rhythm. I nearly throw up. "I have to go," I tell Soup, or at least I think that I do. I say something about math. I feel like I'm talking in the wrong language. I don't understand myself. The phone buzzes again. "Hello, Sloane" over and over and over again. I start to walk away. I start to hurry. I turn it off while I walk. I make it stop.

I make him stop.

I have to tell but I can't. Who will I tell? Detective Marcus? Soup?

I'm going to puke. I'm going to be the kid throwing up on my desk but we're too old for that now. No one pukes on their desk in twelfth grade. *Piper Puker, puked a pack of pickled peppers*, my memory chants.

In the familiar classroom, I sneak into my regular seat, perched on the edge of it in case I suddenly have to run out. *Poised for flight*, I think in my narrator voice, *Sloane hides her true fear behind a tough new exterior. Like the chameleon, she can change her colors. She* has *changed her colors. She is untouchable now. She is fierce and strong.*

I smile a tiny bit. Fierce.

Alive.

I try not to notice everyone staring. The desks here are so old they still have inkwells in them, holes that people drop chewed gum and mint wrappers into. I trace my finger over someone's old initials. The janitors must hate us.

I touch something. (The carved desk.)

I see something. (The back of the head of the kid in front of me, a sprinkle of dandruff on his black T-shirt shoulders.)

I smell something. (Toothpaste, deodorant, dust, and chemicals.)

I feel something. (Scared.)

I press my fingernails into my palm.

The minutes stutter and speed up and slow down and people keep swiveling to look at me.

Ice runs through my veins. I blink hard.

What if they let him out?

What if he's going to kill me, too?

"I don't feel well," I say out loud precisely as the bell jangles. I jump half out of my seat, dropping things: my phone, my pen, my backpack.

Miss Draper calls me up. "I put together a package of what you missed," she says. "Are you feeling okay? You look pale. You may need a tutor to catch up."

I smile and nod, even though puke is rising in my throat.

"Okay," I say. "Sure, okay. A tutor. I'm sorry, I have to go. I have to go home now." I grab the papers out of her hand and practically run out the door. I make myself slow down in the hallway; I try to look normal.

On my way out of the building, I pass the principal's office and there is Soup, head hanging, his mom next to him, and Fatty, his face looking like a steak, his parents looking self-righteous and indignant.

Go to hell, Fatty, I think.

I throw Soup a sign to try to show him that I see him. I get it.

Soup won't look at me. Mr. Stewart is scratching his beard. Fatty's dad looks pissed off.

Math is the answer, I think.

I must catch up on math, I think.

The derivative of us *is* Piper, I think.

I push through the doors and start walking home. The sky is streaked loosely with white clouds. The leaves on the tree are edging toward yellow and orange from green. For a second, I'm surprised.

The season is changing.

Without Piper.

Well, duh.

I take my phone out of my bag and call my mom.

"Sloane?" she says. "Are you all right? Why are you calling me in the middle of the day?"

"I . . . ," I start. "I think I'm getting a migraine, so I'm going home. I wanted to tell you, to let you know, not to make you worry."

She sighs. "Too soon, huh?"

"Mom, it's just a headache. No big deal." But saying it has brought a headache on and maybe it is a big deal. My brain clenches and tightens and then begins to slowly ache and flicker.

A car slows next to me. I glance at it, but I don't recognize the driver. He grins at me. A man. A boy. He whistles. I pick up my pace and he honks and squeals away.

"What was that?" Mom asks.

"Nothing," I say, breathing faster, speed-walking now. Everyone is a James, potentially.

Right?

Especially James.

But he's in jail.

He's not ever going to get out.

Or is he?

You have to tell, hisses Piper. *You have to tell them about James Robert Wilson.*

"It won't make any difference!" I say. "They know he did it! He's going to jail! It doesn't matter what I say!"

"You're cutting out, Sloane. Sloane? What are you saying? It didn't make sense. What won't make a difference? Honey? Oh, it's getting worse. Call me when you get home so I know you're safe. Elvis is there today. Elvis can call if you need him to." She shouts the last part, like that will help me to hear her.

"Mom, you sound fine to me. I can hear *you*. Don't shout! And I don't need the housekeeper to dial a phone for me."

But she's hung up already.

I switch my phone off and try to remember how to keep walking, but my stupid shoes are hitting the ground too hard, jarring me all the way up to my pounding heart, and the lights of the descending headache are flickering across my vision like jumped film and Piper isn't here to help me and I have to get home. My phone buzzes but I don't reach for it. I can't. I won't. Not now. Not ever.

SOUP

I WENT ON MY DAD'S FACEBOOK PAGE
again last night. I scrolled through his new pictures. He's posted
photos of his drum kit and the playlist. He posts photos of the
crowds: musician's-eye view. There's nothing about his photos
that tells me who he is or why he didn't know about me.

Or that he did know and didn't care.

I need an answer so badly, I feel like something inside me
is pulled taut, vibrating.

There are no answers on his wall.

I keep looking. Reading post after post after post. I don't
know what I'm expecting him to type that will change anything.

I don't know who I'm expecting him to be.

*　*　*

I water the lawn. It's amazing how quickly it's coming back to life, greening up. It's been raining, too. The rain has changed everything. The air. The season.

The wind blows the spray back over me, freckling me with a cool mist.

I go back inside. I can hear Mom getting ready for work, the sound of her hair dryer going off. "Going to school, Ma!" I yell.

"Don't hit anyone!" she calls back.

"Ha ha, funny," I say.

"Seriously," she says, stepping out into the hall to give me a quick hug. "Don't look for trouble."

"Like I have to look for it," I go. "It finds me, Mom. I can't help it." I try to make it into a joke by making a gun with my finger, but I don't even know what I mean by that. I put my hands back down by my sides.

"I know, I know," she says. "Hurry up, though, you'll be late."

"Going." I grab my backpack and my board.

"I love you," she yells.

I lift my hand in response. My car mocks me from the driveway. I don't know what's wrong with it. It won't start. Won't even turn over.

Just one more thing in my life that's dead.

After school, maybe, I'll take it apart again.

I roll slowly down the sidewalk, my old skateboard bumping over the ruts and cracks, the sidewalk skittering under my wheels. I feel the vibration in my teeth.

It's not exactly cold but it's rainy and gusty. The rain falls harder, in little bursts.

I stash my board under the front stairs of the building. I have that feeling that I sometimes get when I stop rolling, the feeling that I'm still moving, that I haven't stopped. I wait a few minutes for it to pass. I sit on the steps.

I try to remember what used to happen when I got to school.

I try to remember who I used to talk to (Charlie). What I'd say (nothing special).

Then I force myself to go through those ugly school doors, past the terrible teddy bears and flowers that don't ever seem to quit appearing, then inside. Somebody taps me on the shoulder from behind. I'm so tense, my shoulders are up near my ears.

I will not punch anyone in the face, I will not punch anyone in the face, I will not punch anyone in the face, I will not punch anyone in the face.

I turn around.

Fatty.

I clench.

He looks nervous.

"I'm sorry," he says, and that's it.

"I'm sorry, too," I say, surprised to mean it.

"Dude," he says. "That's enough. Don't get emotional."

I almost, but not quite, start crying. I swallow quickly, three times in a row—Piper's old cure for hiccups, but it also works for sobbing, I've figured out.

"Are you done with punching me?" he says. "You broke three of my freaking teeth, you know."

"I think I'm done. Yeah, pretty much."

"Good," he says. "It's been a messed-up time."

"Yep."

He grins. Then he tips back his head and howls, "Ah aha ha whoooooooooo!"

Everyone is staring.

"You are seriously weird," I say.

"Yep."

I turn my almost crying into an almost laugh. "Looks like your face healed up," I manage. "Ugly as ever."

He belly laughs. "Don't push it."

The bell sounds and we start heading for our lockers, just like before, like everything has settled back into normalcy, like Piper's death was just a flurry, a storm that's passed.

Is it that easy? I think. *Does it just go back to how it was?*

Maybe I've just overthought it. Maybe none of this has to be so hard.

I sit through math, staring sideways at Sloane, trying not to lean forward and just breathe her in. Her hair is different again. Reddish brown now, a fading color that's somehow perfect. It makes me think of some kind of bird, a starling maybe. She's done it differently. It looks looser. Softer.

Feathery.

I force myself to look away. I've missed too much to have a clue what's going on. I look out the window. The wind is pushing clouds so quickly past the glass that it makes me feel like time has sped up but the class drags on and on and on and it's just an illusion.

Sloane turns to look out the window and scratches the back of her neck, parting her hair there so I can see the skin. I want to reach out and press my fingers to that spot so bad. I put my head in my hands and force myself to look at my paper. I haven't written anything.

What does it matter? Everything has already been written, right?

Everything has already been done.

*　*　*

The color of Sloane's hair looks like sun shimmering on fall leaves and I'm really far gone because I'm thinking crap like *Sloane's hair looks like sun shimmering on fall leaves.*

I take out my phone. I text her, "R U OK? Answer me or I'll make a scene."

I see her feeling her phone vibrate. She takes it out, looks at it. Frowns.

She types back, "FINE." All caps, like that.

"GOOD," I type back.

Her shoulders shake a little. I hope she's laughing.

"Later, OK?"

"OK," I type. Then before I can stop myself, I add a row of smileys. "Later, gator hater."

I want to take that last part back. That was a mistake.

But she plays along. "While, vile dile," she types. Then a smiley for good measure.

I feel something inside me relax. I feel something inside me click into place.

A loud bang makes me look up.

"A bird!" someone yells.

"Crow," says someone else. Someone makes a loud cawing noise. Sloane gets up and runs to the window, where there is a smear of red. The crow's blood. I don't have to look; I know it's dead.

"Gross," someone says.

Sloane puts her hand against the glass. She stands there for ages, looking down, motionless as a statue. Then, finally, the teacher says, "Calm down, everyone. Please go back to your seat, Sloane. Now let's go through the problem on the board. Any volunteers?"

I write the problem down and start working it out. It's only when I look up at the end of class that I realize Sloane's page is still blank.

SLOANE

AFTER CLASS, I GO DOWN AND PICK UP the dead bird.

I've never held a dead bird before. They don't weigh anything. It's like holding a piece of cloud in your hand. You can see that it's there, but you can't feel it. I would have thought a crow would be heavier.

Up close, their details are incredible: dark blue feathers, not black. A shining midnight blue.

I empty my backpack of everything and put the crow in it. It's still bleeding. Even while I'm doing it, it feels wrong and creepy, but I can't stop. I carry it around all day and no one knows.

"Piper," I say to it when the last bell finally rings and I can be alone. "Pipes, are you gone? Was that you?"

She doesn't answer.

I think she's gone.

I don't know whether to be relieved or sad.

There's a buzz in my ears, white noise in the place where Piper used to be.

"Come back," I say quietly. "I'm not ready."

But she doesn't.

I take the crow home and bury it in the front garden, in among the fading roses. It's almost October. The flowers are losing their color and the sun is losing its heat and the sea is losing its blueness. I haven't seen a washed-up jellyfish for days. I think they're gone.

I think she's gone.

I'm losing Piper.

I've lost her.

I shiver. It's so cold. I go inside and upstairs and I run a hot bath. I watch as it fills, adding bubbles. I sit on the edge of the tub and think about Piper cutting my hair. I think about how it fell to the tiles, how we stood on it, how slippery it was, how for weeks, I kept finding long hairs stuck to all my socks.

I text Soup.

"Can we talk?"

I'm not going to tell him; I just want to know that I could if I wanted to.

I knew James, I'll start. *I* know *him*.

The air is thick with steam. I let it hide me. I sink into it. Deeper and deeper. The air is like water. A person could drown in all this water. A person could die this way.

My phone chimes.

"Yes. When?"

I type a response and then turn off the phone. I can't leave it on anymore, because I don't know if James will text again. Does he have a cell phone in prison? Is that allowed?

"Hello, Sloane," it will say in a drawl. I fight the scream that wants to erupt from my throat. Instead, I take the phone and I drop it into the bathwater. I watch it sink under the bubbles. I remember, too late, that all my pictures of Piper are in there; I haven't uploaded them to my computer. But it's too late. They're gone. Everything's gone. I can't even cry.

"It's over," I say. The mirror is steamed up. I can't even see myself. "But it's never over."

I soak in the bath until the water goes cold, the now-useless phone somewhere in there with me, occasionally bumping my leg like an errant bar of soap.

SOUP

"—SPECIAL TRIBUTE TO PIPER AT THE FALL Fair," Mr. Stewart is saying. "It will raise money for the children's hospital."

"Children's hospital?" Sloane asks. "What does that have to do with Piper?"

"The Asteroids have agreed to play," says Mr. Stewart. "They graduated from here, did you know that? Back in the eighties."

"I don't get it," I say. "So it's a fund-raiser for the children's hospital? And my dad's—I mean, some band is playing? How is that about Piper?"

"We, as a school," he intones as though he's speaking in

front of a crowd. He gestures with his hand. "*We* think it's important to acknowledge and remember Piper Sullivan."

I make a snorting sound in my throat.

"Philip?" Mr. Stewart says. "Did you have something to add?"

"I don't," I say. "I mean, no."

"We had to pick a charity. All this kind of thing brings in money. So we picked one that we thought Piper would support."

Sloane chokes out an inappropriate laugh and covers it up by pretending to cough.

"Excuse you," I say. Then, "Piper was never in the children's hospital. She wasn't sick. I don't even think she ever knew a kid who was sick."

"I was sick when I was a kid," says Sloane.

"Were you?"

"Migraines." She grins. "Not a tumor."

"That's not the point," Mr. Stewart interrupts. "I know you do art, Philip. We were hoping that you would paint something."

"It's Fall Fair in, like, two days," I point out. "That's not enough time."

"Of course it is!" he says, looking surprised. "We're not asking you to paint the Sistine Chapel! Just a portrait of Piper."

"Um, I don't know," I say. "I don't know if I—"

"There already is one," says Sloane abruptly. "Piper's mom must have it. From her birthday. Soup did one for her birthday."

"How wonderful!" Mr. Stewart claps his hands, as though he can't even contain his delight. "Thank you, Sloane. I guess you're off the hook, Philip."

"Terrific," I say.

"This is nuts," Sloane says. "This is totally ridiculous. This isn't anything to do with Piper. She was murdered! Maybe you should raise money for murder victims! Or maybe you shouldn't use her death to raise money! It's *disgusting*."

"Hey, hey," says Mr. Stewart. "Come on now. It's a memorial. People want to DO something when things like this happen. It's human nature."

"A concert by some people she didn't know to raise money for a cause she wasn't involved with doesn't have anything to do with remembering her."

"I'm sorry?" he says, like he hasn't heard her, when he clearly has.

"I think she means—" I start to try to explain. "It's a bit weird. Sir. I'm sorry. It really is, Mr. Stewart."

Sloane gets up and picks up her bag, slings it over her shoulder. She opens the door calmly and walks out.

My ears are ringing and I have that in-between feeling you

have when you first wake up and you're not sure if you're still dreaming. Is this for real?

My dad is playing a memorial to my girlfriend.

The portrait I painted for her birthday is now her death celebration.

Life has never made less sense to me than it does at this exact moment.

Mr. Stewart sighs. "Thank you, Soup," he says. "Or I should say, Philip." He shakes his head. "I'm sorry, this *has* been a really difficult time."

"Yeah," I say. "It sure has."

He leans forward. "Hard for all of us. Hard for everyone."

"Sure."

"Anyway, technicalities." He claps his hands together, this time with a briskness that suggests the meeting is ending. "It would be great if you and Sloane could say a few words about Piper, or maybe even sing with the band."

"I don't think she sings," I say. "I don't sing. Neither of us sings. We aren't singers."

"I see. This has been a *difficult* time."

I give him a weird look, which he doesn't pick up on. I wonder how many times he's said, "This has been a difficult time," throwing an emphasis on a different syllable each time. I want to buy a T-shirt, paint that on the front, and anonymously give it to him. I have a hugely inappropriate need to laugh. I haven't needed to laugh this bad since Old Yeller died when Mrs. Moffat was reading out loud to us in third grade, and *that* didn't make sense either. Everyone else was crying, like normal people do when a dog dies.

I grab my stuff. I'm texting Sloane before I'm even out of the office: "He wants you to sing."

I type a smiley emoji.

She doesn't answer.

Mr. Stewart is right. This *is* a difficult time.

I fill a whole screen with laughing emojis and hit send. I might not laugh out loud, but at least I can put it out there, I can give it to Sloane, I can show her how weird I truly am and see if she still wants to have anything to do with me.

Not that she wants anything to do with me now, but still.

SLOANE

SOUP CATCHES UP WITH ME IN THE foyer. He looks amused, like he's about to say something I don't want to hear.

"Later, okay?" I say.

He winks and nods. "You've said that before. This time, for real?"

I make a sound somewhere between a sigh and a groan. I remember the text. I was hoping that *he* didn't.

"I texted you," he says. "Just now. You're not answering anymore?"

"Oh, I dropped my phone. In the bathtub. I just haven't gotten around to replacing it yet."

"Did you put it in a bag of rice?"

"I don't think that really works. That's an urban legend."

"It might; doesn't hurt to try."

"I don't even know what happened to it. Elvis probably recycled it."

We stare at each other.

"Look, I have to get to class," I say, breaking the silence.

"Oh! Sure. I mean, are you really going? I thought you were leaving. I'm leaving."

"I'm going to class. I'm here, might as well. And I'm late," I remind him, but I don't move. "Have you ever even heard of that dumb band? Where did they dig them up from, 1996? Piper would be rolling her eyes so hard."

"Oh, yeah." He clears his throat. "They're good. I've heard of them." Soup looks shifty. "They're not super famous. They're okay."

"They're okay? They're a bunch of fat old middle-aged guys! This is the most messed-up memorial anyone has ever planned, if you ask me."

"You could come with me?" he says. "Let's go somewhere and talk."

"No," I say.

Panic clenches at my throat. I can't breathe.

I don't want to go with Soup.

I can't go with Soup.

If I go with Soup, then *Later, okay?* will be now and I'll

have to tell him, and I'm not ready to tell him and I don't know how to tell him. I feel like I'm not breathing. I take a huge deep breath and hold it, like Mom said, until I have to breathe.

He looks at me strangely. The air between us reminds me of when it first starts to freeze in the winter and the water forms a lace of ice.

The ice between us crackles. It shatters on the floor around our feet.

We both pretend not to notice.

"Well, see you '*later, okay*'?" He makes air quotes with his fingers for emphasis, but he's not laughing. "I'm out of here."

"Later," I echo.

"Yeah, so you said," he says, not turning back, not looking at me.

"Bye," I say, but I still don't move. I watch him walk away. He doesn't look back, not once. Then he calls over his shoulder, "The drummer is pretty good! You should download some of their songs."

"Not," I call, but I'm smiling. "Besides, my phone is in the garbage, remember?"

"Get a new one!" he calls, then he's gone.

I shouldn't be smiling, but I am.

The ice on the floor melts.

The ice on the floor steams.

The ice on the floor evaporates into something I've already forgotten.

I find Soup in the Tube after school.

This is it.

This is *Later, okay?*

Not having a phone means that I couldn't exactly ask him to meet me there, but there he is, like he knew, too. He's painting graffiti on the wall. I watch while he makes a huge arcing streak of orange flames.

"So," Soup says when he's done, sitting down beside me, wiping his face on his sleeve.

"So," I repeat.

There's too much *him* in this small space. I'm not sure if I'm breathing properly. I definitely shouldn't have come. I can't faint, that would be ridiculous, but I feel woozy. Light-headed. I have to tell him.

He clears his throat. "Hey."

"So." I force the word out again, long, drawn out. I can't look at him, so I don't. I think about how much actual dialogue consists of the words "hey" and "so." The whole conversation takes place in the tone. Not so much in movies, but in real life, sometimes those small words say everything.

Our tones match in a harmony.

We are both breathing.

We are both alive.

His arm is touching my arm and my arm is steel and his is a magnet and I don't have any choice; they can't untouch. Where they meet, there is a humming that I can feel. This is *chemistry*, then. This is what they mean. They've got it wrong, though. They should have said *physics*.

Magnets.

Force.

The silence between us stretches like a cat in a beam of sun. Settles in. It's stopped raining and the quiet makes the echo in the Tube seem loud. He coughs. Once, twice. I breathe too deeply.

I can't hyperventilate, not here. Not now. I don't even have a paper bag.

The paint fumes are starting to give me a headache. I press the web between my thumb and my pointer finger, which is supposed to ward migraines off, but it does nothing. I wipe my nose on my sleeve.

"You probably think," I start to say, "that I'm—"

At the same time, he's saying, "So I have to tell you that my dad is in the band that Mr. Stewart hired to—"

"I didn't know you had a dad," I say at the same time as Soup's saying, "Sorry, you go first."

And then he's kissing me and whatever I was planning to say is blown out, like wind extinguishing a fire. There's smoke, and then there's nothing left but a burning smell.

"Do you smell something?" he asks, pulling away.

"Yeah. Paint." I lean back in.

We kiss forever. We don't stop kissing. We kiss until I feel like a whole day and night must have passed.

Then we stop.

"So," he says.

"Hey," I say.

"We're really eloquent." He grins. "Someone should write this down to use in a movie later."

"Probably. I should have brought my camera and filmed it so we could transcribe our brilliant dialogue."

He laughs. "Where *is* your camera? I don't think I ever saw you without a camera, you know, before."

"Before," I say flatly. I shiver. Then, "I know."

"Aw, I'm sorry. I didn't mean to bring Piper into—"

"It's fine," I interrupt. "Forget it."

Some things don't go away when you close your eyes.

I should get up and leave but I can't. There's the situation with the magnet and the humming and the physics.

A rat runs between us, his tail brushing over my toes. I scream.

"It's a rat," he says.

"Oh," I say. "So you're in charge of stating the obvious, I guess." I mean it as a joke, but it comes out wrong. Sharp and mean.

"I'm not funny," I add. "I'm sorry, that was meant to be funny."

"You are funny. Usually. Maybe not right now. I won't even make the joke I was going to make about rat traps."

"It's been a *difficult* time," I say, mimicking Mr. Stewart.

Soup laughs without moving his mouth. "Better," he says.

Neither of us moves. The sun pushes through somewhere and the fallen raindrops start sparkling in the waning light of the day. I can't tell what's real shimmer and what's a migraine aura, threatening. Across the street, a thick stand of trees rustles. It's really more beautiful than it should be. *Look at that*, I want to say. *The beauty*. I also want to smash the whole image with my fist. I can feel the *waiting* inside me, compressed and wanting to unfurl.

"Touch me," I say.

"What?" Soup asks.

"Forget it," I say. "If you say 'what' when you heard me, then it wrecks the moment."

"Sorry." He gently rests his hand on my shoulder.

I stare out onto the wet road, the occasional car going by and spraying water in arcs from the deep puddles. A crow swoops low, a McDonald's wrapper in his beak. Somewhere

344

in the distance, there's the sound of music blaring up and dying away. I hug my legs without moving my shoulder. I don't want to move my shoulder away from his hand.

An image of James, over me, his mouth hanging open.

The way he grunted.

The look on his face.

I cough, gagging a little bit.

"Are you choking to death?" he says, patting my back.

I shake my head.

"I miss her," I say. "Don't you?"

He doesn't answer for so long, I wonder if I really asked it, or if I just thought it.

Then, "Yes. But it's different. You were best friends for your whole life. She was only my girlfriend for a few months."

"Almost five." My voice is so small, it might not even come out. I have goose bumps rising everywhere.

He shifts himself a fraction of an inch closer to me.

And then suddenly, we're kissing again.

My lips, his lips, him, me.

I push him away. I have to tell him.

"Hey," Soup says.

"Sorry. Sorry, I'm so sorry, I'm sorry. I have to tell you something."

"Okay." He pulls back a little bit, eyebrows raised. "Sloane? Are you all right?"

"I don't know if I can say this."

"Try." He picks up my hand and squeezes it. I can feel my heartbeat all the way down to my fingertips.

A cyclist rides by, a spray coming up from his wheels. In the distance, a dog barks.

I take a deep breath.

"I know him," I begin. "I know James Robert Wilson. So does Piper. So did Piper. She met him at work. He worked at the movie theater. He was the one. He was the one who I slept with who wouldn't leave me alone. It was him."

Soup is watching my face carefully, like I'm something fragile that might break.

"I'm fine," I say. "I'm going to tell you all of it. I have to tell you all of it. Okay?"

"Okay."

So I do.

SOUP

I WANT TO DO IT AGAIN AND AGAIN
and again and never do anything else, ever.

That's the truth. That's what it's like, kissing Sloane. It's like falling into something and getting stuck there: quicksand or tar. But a good kind. I don't know how to make the right kind of metaphor; I know that with Sloane, it's right. She's what matters. Everything else is noise and stupidity.

Nothing else matters.

Not even my dad and why I know he exists and he doesn't know who I am.

Not even what she told me about James Robert Wilson.

Which was shocking, don't get me wrong.

I don't exactly know what to do with it, so I've wrapped it

up and stored it somewhere deep in my brain, a place that I imagine looking like a messy art room. I put it in the corner where I don't have to think about it right away.

I lie on my back on the cool, wet concrete. I look up at the roof of the Tube and see layers and layers of paint that I've added over the years, one on top of the other, overlapping swear words and art, the round canvas of it, the layers of everything I've ever felt.

I'm on a rocket ship to a planet where nothing matters but love and art and no one is dead.

Not Piper, not anyone.

I rub my hands over my arms, touch my face. My skin tingles.

The skin feels stubbly on my chin.

I kissed Sloane. Again.

It's so good, kissing Sloane.

Do I deserve something so good?

I take out my tin of red and I spray until nothing is left, the mist of the paint freckling into the air, probably into my lungs. I can taste it on my tongue. I turn the painting into a setting sun.

Sunsets are cheap and easy with spray paint.

Try it one day. You'll feel like freakin' Van Gogh.

SLOANE

I'M WALKING DOWN THE HALL WHEN THE
fire alarm goes off like a message from the dead.

From Piper.

It's shrill and deafening.

It takes me a few seconds to figure out what it is; mostly it
feels like a cacophony that's coming from somewhere inside me,
the pain that's trapped in there, the sound I can't bring myself
to make.

Or the warning bell of the zombie apocalypse.

No one is panicking, except me. Kids are slowly wander-
ing to the exits, talking and laughing.

I can't move.

"Sloane froze in the hallway," my imaginary narrator's voice intones, "while the building burned around her. No one knows why she ignited, but she took the building down with her. The other students escaped, but the school was destroyed." A pause. "The source of the blaze appeared to be the girl herself."

I check my arms for smoke.

No smoke.

No sparks.

No flames.

Maybe Piper's not mad anymore.

Maybe Piper's gone.

I put my hand over my own mouth, not sure if sound is coming out or not. I need the noise to stop. It reminds me of something. It reminds me of everything. A cigarette in my hand, my phone in the other one, the crunching sound of the car pulling into the driveway, Piper's mom's voice, the sound the sky would make if it shattered and fell, and I'm breaking into a million pieces, frozen in place, my mouth opening and closing, opening and closing. Everyone has left, but I can't move.

I'm stuck.

"James," I say out loud.

A hand on my shoulder.

I jump and scream.

There's no one there.

"Leave me alone," I whisper. "No one knows, so it didn't happen."

But Soup knows.

The alarm stops.

Kids start coming back inside, still joking around.

The bells still echo in my head.

There's something I have to do. It's time to tell.

I take out my new phone. There's only one number programmed in so far. I use it to text Soup. "Police station. After school. Come with me?"

"Confirmed," he replies quickly. I slip my phone back into my bag. The other kids are disappearing into classrooms. I straighten up and I turn to go down the stairs, hurrying so I'm not late.

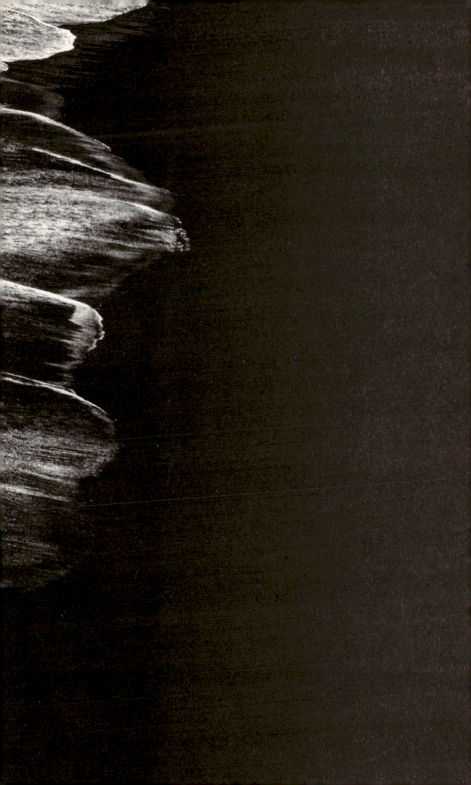

PART THREE

BEFORE

THE PILE OF NEATLY FOLDED CLOTHES sits on Mr. Aberley's kitchen table. "Talk," he says. "Tell me everything, Ms. Sloane."

"I don't know if I can, Mr. A," I say. "I don't know how to say it."

"Did you ever wonder," he asks, "what I do all day?"

"Not really," I mutter. "I mean, I don't know. Nap?"

"My dear Sloane," he says. "I'm tired. It's true, I've been alive for a long time. But I do more than nap."

"Oh," I say. I sneak a look at the pile of clothing. The jeans are frayed. A few white threads stick out. The T-shirt looks as though he's ironed it. On the top of the pile, there's a wallet.

Of course there's a wallet.

Boys always have a wallet.

Men always have a wallet.

"The fascinating thing about being old," he goes on, "is that people are unable to imagine that you were ever anything else. Certainly not that you were once a baby, and then a child, and then a teenager." He pauses. "Teenagers are the worst at it, I think. They think of themselves as a species. Maybe they are a species. Perhaps they are a species that goes extinct as soon as they become adults. Of course, that's not possible. We are one species."

I yawn without meaning to. I'm not bored, but when I get anxious, I can never pull enough air into my lungs.

"I'm interested in species," he says. "It's something you and I have in common, remember? The talks we've had about the flocks of birds, the whales washing up on the beaches. Speaking of which, three dead humpback whales just this week. Did you read about that? Trapped in those ridiculous nets at the fish farms." He pauses. "Murderers. Blood on their hands."

"Three?"

"Three," he says. "It's a terrible thing."

"Totally," I agree. "Anyway, I don't think like that, that all old people are just old people. Grandma was amazing. When she was young, she was really successful."

"But she stopped being a powerful businesswoman when she became old. And because she was old, she only had two dimensions to you, like she was simply a photograph of herself."

"Mr. Aberley," I say. "Come on. I loved my grandma."

"I know. But I don't think you knew her very well. In any case, that is neither here nor there about these clothes."

"I'm trying to figure out how to explain." I look out the window. The sea looks gray and cold today. Unwelcoming. I think about the dead humpbacks and I feel like crying. In the distance, a wave rises like a whale's back.

Mr. A blows on his tea. I can smell his breath, which is musty like mothballs.

"My point—and I do have one—is that old people are also young people. We are the same as we've always been, it's just our housing that's changed," he says. "If you think about it— and I do think about it a lot—our bodies are the carriers for our souls. Do our souls ever really change?" He stares out the window, his blue eyes seeming to almost fog over.

"Mr. A. The thing is—"

"I'm not finished," he interrupts, his voice stronger now. "I understand why someone might want to take a boy to an island in her neighbor's boat. I understand why she might want to do that, to be alone with him. I understand she might not be aware that her neighbor has a rather large collection of telescopes. Because he enjoys seeing things: the whales while there are any left, and the birds, of course, but also the changing tide, and the shape of driftwood on the beach." His blue eyes look directly at me. "Sloane, I'm not judging what you do, but I feel the need to warn you about something that I know. That young man whose clothes these are is not a boy. He's a man. And there is something about that particular man that I recognize, being a man myself. After you tell me where I can find him, I'm going to return these things to him and then you aren't going to see him again."

"I don't want to see him again!" I blurt. "I want him to disappear."

"I see," he says. "People tend to not disappear, you know. Especially the ones who you hope will go."

"I know. I know he won't really." I spill some sugar on the table and trace my finger through it. "I know he won't vanish, but I'm not going to see him again. You're right. It was a mistake. It was all a mistake." I pause. "How much did you see?"

"I hope it's not a mistake that comes back to haunt you," he says, not answering. "I hope you'll be more careful in the future. I hope . . ." He trails off, and his head drops forward slightly.

"Mr. A?" I say tentatively. I push back my chair and stand up. I go around to his side of the table, put my hand on his shoulder. He jerks upright.

"Your grandmother's funeral is when?" he says. "That's what you came to tell me, right? Perhaps you can drive me. Perhaps on the way, we can drop these items at your friend's home."

"I don't know where he lives," I say. "I know where he works."

"Close enough," he says. "What you did, leaving him there like that. That was dangerous, do you know? I know people are always blaming young women for things, saying they asked for this and they asked for that. You didn't ask for anything, but I also don't think you understand young men. At least, not angry young men. I'm not sure of the answer. You had to leave the island when you did. I understand. But you opened yourself up to be on the receiving end of his anger. He will be righteous about it because that is how he's wired. It's all predictable. And terrible. When I drop the clothes, I will tell him to stay away from you. But I don't know if he will. I suspect he will think that I'm a joke."

"Mr. A. No. Don't. If he is angry . . . I don't want him to take it out on you."

"I'm not a threat to him. Not in the way that you are. You don't understand. I know you don't. I wish you didn't have to. I'm afraid you will soon enough. Now, I'm tired. I need a nap. See you tomorrow, Sloane."

"See you, Mr. A," I say. I leave the clothes on the table. It will be hard to explain to Mom and Dad, who will be driving, why we're stopping at the multiplex on the way to Grandma's service, but maybe they won't ask. Maybe they won't notice how strangely I'm behaving. Maybe they won't ask me anything at all.

NOW

THE DAY AFTER SOUP AND I GO TO SEE
Detective Marcus, I skip school. Mom and Dad don't ask
when I say that I'm staying home; they just look at each other,
something passing between them that I don't want to see.
They are going to know now. *Everyone* will know now.

Everyone will know what I did.

Everyone will know who I am.

I deserve it. Piper doesn't. She definitely doesn't deserve to
be dead.

On the other hand, it was all her idea.

Is that victim blaming?

Her tongue on her lip. Twirling while she modeled a cashmere sweater. She's the one he wanted all along.

Obviously.

I knew that.

I should have known that.

I should have guessed.

I was a Piper substitute.

Instead of going to school, I sit on the rocky beach.

The sun is warm in an inadequate autumnal way. It's high in the sky, which remains blue as ever, an illusion of heat. The season is turning the furnace down gradually, slowly reminding us that winter is coming.

I am like the sky: I look the same.

But I am different.

I take a stick and flip a grounded jellyfish back toward the water, just in case it's not quite dead. It's hard to tell the difference between a live jellyfish and a dead one once they've been beached. Sometimes when I get them back into the water, they fan out and start to float again.

Sometimes.

Not very often.

Mr. A was wrong about the whales. Only two of them died. The third one lived. After they untangled him, he swam away, rising and falling like the waves.

I've been reading the websites again.

They shot a mountain gorilla in an American zoo because a boy fell into his enclosure and they were worried, they said, for the child's safety. There are only eight hundred mountain gorillas left in the world. Well, seven hundred and ninety-nine now. They are counting down to extinction.

If I were to make a documentary about that, I'd interview people on a busy street, traffic zooming by in the background. I'd take my camera on a plane to wherever the remaining wild mountain gorillas live. I'd crouch in the long grasses and point my camera lens shyly in their direction. I'd stay still and film their quiet faces.

Piper, I say to the waves, but there isn't an answer, because she's gone, really gone, all of her dissipating into the hugeness of the sea. Her mom told me that they scattered Piper's ashes in the ocean. *She hated the water!* I wanted to say. It made it extra sad, somehow, that Piper is dead and her mom thought that's who she was, a kid who loved the water, and she was so wrong.

"Goodbye, Piper," I whisper to the sea. "I never liked you anyway."

Then I add quickly, "I *loved* you," so her ghost doesn't misunderstand my joke.

I want to get into the water and drink it so that I can hold her in for longer.

I wade in up to my knees and the cold water sinks into my jeans like it's been waiting for me. I can't hear her.

I wade in up to my waist. It's so cold. This time, I can feel the current, tugging at me.

I deserve that.

I should let it take me.

Why not?

I took his clothes.

I humiliated him.

I triggered something. It might have happened anyway, but also, it might not have.

What if I'd fallen in love with him? I'm sure people do that all the time, save someone from becoming a killer by loving them before they kill anyone. Maybe everyone is capable of loving a murderer.

I don't know why I couldn't.

I could have saved her.

I've been so stupid.

My legs are aching from the cold.

I turn around and face the house. I slowly walk back up to the beach. The sun is fading. The blue is bleaching away to a thinner gray. I start counting the jellyfish: one, two, three. Seventeen.

Odd, unlucky. That's what Soup would say.

A splashing makes me turn around. Mr. Aberley. "Sloane?" he says. "I haven't seen you for quite some time. I've had a lot of tea that hasn't been enjoyed with company lately."

I cringe guiltily. "I'm sorry, Mr. A."

"Cold in there today!" he says. "Too cold for swimming.

Go warm up inside! I've got to get rowing now. Keep my girlish figure."

"Looking good, Mr. Aberley," I say. "You still look good."

I make my way up to the house. My legs are so cold I can't even feel them. The migraine pills are making me feel spun out, thin, like the sky. I don't even know if I have a migraine or if I took the pill because I wanted to feel less substantial, if only for today.

I climb up onto the deck and go up to the old chair. It looks like it hasn't been sat in for years. But it has. That's where I was sitting when everything changed.

Prosti menya. Anteeksi.

On the arm of the chair, there's a black burn from my cigarette in its elephant tusk holder. There were only seven people at Grandma's funeral. There were hundreds at Piper's. Maybe if you live to be old, you have enough time to alienate all your friends. Or maybe she just outlived them. Piper didn't have a lot of friends, but she sure brought a crowd to her service. "Life is weird," I say out loud.

There are cobwebs everywhere. I hate the way they stick to me but I sit down anyway, feeling them in my hair, on my skin. Piper hated cobwebs. If she ran into one in the woods, she'd scream and scream, pulling it off her.

"You sound like you're being murdered!" I'd laugh, helping her wipe them away. "There's no spider."

"I'm not scared of spiders," she'd say. "It's the sticking to me, the way I can't get them off."

I look down at the beach, at the waves, at the same things that are always there but never the same. Only me and Mr. Aberley really exist here; he is in the background of so many scenes of my life, like parentheses around sentences.

A seagull flies by, but there is no joke to be made.

My phone plays the standard ringtone that it came with. I haven't changed it to a meaningful song yet. I turn it off without answering.

The sky is thickening now, with gray clouds.

It seems heavier.

It's weighing down on me.

Fall Fair will be chilly. There isn't enough blue left in the day to last into the evening, to keep it warm.

I have to go to it.

I can't miss her "memorial" even though I want to miss her memorial. I search my skull for a migraine but there's nothing but the flat echo of the pills.

I can do this.

I can get through it.

For Piper.

"This will be goodbye, okay?" I say out loud.

Nothing.

"Tell me that it's going to be okay," I plead to a crow, but when the words leave my mouth, I realize that there's not one crow, there are fifty, at least. A murder. They are perched on the roof, heads cocked, staring at me with their black marble eyes like they are trying to figure something out. "I'm not dead," I tell them. "I'm not going to die. You're safe."

Crows investigate dead bodies, looking for the danger so they can protect themselves and one another if they find the source of the risk. The crows understand that extinction is at stake.

One squawks and the others rise as a group, wings flapping noisily, settling a few hundred yards away in a leafless tree, calling out to one another.

"Piper," they say. "Piper, Piper, Piper."

My documentary will be called *Crows: Murders and Ghosts*.

The wind picks up, blowing noisily through the half-leafless trees, the evergreens, pushing waves up in the bay. Mr. Aberley hasn't rowed back yet. I stand up and see if I can spot him. For a minute or two, I can't see him, and I start to panic. Did he sink? Did he die? No one else can die. There can't be any more blood on my hands. And then there he is, slowly making his way back across the bay.

Just like every other time, heading back home, keeping his girlish figure.

* * *

I choose my clothes carefully. Going to Fall Fair without Piper feels unthinkable, but Piper is dead and I'm with Soup and James Robert Wilson is being held without bail and the sky hangs lower and lower over the house, grayer and heavier with each passing moment, and full of storms and judgment.

In the mirror, my hair looks longer.

I look in the mirror. It's me. Just me. Sloane Whittaker, age seventeen.

I imagine Piper, slipping deeper into the sea, reaching up to the sky, trying to get out. The sky is the future. Outside, the sea has risen in whitecaps. The wind whips the curtains against the walls, stirring up dust and feathers and the old nicotine smell of them from when they were in Grandma's room.

Soup will be here any minute.

I'm going to tell him we can't see each other anymore. We can't keep kissing. We can't.

Slut and lust are really the same word.

I'm wearing a heavy knit sweater, a thick scarf. My hair is almost fire-red now. Instead of fading, it seems to be getting brighter. My freckles stand out against my white skin. No matter what angle I look at myself from, I can't see the phantom of Piper.

She's really gone.

"I hope you die, James Robert Wilson," I say out loud. "I hope they kill you in prison."

I have to think about what I'll say to Soup or if I'll say anything at all.

Soup honks once, twice, three times.

"See you later, parents," I call, passing through the kitchen on the way out.

"Home by midnight!" Mom says.

"Mom, no. Please, no curfew tonight."

"Twelve thirty," says Dad. "You get a bonus half hour."

"Gee, thanks." I give him a quick kiss on the cheek. His skin is as smooth as a girl's. "Nice shave, Dad."

"Yeah, yeah, off you go, kid," he says. "Have fun."

"But not too much," says Mom. They laugh like she's told a hilarious joke. They've done this routine for as long as I can remember, but recently, they haven't had much of a chance to use it.

"You look nice," Mom adds. "Like a model in a catalog for fall clothes."

"Thanks, Mom," I say. "Not high fashion enough for *Vogue*?"

"Your clothes are too normal," she says. "Maybe if you wore a cape?"

"Do you have one?"

"Nope. Guess you'll just have to go as a normal person."

"It's a good disguise," I go. "No one will guess the truth."

"You'll fool them." She holds on to my hand for a second and smiles, then lets go. "Now get going! Dad and I are coming for the tribute. It starts at six, right?"

"Right," I say.

Mom looks at my face. "It's not like the funeral," she says. "It's meant to be a celebration of her. Try to look at it that way."

"Trying," I say. "Not understanding, but trying."

Soup honks again. "I'm coming!" I yell. I roll my eyes for my parents' benefit. "Don't do anything I wouldn't do while I'm gone."

I run down the front path, the gravel crunching under my feet.

The sprinklers come on. I pause for a second and look at the rainbows in the spray. I can feel the mist on my skin.

In the distance, a seagull calls.

I open the door of Soup's car and I slide into the passenger seat.

It feels like my seat.

It feels like home.

It feels safe.

Soup reaches over and squeezes my hand.

"We're doing this thing?" he asks.

"We're doing this thing," I say. It starts to rain as he pulls out of the driveway onto the road, big plopping drops of rain. The trees shiver in the wind.

"So what are you going to say to your dad?" I say.

The music on this ride is too loud. It's deafening and it's inside me, churning my guts around, and I'd throw up if I'd eaten anything, but luckily I haven't. Soup's leaning on my shoulder in a way that is making it hard to breathe, so I hold my breath, which makes it worse.

The music is too loud. I don't belong here. I don't want to be here, the music beating through me like a pulse. I don't know why I haven't gone home, climbed into the familiarity of my bed with its entangling sheets that Elvis has probably pressed flat and smooth again, safe and cool.

The ride speeds up and speeds up, spinning me around and around. Spinning me through the life I had before and the life I have now and the way that I'm here with Soup and how much I miss Piper and then, when I think I can't stand it, the ride slams to a halt. The music is so loud now, and the sound of it is making me dizzier and dizzier. The ride grinds into reverse, faster than I'd imagined possible.

My eyes are tightly shut and I think about the antelope, dropping dead on the savanna, corpses rotting in the sun for ages before anyone realized, before someone found them, all dead.

People die on fair rides, even the ones that feel safe. Just last week, a family of four died in Australia on a slow-moving river ride that slowly turned over and slowly trapped them against the conveyor belt, slowly but surely killing them.

Everyone dies.

When the ride finally stops, I can hardly stand up and walking feels impossible but there's the announcement. "PIPER SULLIVAN," it says. I catch the words "memorial" and "asteroid."

I lean hard on Soup. "Hey," he says.

"Hey, yourself," I murmur. "This is it. Piper Sullivan's Memorial Asteroid."

"You're such a weirdo," he laughs. "But I like it. Piper Sullivan's Memorial Asteroid makes as much sense as a title for this show as anything else."

"She'd like it."

Mr. Stewart is already talking but the speakers aren't working properly. I can't really hear him. Someone shouts, "LOUDER!" He keeps talking. The words "children's hospital" come through. And then "cancer." He's conflating all the deaths into a charity grab. It's terrible and amazing at the same time.

I lean over to make a comment to Soup but then the screen

suddenly fills with a huge version of Soup's birthday portrait of Piper. It's so beautiful. It's like fireworks. It's like flowers. It's like everything. I gasp. "It's amazing," I say.

"You'd already seen it!" he says.

"I know," I say. "But look at it. It's really amazing."

"Thank you," he whispers, right into my ear, and I feel a shiver go all the way to my feet. A good shiver.

"This has been a *really* difficult time," says Mr. Stewart. Soup pokes me in the ribs and makes a face. I giggle.

"Don't make me laugh!" I say. "We can't laugh at Piper's Memorial Asteroid!"

"She'd want us to," he says gravely.

There's a smattering of applause. Mr. Stewart waves a donation box that's shaped like an enormous piggy bank. Behind him, four guys come onto the stage with instruments. A drum kit appears. There's some shuffling. I look around for Mom and Dad. They must be here somewhere, but it's so crowded, I can't see them.

"PIPER SULLIVAN!" the lead singer shouts. "THIS ONE'S FOR YOU!"

They start playing, but with the misfiring speakers, it sounds like screaming.

It sounds like a cry for help.

I catch Soup's eye. I point at my ear.

He makes a face.

Shrugs.

"That's my dad," he shouts into my ear.

"What?" I ask. "Where?"

He points at the stage.

"The drummer?"

"Yes," he yells.

"He looks like you," I shout.

"You think?" He smiles a little. "Yeah, he does a bit. They're really loud!"

I wait for a break in the music, then say, "What are you going to do? Are you going to introduce yourself?"

Soup drapes his arm over my shoulders. "Not tonight," he says. "I want to show you something."

He leads me through the crowd by the hand. He walks me down to the edge of the water. This is not my beach. This is not the island. This is not where she died. This memorial has almost nothing to do with her.

But unlike at the funeral, I can really feel her. I can't explain it, I just can.

"Piper?" I whisper.

"Look," Soup says. "She's here." He takes a stick and drags it through the water, and like magic, the water lights up in the moonlight.

"Oh!" I say. "Oh."

In silent agreement, we sit down on the sand and take off

our shoes. We roll up our jeans. The rain has stopped and a cold wind is whipping against the water, making ripples. It's hard to remember the heat wave now, how even at night it felt like it would never cool down.

We wade into the water up to our knees, our feet sinking in the soft sand. We're kicking up huge sprays of phosphorescence, making arcs of magical light with every step, with every move that we make, with the way our bodies move together in the moonlight.

"Goodbye, Piper," he shouts, his voice soaring over the water like wings, like a bird.

"Goodbye," I yell. "See you later, alligator hater."

And I know it can't be true, I know she isn't here, but I swear I hear her, faintly, behind the driving beat of the music; I think I hear her say it. *In a while . . . vile . . . crocodile.*

It could just be a voice from the crowd behind us. It could be a bird. It could be anything, but I *know* it's her. We're connected that way.

Always.

Forever.

That's how it is with us.

That's how it will always be.

EPILOGUE

I've lost track of me, blown free from myself, yet I'm still in the water and not in the water. I'm in Sloane and in Soup and in my mom and in everyone who I ever breathed on and touched and hung on to, each time leaving tiny bits of me with them, like they left themselves with me, too. So in the water, there are parts of Sloane also twirling in the light, different colors of blue and green and white and Soup and Mom and everyone everyone. We're all in the water: me and James on the island where he said I love you, you know. I felt so strange and I laughed and I laughed and I said no to him, no you don't and no I don't and no, and do you ever stop taking yourself so seriously. And he said love is serious. And I said do you see the whale? The fin of a humpback rose up in the moonlight.

And now I am the whale and the moonlight and the sea but then I was just me and I turned my back on him and then there was the feeling of him behind me and then something around my neck. There was the lace around my neck.

And his whisper in my ear, all the molecules of that wet whisper of that one word, "Monster," which was also one of the last words that I said to Sloane, the slap of that one word, which is still in her and will be in her forever. I regret. I regret. I regret.

Fault is impossible to find. A crack in his brain, an emptiness in my heart, a nothingness in all of us.

And I'm slowly and quickly forgetting how words are letters joined in sound to make a feeling, which is that lace tightening around my neck in such a way that I didn't have as much time to be afraid as to be surprised. And I thought about how he had a choice, everyone has a choice, and the part of me that I left with Jimmy, the word no, that I put inside his ear and his brain will one day turn into a tumor that starts to grow behind his left ear and eventually will cost him his face and his mind and only then his body and he will die and his cells will drift apart in this same way and each bit of him will become a bit of something else.

And in this way, in this way we are all lovers and loved and murderers, too.

And from here I can hear just the sound of the fair that echoes through the surface and makes a vibration that's shifting the last of my cells apart.

And Sloane is with Soup is with me and us and we and I am not here not anymore and none of it was important.

Only that word no.

And I want to go back and to say no for Sloane and for all the girls who need to know they can say no and should say no and all of us are saying no.

And I've forgotten I've forgotten I've forgotten everything that was anything but love and I love you Sloaney and I love you Soup and I love you Mom and I'm sorry anteeksi.

And now I am anteeksi *spread out in the waves being pushed gently on to the shore leaving white bubbles and froth and I'm here and I want them to see me to drag a stick through the water and see me glowing no and I was right to say no because sometimes no is the only answer, say no, Sloaney. Tell them all no or tell them all you love them.*

Tell them all I was here and I loved you and you loved me and we were us.

And goodbye Sloane and all that was and all that never is going to be and goodbye I never really liked you goodbye I love you forever and forever goodbye.